ALSO BY STEPHEN FOREMAN

Toehold

WATCHING GIDEON

Stephen Foreman

Simon & Schuster Paperbacks
New York   London   Toronto   Sydney

Simon & Schuster Paperbacks
A Division of Simon & Schuster, Inc.
1230 Avenue of the Americas
New York, NY 10020

First Simon & Schuster trade paperback edition November 2009

SIMON & SCHUSTER and colophon are registered
trademarks of Simon & Schuster, Inc.

For information about special discounts for bulk purchases,
please contact Simon & Schuster Special Sales at
1-866-506-1949 or business@simonandschuster.com.

The Simon & Schuster Speakers Bureau can bring authors
to your live event. For more information or to book an event,
contact the Simon & Schuster Speakers Bureau at
1-866-248-3049 or visit our website at www.simonspeakers.com.

Designed by Jill Putorti

Manufactured in the United States of America

10 9 8 7 6 5 4 3 2 1

Library of Congress Cataloging-in-Publication Data is available.

ISBN 978-1-4391-3574-7
ISBN 978-1-4391-5358-1 (ebook)

For my children
Sevi D and Madden Rose
My "Absolute little gods of the moment."

And for my wife
Jamie Donnelly
Who watches over us all.

WATCHING
GIDEON

PART 1

One bright day, shortly after Seaman First Class Jubal Pickett returned home to Natchez, Mississippi, from the war, he and his son, Gideon, going on three, went for a walk. Gideon wrapped his chubby little hand around Jubal's trigger finger and lurched along beside his father with happy determination. It was during this period of time that Jubal had his dream. In his dream, he and Gideon were walking together across a meadow somewhere in Yugoslavia when artillery shells began exploding all around them. Jubal didn't know what they were doing in Yugoslavia, since his tour of duty with the navy ended early with a sucking chest wound at Pearl Harbor, but that was his dream and there they were. In the instant, without thought, without hesitation, Jubal threw himself on top of his son to protect him as the shells screamed around them. In actuality, Jubal's dream was so real he leaped out of bed and cracked his head against the bedside table on his way to the floor. In real life, he would die for his child, and Jubal knew this like he drew breath. The thought came to him that the Old Testament Abraham was one sick son of a bitch. He, Jubal Pickett, loved his son so much that he'd never dare harm him. "Wouldn't give you a nickel for him, wouldn't take a million," Jubal would say with a fond wink in Gideon's direction. As far as Jubal was concerned, a man who'd kill his own son wasn't but scum. Anybody'd do that to his own kid ought to be spread-eagled on top a hill of fire ants with corn syrup poured over his skin and his eyelids held open with cactus needles. The day Jubal realized this was the day he stopped believing in the benevolence of any God who would ask such a thing.

———

Gideon Pickett, sixteen years of age, sat beside his father in the cab of their red, nearly new 1952 Ford Flathead V-8 three-quarter-ton pickup as they left Natchez, Mississippi, behind them towing a used Airstream trailer and heading for the uranium fields of Utah and a future more promising than the past. About the time Jubal's truck had rolled off the assembly line, uranium in the United States had gotten to be more valuable than gold. The bombs that had obliterated two entire cities and forever altered the universe transfixed the nation with the spectacle and promise of atomic power. The press took to calling that radioactive hoard buried somewhere in the vast and treacherous canyon country of southern Utah the Hidden Splendor. Fortune hunters from all over the nation converged on the tiny town of Edom, heretofore unheard of and home to no one but a handful of desert rats. The smart money stocked up on picks and shovels, but men like Jubal Pickett caught the fever like sails catch a gale-force wind. They believed so fervently that hard work and perseverance would pay off in great wealth that they mortgaged their farms and homes and headed into the feverish heat of the desert wilderness to find it. In Jubal's case he sold a forty-acre farm on the river that had been in his family since before the Civil War. His ex-wife, Gideon's mother, referred to the transaction as "forty acres and a fool," but Jubal was committed to a course of action designed to carry him into a future fat with material excess. He would not be stopped by provincial concerns. Gideon would have what he needed: new clothes, travel to exotic places, two-inch steaks fresh from Kansas City. His son would never have to worry about a roof over his head; Jubal would put a palace there. Sure, the man had his dreams, but he prided himself on his practical side as well. He haggled a pretty fair deal on the forty acres with the tenant who'd been farming it for years, anyhow. The man hadn't quite met Jubal's price, but he'd come close enough. Jubal told him throw in the truck and they'd close, which is how Jubal and Gideon came to own the nearly new red Ford pickup. Jubal thought that was some pretty slick stuff. It didn't hurt that Gideon's favorite color was red.

Jubal came from a long line of horse traders, boatmen, roust-abouts, roughnecks, and thieves sometime late in the eighteenth century. His people, originally from the Scottish Highlands, found themselves in the bluegrass country of what would one day become the state of Kentucky, yet they were not bump-kins—peasants, yes, but canny and shrewd. The progenitor of the family, a man named Sid Pickett, came over as an inden-tured servant, but he learned horse trading from his contract master, bested him with cunning deals on the side, and bought his way out before the end of his servitude. An astute observer, he noticed that boats, as opposed to horses, didn't kick, bite, excrete, or eat, and so he became a member of a breed known up and down the Mississippi River as "Kaintucks": hard, wild frontiersmen who trusted no one, who drank, fought, and built flatboats that they floated down the Mississippi River loaded with goods. They'd sell their commodities at Natchez, sell the boat for lumber, stuff the cash in their pockets, and walk home along the Natchez Trace, four hundred and forty miserable miles of footpath from Natchez, Mississippi, through a little corner of Alabama and on up to Nashville, Tennessee.

Not surprisingly, bandits considered the trace a mother lode of opportunity. They were merciless men who took the hard-earned cash of their victims with impunity and thought no more of plucking a person's life than plucking a blade of grass.

More than once did Sid Pickett fight his way out of an am-bush, but only once was he bested. Two men waylaid him and took his money. They'd gotten the jump, and they'd hurt him, but they hadn't killed him, and that was their mistake. He managed to escape and flee, however, and instead of continu-ing home, Sid circled back and tracked them down. One of the robbers had walked deeper into the woods for a little privacy. Pickett waited until the man dropped his leggings and squatted, then he bludgeoned the unsuspecting bastard from behind with a stone the size of a land turtle and damn near tore his head off his neck. He came up behind the other one, too, hammered him with a blow to the back of *his* neck, and tied the stunned bandit's hands in front of him before the thief could figure out what was happening. Then Sid grabbed his hatchet, chopped off both his hands, took his money, and left the poor wretch howling in the woods. There was a dark side to Sid Pickett. He conceived of revenge in tragic proportions.

This incident left Sid thinking he'd had enough of that walk, so he used his profit to buy a hundred acres of virgin forest on the river between Natchez and Greenville, and he put up a trading post not too far from where Andrew Jackson engaged in the slave trade. Pickett was a shrewd trader, and he knew the value of lumber. So he did well enough, though he never became a wealthy man. However, except for a brief period after the Civil War when Lincoln ordered "forty acres and a mule" be given to freed slaves, the land remained in the possession of a Pickett. After Lincoln's assassination, his successor, Andrew Johnson, rescinded this transfer of property, and the land reverted back. Somehow it stayed in the family all the way down to Jubal, though by the time he got it the trading post was a local Piggly Wiggly that leased the land on which it stood, plus the remaining forty acres had so many encumbrances on it you couldn't put up an outhouse without an edict from God. His parents had farmed it, but that's not what Jubal wanted for himself and not what he wanted for his son. There was beauty but no profit in that. You ate what you grew and slaughtered, paid your bills, and started the cycle over. You normally had enough, but there was never more. So he sold it, and there was profit in that.

The only thing Jubal truly knew about his great-great-great-grandfather was his name written in the family Bible, but the patriarch was his blood nonetheless, and, though it had been watered down through all the years and all the begats of Pick-etts, the name still had a good bit of bite to it. The bile had been leached out but not the mischief. Jubal had a heart as big as a Packard's hubcap, but he wasn't one to let unkind behavior go unanswered, and God help you if you bullshit him and he caught you at it. His dreams were a whole lot bigger than he was, but he was just the kind of tough, wiry little guy you'd have to hit with a jack handle to put him down. He had manned an antiaircraft gun on a destroyer during the attack on Pearl Harbor and managed to shoot down two kamikazes while under constant cannon fire from their guns. The medics were astonished at the number of wounds it took to finally stop him.

Usually, though, he went through life with a smile for everyone and kept his energy for what was important. He really didn't believe he'd been tested yet, not like Abraham, anyway. Jubal didn't count Pearl Harbor because he fought on instinct and barely remembered much about what he had done. He had no option but to fight, and to him a true test demanded that the one being tested make a choice between right and wrong, between good and evil. As far as Jubal was concerned, his had been just the usual ups and downs of a workingman's life, but he felt that there was so much of something more out there waiting for him. He felt that what set him off from the other fellows was the sure, firm knowledge, deep in his soul, that he would persevere. Once he put his mind to something, his will carried him along like a leaf in the current. Now the red Ford pickup flew over the road like a magic carpet, and his son was sitting on the seat beside him lost in one of his dreams. Nice, thought Jubal Pickett as he looked over and smiled at the boy. Jubal had rid himself of everything that held no importance. What was left sat beside him or was packed inside the small trailer hitched behind the pickup. Damn, Jubal thought to himself, what a ride! It suited him a lot better than holding a lease. It was exhilarating. He felt like a hawk in free fall.

———————

Gideon's mother (Jubal's wife) never got used to her son and left home before he reached double digits. Gideon was a blue baby born with a caul over his face. He immediately underwent a complete blood transfusion, and, when that condition had been alleviated, the thin sheet of skin was surgically removed. There was no longer any reason to believe that Gideon was anything but a normal child, yet RuthAnn (for that was her name, RuthAnn Porly of the Tupelo Porlys) couldn't help it but her skin crawled when she held him, which happened only when she couldn't avoid it anymore. It wasn't long before he hated to be held as much as that woman hated to hold him. Way before he walked he used his little legs to try to lurch off her lap, time and time again, lurch, lurch, get off me, lurch . . . Then she'd hold him out at arm's length as if he had a bad smell and yell for her husband to come and take the kid, and Jubal would come and take him and hold him and croon popular songs in his ear, like "Stormy Weather," "I Can't Give You Anything But Love," "Heart and Soul" . . . The intervals between lurches became longer and longer until they finally stopped altogether, and Gideon would sink into his father's arms like a pudding. This would drive RuthAnn mad. Right from the beginning she was certain those two were plotting against her. And then there was the rash.

If a woman can be allergic to her own offspring, this one was. She broke out in the rash the day she discovered she was pregnant, and that rash didn't quit until the day the front door slammed shut behind her a few years later. Gideon was born with the same rash. When his would wax, hers would wane, and they passed that raw, red, prickly thing back and forth so many times that RuthAnn finally felt pushed to within one millimeter of the abyss. It was like having prickly pear cactus in your crotch, but that wasn't even the worst of it.

As far as RuthAnn was concerned and in her heart truly believed, she bore it all with noble forbearance, except for this, what finally broke her: Gideon did not talk, did not even utter a single sound that could be construed as speech or anything else like it. What was remotely close was a gaglike sound that came from somewhere deep in the bottom of his throat and had not a thing to do with his vocal cords. Even when he cried there was no sound other than that same gagging one; it never changed pitch. Old Doc Barnaby assured Jubal and RuthAnn that their baby was in good health—all his nuts and bolts were in place and holding strong—except for this strange thing, what the doctor called a lazy tongue. As he explained it, every once in a while a tongue turns up that failed out of first grade. It never learned what it was supposed to do. It just kind of flops around on its own and makes sounds nobody can understand. He assured the parents that their baby would probably grow out of it, but that never happened. He would smack, pop, and click with his lips and mouth and tongue, but, except for the gag, these were the only sounds Gideon had. RuthAnn felt herself in league with mothers whose children were afflicted with conditions like hydrocephalus, polio, and hemophilia; however, what finally drove her over the edge was the way Gideon and Jubal seemed to understand each other. As the boy grew older, RuthAnn was certain there was a conspiracy going on, that he and his father colluded against her and shut her out, and the truth was, once she was out the door, they barely noticed she was gone.

———

Jubal loved being on the road. It calmed him just as it had always done for Gideon, too. When Gideon was agitated or distraught as a little kid, Jubal would climb behind the wheel of whatever truck he had at the time, put Gideon in his lap, his little hands on the wheel inside his father's hands, and drive them around until they both felt better. Mostly, Gideon's behavior mortified his mother, but Jubal simply took it in stride. He and RuthAnn had one of their worst fights in the car after the birthday party of one of the neighbor's children. Gideon did not want to go, and Jubal saw no point in insisting he do so, but RuthAnn decided to do battle over this one (something about the other boy's mother being a Daughter of the Confederacy), and they all wound up going. When they got there, however, Gideon would not get down from the cab of the truck. He sat back on his knees and refused to budge. RuthAnn came close to assault and battery, so when Jubal said firmly, "Come on, son," Gideon recognized the wisdom of not taking the hard way out. The boy rocked forward so that he was on his hands and knees and climbed down from the truck, face forward. "What the hell is he doing?" shrieked RuthAnn. "He's making like he's a puppy dog," replied Jubal. "How the hell do you know?" she yelled. "Ask him," Jubal said. Once on the sidewalk, Gideon licked his paws and, heeling on his father's left side, headed into the party on all fours. He stayed that way the entire afternoon and even in the truck until they got home. RuthAnn kept excusing herself to go to the bathroom, where she would nip from a vanilla extract bottle she kept in her purse for just such emergencies.

Jubal was thinking about this incident as they crossed over the state line into Texas from Louisiana, and he laughed as he remembered it, but as they skirted the nearby town of Sabine Pass, Jubal began to sense something out of order. A vague dis-ease had sneaked up on him, like a subtle warning before a serious headache, when you can absolutely feel every single follicle on your scalp. Normally it amounted to not much more than a sign that Gideon was getting hungry or that a cold was just starting to manifest or, when he was a baby, that he was teething. This time, however, it came on so suddenly that Jubal snapped a sharp look over to his son. Probably nobody else would notice the difference but Jubal spotted the tightening of the boy's mouth, a slight compression in the far corner of his right eye, his chin tucked down. He had seen this face before. Anybody else looked at Gideon what they'd probably see was grit, but Jubal knew different. It was the boy's pain face. It meant that he was hurting but not about to admit it, not about to give in, either. The boy was not immune to pain—he'd move his fingers away from an open flame, no problem—he just wasn't about to show it. His mother, who shrieked in panic at a hangnail, was sure there was something seriously unreal about the kid. This was one area—probably the only area—in which Jubal believed she had a point. Gideon kept the stuff that hurt in a very small place. It was always there, but sometimes he could put his hands on either side of it, lift it like a medicine ball, and put it aside. His father witnessed the boy's daily struggle and did his best to take it on, but there was a core in the boy that never melted, and that saddened Jubal because he suspected in his heart that it never would.

Gideon attended school but not class with regular kids. He was in what they called the "opportunity" class: feeble learners, borderline retards, low IQs. Gideon's world was not the world experienced by his peers. He figured out that his tongue never worked the way he wanted it to. He heard them say "lazy tongue" but for him it wasn't so much lazy but the opposite. It flapped around in his mouth like a flounder on a hook. It wasn't just that his tongue was lazy; mostly he also didn't hear words the way other kids did. Only sometimes he did. What happened inside his head was that words separated and turned into noises, so that bunches of words became bunches of sounds—rusty bolts banging about an empty bucket—and when that happened, the boy had no words anywhere at all. He never played with the regular kids at recess either, never played with them before or after school. His father dropped him off and picked him up, and, during recess, his teachers kept the "opportunity" class kids in a cluster away from the others.

It happened that on a certain day Jubal was about an hour late to pick up Gideon, and, when he got to the school grounds, Gideon wasn't waiting where he usually did. It was in the fall, not too many days into the new school term. It was also football season. Two pickup teams of neighborhood kids were playing on the field behind the school. Jubal parked his Ford V-8 and went inside to look for his son. Nobody had seen the boy since class let out, but the janitor suggested that Jubal should look out back. Maybe he was watching the game.

There had been a lot of rain that week, and a playground full of boys kicks up a lot of mud. The kids were covered with it, and Jubal wished he could join them; it seemed like so much fun being a kid just then. Right now all he could see was a pile of struggling, muddy bodies. Then one of the players spurted out from under the pile like a loose ball, only this kid had the football tucked into his midriff as he barreled forward, and nobody could stop the guy even though he was at the low end of normal size. He ran with no finesse whatsoever—he only went straight ahead—but he ran with such power and focus that he went right at and over the other boys, and they simply could not stop him. It wasn't that he aimed for anyone—he was not a vicious player—but if you were in his way you went down and it hurt. Low end of normal size? At that instant, it hit Jubal: he had just witnessed his son, Gideon, score a touchdown, and, he soon found out, it was not the boy's first. Gideon could not catch the ball at all, but tuck it tight into his midriff and step aside. In the hour since school let out he had scored five times, and everyone else wore a helmet and shoulder pads while all he had was himself and his Keds.

Jubal was to take Gideon to the doctor that afternoon (he was due for a polio shot), and they were already late, but Gideon refused to leave the field. Jubal thought he was going to have to cart him off bodily, which, if he weren't lying, he wasn't so sure he could do anymore, not without damage anyway. The boy finally did what his father asked him to, and as Gideon limped beside his father back to the truck, Jubal realized that his son had taken a hell of a beating. The doctor took one look at him and made him get up on the examination table, where it was discovered that he had played with two broken ribs and a broken left foot. But the only thing that stopped that boy from getting out on the field the next day was the bulky plaster cast on his foot. His father knew that once Gideon healed he would be back on that field, so he managed to find the boy a secondhand set of pads and a helmet at a pawnshop in Natchez. Gideon played football every chance he got until he was sixteen and didn't have to go to school anymore, but then he had to give up the game because only bona fide students were allowed to use the playground. Gideon had been about as upset as he'd ever been, but the timing was right: he and his father slammed the door on Mississippi and hit the road for Edom, Utah.

Now they'd passed into Texas, and something was wrong. Jubal looked over at his boy. He couldn't see his face because his son's body was turned away from him. Gideon was leaning against the truck door with his knees pulled up, his back taut. Definitely wrong. "What is it, pup?" asked Jubal. When Gideon turned to his father, Jubal saw the face, the pain face. "What, kiddo?" asked his father. "You want to get out, stretch, walk around a little? Let me pull over." Jubal left the blacktop and came to a stop on the shoulder of the road, but Gideon didn't make a move to get out. "You about to tell me where it hurts or what?" asked Jubal, then, alarmed at having no answer, he climbed down from the cab and went around the front of the truck to open his son's door. When he did, the boy pitched over into his arms, weak and barely conscious. His breathing was shallow, and the heat coming off his body alarmed his father even further.

"Jesus," he said, "we gotta get you to a doctor." He tucked his son's body back onto the seat of the truck, took the wheel, and stepped on the gas. The truck spit gravel from the shoulder and peeled rubber another ten yards down the blacktop. The house trailer thrashed behind them. Jubal damn near stood on the gas as he raced to Sabine Pass. He reached town still running hard and careened onto Main Street at a good fifty miles per hour trying to spot a hospital or a doctor's office. He took the turn on two wheels. The trailer swung violently back and forth. Just as he fought the wheel and straightened out, Jubal heard a siren and looked in his side-view mirror to see a police cruiser, lights flashing, bearing down on the tail of his trailer. Jubal never questioned what he had to do. He wasn't stopping any truck 'til he got to a doctor.

The cruiser stayed right on him as he shot by the hardware store, the drugstore, and the doctor's office on the other side of the street. Jubal caught it and hit the brakes. He hung a U-turn, nearly jackknifed, and screeched to a stop in front of the office. The police cruiser hung its own U-ball and cut off the truck. Both officers jumped out with their guns drawn, but Jubal had already gotten to his son's door by the time they ordered him to halt. "Don't move!" Jubal had Gideon in his arms and was heading for the door with the shingle. "Open the goddamn door," he bellowed. About a second before they pulled their triggers the police got it that this was an emergency. They helped him through the door and stood behind him in the doctor's vestibule as Jubal, his son cradled in his arms, begged for help. Where was the doctor? "My son needs the doctor!" But the doctor had taken the afternoon off to go quail hunting, and there was no way to reach him. The woman behind the desk was only a receptionist, but it was obvious to her that this was an emergency. She asked had the boy ever had his appendix out, and, when Jubal told her no, she told the policemen to get this child to the emergency room in Port Arthur to the north, fifteen miles away, the only hospital around. Pronto. So, with the police cruiser in the lead this time, Jubal raced to Port Arthur knowing that his beloved son was going to die if he didn't get help soon, and might die anyway. When he reached the hospital, Jubal was out of his truck and attempting to cradle Gideon in his arms before the policemen could reach him. "Sir! We've got help now! Sir! Let us take him." Orderlies took Gideon from his father and rushed him inside on a gurney, where a nurse said, "Please, sir," and tried to lead him away, but she might as well not have been there, as Jubal followed the gurney carrying his son into the examination room. By then Gideon's eyes had rolled back into his head. A nurse drew the curtain around them.

"Where's it hurt, son?" asked the young resident.

"His stomach," said Jubal.

"Let him tell me," said the doctor.

"He don't talk," said Jubal.

"What do you mean?"

"I mean he don't talk, goddamnit!"

"Call the OR. We're bringing him up."

"What're you gonna do?" asked Jubal.

"You can't come with us, sir," a woman's voice said.

"Tell me what you're gonna do!"

"Everything we can, sir." Jubal touched his son's head as they pushed the boy out of the examination room. It felt like the boy's brain was baking in a clay pot. A woman's voice suggested he follow her and would he like a cup of coffee? Was he all right? Was who all right? Who were they talking to? Jubal Pickett moved through a fog. He couldn't see a thing, and everything he heard sounded as if it came from somewhere else.

Gideon's appendix had ruptured. His insides were infected by the pus discharged into his system. The medical staff was amazed that the boy withstood so much pain. Would he live? They told Jubal everything but that. It could be days. No one knew.

Jubal stood by his son's bed day and night without knowing what passed or which was which. His job had been to take care of the boy, and look what he let happen. When Gideon was an infant Jubal never once slept on through the whole night. A piece of him was always listening for a sound from his son's room. His hair would feel as if it were crackling with energy, wired to keep him alert. Now the stricken man lacerated himself without mercy. In his mind he begged to be beaten. If his son died, he would die, too, would take his hunting knife and eviscerate himself in the same room, die with his eyes fastened on his dead boy's body.

PART 2

The year 1953 began with the death of Hank Williams and ended in December with Marilyn Monroe as Playmate in the first issue ever of *Playboy* magazine. In the meantime, the Korean War came to a halt, and Abilene Breedlove left her common-law marriage in Muskogee, Oklahoma, and headed south on her lonesome. She'd caught that two-timing bastard between the thighs of her then best friend and came about that close to driving the pointy end of a pickax right through his chest and clear into his cheating heart.

Twenty-eight years ago, Abilene's father named her after the town in Texas where he had left his only true love. That he left her in the arms of another he used as an excuse to act like a reprehensible bastard for the rest of his life. People sent him into a tirade when they pointed out that Abilene wasn't any kind of girl's name. "Goddamnit," he said, "if some low-order

son of a bitch can name his daughter Charlene, Carlene, Marlene, or Darlene, then I can damn well name mine Abilene.
Read your Bible. Ain't no Marlene Darlene there." Then he'd
add, "Abilene's there, numb nuts, chapter and verse. And don't
you dare call her Abby neither!"

Abilene hated her old man so much she ran away from
home at the age of sixteen with one just like him. He called
her Abby, and she fell in love like laundry down a chute. He
didn't last long. Nobody else did, either. "What's a man got in
common with a Good Humor bar?" she'd come to ask. "Once
you lick off the icing they're all the same."

When you grow up with carnage you don't know carnage.
It's not that you don't mind it. You don't *see* it for what it is
or much of anything. You look right through it as if it isn't
there, because it isn't. It's just people in your house doing
the stuff they always do. As for men, you get to understand
that if you're around one long enough, he'll eventually take
a swing at you. What happened after that was up to you.
There were still places in the world where if a man catches
his wife with another man and shoots her, they let him go
free. If he shoots them both they make him mayor. Muskogee was one of those places, but Abilene wasn't convinced
the same rules applied to her. Impaling your ex and his mis-
tress with a pickax would, she was sure, be frowned upon
even though the thought of it was juicier than a Christmas
turkey.

She'd actually had real hopes for this last one. By the time she finally got to him, she'd learned a few things about men, having never been without one more than a few weeks, and that was stretching her to the limit. She felt the need to tote up and start over, finally take the time to think it all out. She kept a pad with her so she could write down things when they came to her, like a list of what she had learned from men. For starters, if a dog don't hunt, you shoot it. That had logic, a dog being a tool, and a tool being useful, or what else did you need it for?

That a man and a woman can look at the same thing and see something entirely different was another thing she learned fully and completely. She might could see Earl's point but that isn't what she'd've done, Earl being the guy she was with at that time. One night they were parked on a hill overlooking an excavation site that was in the process of transforming the countryside into a giant housing tract. Abilene leaned back against his shoulder—Earl's right hand set to slide over against her breast first chance he got—took a swig of vodka, and began to muse about what she'd do with all that land if it was hers. She went on about how she'd put a house close by the river, where she'd put the garden and the apple orchard, but Earl, who loved to work on cars more than anything in this world, Earl looked out on the empty landscape and imagined it filled with junk cars, rows and tiers of them, his idea of consummate beauty. Abilene liked it empty. "But there's nothin' there," yelped Earl. Exactly.

Something else she learned living in the Five Civilized Tribes territory of Oklahoma was that half the men at the bar proudly claim a Cherokee grandmother or a Creek great-grandmother somewhere down the matriarchal line but never a grandfather, never anything with a penis, not an Indian penis, that's for sure. Wouldn't be any family tree with a white woman and an Indian man. Just wouldn't. There was other stuff, too. For a long time Abilene questioned none of it. It was what it was, not so much an issue, and then life served up Ron Don Thompson.

PART 3

Ron Don Thompson was into real estate and community entertainment. He had been stationed in Berlin after the war with the occupation army, quartermaster corps, a cash cow for a farsighted businessman who sensed an opportunity and pounced on it: cigarettes exchanged for a case of Rhine wine, nylons when needed, razor blades for perfume, money paid for money, dollars on demand. He deemed himself an entrepreneur with bigger dreams in mind. Once honorably discharged, he brought his vision back to Muskogee, Oklahoma.

By the time Ron Don Thompson walked boldly through the front door of the Five Tribes diner, Abilene believed she knew a few things, and character was one of them. She stood behind the counter and watched him give each stool a little spin as he walked by. When he chose a booth Abilene gave the girl on the floor five dollars if she switched places with her. "I just got this feeling," she told the girl, checked her lipstick, and walked over to take the man's order. Before he left that booth again he had a T-bone steak, baked potato, apple pie, coffee, and Abilene's phone number. He asked her for it, and she wrote it down on a blank check.

The next day he came to the diner at the same time, and the day after that he came in when she got off, so they had dinner together, which led her to begin to recognize this man as an opportunity different from the others thus far. He had ideas, dreams, plans, and he seemed to want to share them with her. There was something of the pioneer in him. Abilene could see Gary Cooper playing him in the movie.

One evening he invited her back to his place to see some movies he'd brought over from Germany. And then he said the words that really endeared him to her: "Trust me. They aren't blue movies. I respect you too much for that." Good. Abilene was sick and goddamned tired of the grunt 'n' rut school of courtship. It'd been a while since she met a man who was so considerate. She couldn't even think of one.

Ron Don hadn't lied, but what she saw heated her blood nonetheless. The black-and-white images on the portable screen had been taken with a home camera, the kind of rig GIs could buy at the PX on base. They raged and snarled like gigantic leaves swirling in a windstorm, two dogs (she thought they were wolves) fighting with such base ferocity that it was frightening to see, yet when she turned her head away she felt compelled to turn it back. She could not look away for long. The dogs were on their hind legs, each attempting to get its jaws on the other's throat. The smaller and quicker of the two suddenly dropped to all fours and grabbed the larger's left rear leg in its jaws. Abilene found herself rooting for it. She wanted the bigger one down and vanquished, wanted the danger to her side over with. The bigger one dropped and twisted on its back; the match was over. Men and women in the crowd exchanged money and toasted each other with vodka. The film ran and flick-flicka-flicked a blinding white light upon the screen until Ron Don got up to turn it off. When he turned back to Abilene she saw his face as she had never seen it before. Pure desire fixed her. It seemed to her that he leaped across the room in a single bound and took her down. She just lay back her head and howled.

Afterward, he explained the whole dream as she lay exhausted back against her pillow. Ron Don was hardly out of breath. See, the whole idea, he explained, came from him putting two and two together. What she had just witnessed were film clips smuggled out of Russia from a forest south of Moscow. For hundreds of years sheepherders in Russia had to breed and train their dogs to dispatch wolves. Hardscrabble people need a hardscrabble sport. Every year they had contests like these all over the mountains to see what dogs were the toughest. "Yeah," offered Abilene, still murky. "Wolves. Where?"

"That's the beauty part: we don't need wolves. We got pigs!" Ron Don looked as if he expected Abilene to jump up from bed and click her heels over something, but she didn't get what. "Hogs! Wild hogs," he brayed. "That's the secret ingredient."

"You're makin' me feel too stupid," said Abilene.

"Hawg-dawgin'," he said, holding his hands out as if it were too obvious for more words. Abilene still didn't get what this man was telling her, but she had to credit the energy it gave off as fantastic. Oh, God, it don't get much realer! "There's history here," claimed Ron Don with the passion of the true believer, and he set out to educate Abilene Breedlove in the ways of business. Pacing back and forth as he talked, she could tell he was onto something.

"I'm tellin' you, Abby, this thing is so big it's gonna knock baseball right out of Oklahoma. Hawg-dawgin', sweetheart. Hawg-*dawgin'*! Can I spell that right out there for you? H-O-G-D-O-G-G-I-N-G. What's the biggest pest around here? What eats the crops what it don't shit 'n' piss on? And what's mankind been doing about it since time irrememberable? The answer to the first question is hogs, and the answer to the second question is hogs, and the third answer is we hunted them. Now, listen up: this is history. We're getting into roots here. Couple hundred years ago. Maybe more. Conquistadors brought pigs with them as a food supply, then those same pigs went wild. Professors at the university level call them 'feral.' I call 'em the future. Are you with me, Abby? Still with me, baby?"

She wasn't sure she was but she tried very hard to look like she was.

"Follow me down the road, Miss Breedlove," he went on.

Well, hell, she thought, and went right along with him.

"Your daddy did it. His daddy did it. Everybody's daddy did it. Thousands of daddys, thousands of hogs, and thousands of dogs, every one a family favorite, every one bred tough as nails, every one of 'em got pig fever in their blood. Can't you just see it, Abilene? The hog-dawgin' championships in greater

Oklahoma, Muskogee as the very juggernaut of a new breed of fightin' dog. A killer pig with three-inch razor-sharp tusks and a hide like plate armor against the best of breed in Oklahoma. We'll be the Vegas of hog-dog fights."

And then it did, it just fell into place, and she saw it, too. "Have a family night," she said. "Kids under twelve get in free."

"I like the way you're thinkin', Miss Abilene Breedlove," he said. "It's brutal out there. Get the kids used to it."

"Folks can afford this," she said. "Call it the Pig Palace." And the two of them went on dreaming like that deep into the night. They sifted through lots more names—Pig Paradise, the Pork Shop, Pig Pen Productions, Pig in a Poke, the Polish Pig, and more. They rejected Pig in a Poke because nobody knew what a poke was, and they rejected the Polish Pig because nobody was from Poland. Kids would be free; they decided certain on that, a family business, cheap and wholesome entertainment being the best way to go. Yes, it was a brutal sport, but, hey, so's the world, buddy, so our kids best be getting used to it. The house would not sponsor gambling, but if folks wanted to make a little side bet with their neighbor, that was their right and business. And if they wanted to leave 25 percent of the wager as a gratuity to the little lady manning the refreshment stand (that'd be Abilene), well, that would be much appreciated. They'd even have greased pig contests for the kids, probably the ones too chewed up to fight anymore, and how about a gift shop, sell pens with the name Pig Pen on it, key chains, stuff like that. By the time Abilene slept she, too, was convinced that Ron Don Thompson himself was gonna do for Muskogee what Mr. Henry Ford done for Detroit.

Now, why'd that dumb bat-shit bastard have to go and fuck things up? Dumb. Dumb. D-U-M-B! She'd thought they were doing pretty good together. Sometimes she'd hand him a Phillips-head screwdriver when he wanted the other one, but, mostly, pretty good. He liked her idea about getting a discount from Dr Pepper if they'd hang a sign and told her to get on it. The gift shop would be hers to set up whatever way she wanted. He'd start lining up the fights. So what the hell went and happened was that he could not keep the one-eyed pig in his pants.

The first time it happened Abilene could kind of sort of understand that. It was with his old girlfriend, and everybody knows damn well that people get so used to having sex with each other then they can't stop when they should stop. She had no intention for their discussion to turn into a heated argument, but turn it did. He shook his fist at her, and she told him if he hit her he'd better damn sight never close his eyes again because she'd burn him to death in his bed. It got nasty, but they'd got through it.

Things after that did get back to being pretty good. Dr Pepper agreed to a discount. She took to signing her name "Abbi." Ron Don was getting calls and letters all the time. People were frothing at the mouth to pit their dog against another's. It looked like they'd hit the jackpot. He took to saying that a good idea sells itself, and he made certain the counter at the refreshment stand was just the right height for Abbi. She began to see how good life could be. Yeah, so then why'd that stupid son of a bitch once again have to blow their boat out of the goddamn water? And with her best friend! My God, the bitch had oatmeal on her thighs and "bacne" (which is how Abilene referred to pimples on your back), not to mention the loyalty factor, or lack thereof! It went through her mind that maybe it was just a mercy fuck, but then so what? Did he even care who it was? Apparently not is how it turned out. "Old enough to bleed, old enough to butcher" was his motto, which is what Abilene found out, so by the time she caught RD and her best friend she was truly boiling. They were butt naked in the middle of the day, and he was pumping away like an oil rig when Abilene bounced a can of fruit cocktail off the back of his head. He howled and rolled off the bed, whereupon she leaped on her ex–best friend and tried to smother her with the pillow that had been under the woman's ass. But RD came up off the floor and stunned her with a blindside right, at which point he and the girl bolted out the door still naked.

Abilene tore the place up, *tore the place up*! A rampage is what it was. She squirted charcoal lighter fluid all over the mattress and lit it. Then she took the scrapbook she'd been saving with all their pictures showing how far they'd come and tossed it into the flames.

The fire department trucks and two squad cars arrived at about the same time, sirens wailing. It sounded like an air raid in the neighborhood. Smoke boiled out the bedroom window. Burning newspaper clippings rose over the roof. Neighbors gawked as Abilene was led away in handcuffs. RD pressed charges. Malicious mischief and battery got her six months in county jail. When she was released RD hit her with a restraining order that forever kept her off the premises. He gave her nothing. Everything was in RD's name, and she could go ahead and sue if she wanted to, she wasn't going to get a goddamn penny. Abilene had given her all to their joint enterprise, and what she got back was a dump truck load of grief. The last she heard his creditors were chasing him, and the SPCA and the health department were each trying to shut him down, but she thought anything short of injecting him with the plague was not punishment enough.

PART 4

Jubal Pickett continued to stand watch over his son's hospital bed like the angel with the flaming sword guarding the gates of Eden. He knew he could not weaken because if he weakened his boy would die, so he sought images of strength: himself stiff and straight as a pike, himself wrapped tightly in baling wire, himself a block of reinforced concrete. He could not and would not come undone. A beard does not grow if you are dead, so each morning he would take heart from the few scraggly hairs on the boy's soft face. Only once in days had the boy opened his eyes, and then the expression on his face—eyes wide, pupils rolling up—was as if he'd seen something hideous crawling up the opposite wall. Jubal called his name— "Gideon"—and the boy's head rolled toward his father, the eyes went wider—"Gideon"—then relaxed into . . . It was as if the boy reached for a smile and could not quite get it, but that was close enough for his father. The eyes closed again. A small sign. Some hope. Jubal held tightly to his son's hand.

She had been watching him for a while now from her position at the sixth-floor nurse's station. When he slept she did not know. What he ate she did not know. She once brought him a Coca-Cola, and he thanked her for it, but she didn't think he knew who gave it to him, whether it was a man or a woman or whatever it was. Before he even took one sip he wet a corner of a clean washrag with cola and touched it to the boy's lips. The kid was burning up, and the poor man stood by unable to do one single thing about it. The boy had got poison all over his insides when his appendix blew. Pretty much every case she ever heard of the patient died, not that her medical experience was so vast, because she'd only been the sixth-floor receptionist a month or so, not full-time either. A floater.

Although she'd been on the job only a few weeks, Abilene had actually been in Texas for three months, going on more. The timing had been right. Her second cousin's husband down in Port Arthur walked out on her about the same time Abilene was trying to put as much space between herself and Muskogee as possible. In a letter to Abilene, her cousin, Corinne, wrote how her husband had "left me rattling around alone in this great big double-wide with nobody in it." She was really more like a sister than a cousin. They had grown up together in Muskogee before Corinne got married and moved away. She practically said she'd pay Abilene's way to come see her. "Come on down, sis, and let's us do some serious damage," she wrote. Abilene didn't think the offer sounded half-bad. "You don't have to worry about a place to stay, and I've got plenty of Twinkies in the fridge," continued the letter. So Abilene packed what she could carry and hopped a Greyhound south.

Did Abilene and her cousin do some damage? For a while there, it was batten down the hatches. Abilene wasn't off the bus an hour when she and Corinne were hoisting chillies and dancing Texas swing at the local honky-tonk out to Sabine Lake, where her cousin toasted the whole goddamn barroom at the top of her lungs, "Here's to the bee what stung the bull what got the bull a-buckin', and here's to Adam and Eve, what got the world a-fuckin'!" Everybody in the joint drank to that one. Up until that moment, Abilene hadn't known she'd signed on for hazardous duty, but she vowed to take it like a man. Lord! The taste of freedom! Move over, Kitty Wells. Make room, Hank Williams. Here's two more honky-tonk angels. I shake out my hair the way men like, and he notices. Do I need a light? Sure, cowboy. Light me. I smoke Luckies. You? asked with the head slightly cocked to the side, lips just open, as if about to blow a smoke ring.

Corinne took a few days' sick leave coming to her from the hospital, where she worked the cash register in the cafeteria but sometimes filled in behind the steam table when they were short. She told Abilene not to worry, she had the tab, then the two second cousins gave their Muskogee High cheer and commenced to do their best to tear up Port Arthur. Which was all well and good. For a while. As far as Abilene was concerned, really, it got old pretty fast, for, irregardless of the fact that RD was a prick, she had come to think of herself as a one-guy gal.

Listen, she reasoned, they're all pricks, but you had to have one anyway. So she had to admit she was relieved when Corinne's husband moved back into the house. At first. But then it got real awkward. Corinne'd had her taste of freedom and cursed the day she ever let that slob come home. In her brief foray into the Port Arthur social scene Corinne had acquired quite a following, and, goddamnit, she wasn't about to give it up. She talked Abilene into covering for her, like, would Abby go to a movie and say the two of them went together, or say they went shopping all afternoon? Abilene wasn't crazy about this setup at all, and she especially wasn't crazy about it when Corinne's husband started acting in a manner designed to pry her panties off and began to make revolting suggestions about the three of them. Worse was the day Corinne exploded because she believed Abilene was playing it both ways (which was not even remotely true). Her and him? What's his name? Tug? Abilene thought the word *oink* had been invented to describe men like her second cousin's husband. How could Corinne even think it? But she did, and Abilene took that as a sign to move on. Which is how she came to her job as a temp sixth-floor receptionist at the same hospital as Corinne.

Corinne had the hots for this doctor who she swore had a cute friend, just adorable, another doctor, a proctologist, so one day these two guys just happened to show up to the house with Abilene's favorite food—Chinese takeout—at dinnertime. Corinne hadn't gotten three bites through an egg roll when she and her doctor disappeared into the bedroom with the hot mustard and duck sauce. Abilene and Connor—that was his name—sat there at the kitchen table trying to pick up rice with chopsticks and feeling really stupid. Abilene was chewing on a water chestnut when she broke the silence by asking him what a prognosticator does. "A prognosticator predicts the future," answered Connor.

"Wait a minute," said Abilene, "I thought you were a doctor."

"I am," he said.

"What's being a doctor got to do with predicting the future? People don't need you to tell them when they're gonna die, do they?"

"A proctologist," he said.

"What?" she asked.

"Not a prognosticator," he explained. "A proctologist."

"What's he do?" she wanted to know, baffled.

"He deals with disorders of the rectum and anus," he said.

That stopped her.

"Actually," Connor went on, "the rectum, anus, colon, and pelvic floor."

"I didn't know my pelvis had a floor," she wondered aloud.

"Everybody's does," he said.

"I guess so," she sort of mumbled. Aw, damn, she wished Corinne'd come out of that bedroom! "Let me know if I got this straight now," she went on. "A proctologist tells the future by looking up a man's ass?"

"Hey," he chortled when he saw the look on her face, "that's a good one."

"And you thought I was just another pretty face," she said, and winked.

"Take hemorrhoids, for instance," he said.

"Excuse me?"

"Hemorrhoids," he answered, warming to the subject. "Inflammation of the veins in the rectum and anus."

"Ouch." She winced and clenched her bottom.

"Very painful," he went on. "But maybe not as painful as anal fissures."

"Hold on a second. Does your wife let you talk to her about stuff like this?" she asked with a sly smile and a very coy spin on her words.

"What wife?" He practically yelped it at her.

"The one you promised to love, honor, and obey. What's-her-name. You know."

"How'd you guess?" he asked meekly.

"It wasn't a guess," said Abilene.

"I should go, huh?" asked Connor, standing up.

"Who's driving," asked Abilene, "you or your buddy?"

"My buddy."

"Looks like you're here for the duration, Doc," she said, "so sit down and tell me something I don't know."

"Like what?"

"Wow, Doc, you want me to do all the work, don't you? OK. Let's play a game. You think of something you've always wanted to tell your wife but you're afraid to because you know she doesn't want to hear it, then you tell me. *I* let you. See? Sound like something you'd like to do? With me? Abilene Breedlove? Tell me anything. It's OK."

"Anything I want?"

"Anything you want," she purred.

"Are you ready?" he asked.

"Oh, yeah, Doc, I'm ready," she assured him.

He took a deep breath and blurted out: "Hemorrhoids changed the face of Europe!"

"Whoa," she said.

"Do you have any idea why Napoleon rode sidesaddle?" asked Connor as if he were about to reveal the word of God.

"Hemorrhoids?" she tendered.

"Yes!" he cried. "Hemorrhoids!" He was ecstatic. "Did you ever think what might have happened at Waterloo if Napoleon'd had his hemorrhoids fixed?"

Abilene had not.

"We'd probably be speaking French and eating frogs, and that's a hell of a way to live."

She guessed it would be.

"God, it feels so good to get this out!" he cried. "Thank you!"

"I'd say 'anytime,' but you're taken," she said as she straightened his tie. "Now, Doc, tell you what you do: you buy that wife of yours twelve red roses and a box of chocolates, then you go home where you belong and the two of you cuddle on the front porch swing."

"We live in an apartment." He shrugged.

"Well, damn it, son, find someplace to sit down, and make sure she gets the one with the cherry in the middle."

Connor was grateful for the advice and proved it when Abilene needed him. He was the one who helped her get her job as a receptionist at the hospital when she left Corinne's house. Abilene had her choice of jobs, but saying hi and showing people the way was more her style than standing at a cash register in the cafeteria or emptying bedpans. For certain, there was no longer any room under the same roof for Abilene and Corinne and Tug.

———————

It just came over her one day while sitting there by the telephone at the nurse's station. Abilene had never seen herself as a deep thinker. She knew she was plenty quick enough to count change and to laugh at a good joke when she heard one, but even back in high school her dreams weren't large ones. She gave some thought to joining the navy and becoming a nurse when she graduated, partly because she thought those crisp, white uniforms the WAVES wore were pretty spiffy, but respect for authority was never high on her list of character traits, so a career in the military was not her best idea. However, nothing else ever really grabbed her interest. She did work in a flower shop for a while, which she liked, but no way could she raise the kind of money needed to go into that business. However, the one big thing she did take away from working with that despicable son of a bitch RD was that she could be a good partner and help a good man make some good money. This would, she knew, take some adjustment on her part, but she vowed to try.

———————

On a slow day in a backwater hospital Abilene was left with nothing much to do except sit there and think, sneak a peek at fan magazines (Jeanne Crain used Lustre-Creme shampoo, too, la-de-da), and look at strange faces. She saw some bona fide lulus, too. One of them was an honest-to-God albino who wore thick sunglasses inside. He had blue irises and beady, red pupils like match heads that Abilene could see when he took off his glasses to wipe the lenses.

But the strangest creature to get off that elevator and come down the hall was, in Abilene's considered judgment, over-qualified for Ripley's. She had gotten so used to the elevator door opening and closing that Abilene rarely looked in that direction when it happened. This time when the elevator bell rang, she didn't know why she looked over, but she did. As the doors opened, a man and a woman got off together, each hold-ing the hand of what looked to be a monkey between them dressed in little girls' clothes like in the circus, a small chim-panzee, to be precise. The problem was that it didn't walk with that rolling, knuckle-dragging, simian gait; it walked like a little kid, a two-year-old, a long shot at two and a half. Abilene was shocked to realize that the reason this thing walked like a little kid was because it was a little kid, a tiny girl, her face, arms, hands, and legs covered with strawberry-blond hair, flaxen in texture, not bristly or wiry as you might expect. She wore a daisy-yellow pinafore and celery-green leggings, but it was obvious that her entire body was covered with hair, flaxen, rich, strawberry-blond hair.

Abilene was cool enough not to recoil on the surface, but on the inside she retched and prayed she wouldn't toss her lunch. When she saw them heading smack in her direction she was hor-rified. Every muscle in her body screamed at her to dive under the desk. It was like this troll had jumped out from under a rick-ety bridge in some forest somewhere and demanded tribute of the most hideous kind from her. What did this creature want?

The little thing stopped at Abilene's desk and tendered her a slip of paper. Abilene took it, and it was like taking something from an animal's paw. The slip was machine printed with the words *My name is* and then, handwritten underneath, the words *Sophie Rose*. Abilene stared at the slip of paper, reluctant to raise her eyes to meet the others'. She kept her face down as she looked for the child's name in the floor's register. Abilene scanned the list of patients top to bottom and back. There was nobody by that name scheduled for admittance, and then it occurred to Abilene to check the floor number on the slip of paper, whereby she discovered that these folks wanted the children's ward and that was another one up. She had to tell them. She had to look up. "Lord, don't fail me now," she mumbled to herself, pulled her head up straight, and looked right into the little thing's eyes. They were a deep green, the shade of a summer leaf. Abilene steeled herself. "Are you Sophie Rose?" she asked. The little thing nodded its head. "See, Miss Rose," Abilene said, "tell your mommy and daddy this says seventh floor but you wound up on"—she wrote out the number six and traced it with her finger like she remembered her second-grade teacher doing—"sixth," she said, and smiled. Who the hell made you Miss Biggety Britches? she had admonished herself. What would you do if it was a puppy or a baby seal? You'd think it was real cute, so shut yourself up, Abilene!

"Say thank you to the lady," said the child's mother.

"Thank you," said the little thing.

"I'll come up and pay you a visit, OK? It's nice here," said Abilene as they turned back toward the elevator. "You take your medicine now."

Later, while leafing through a magazine, she saw that Rita Hayworth and the little thing both had the same color hair, and that's when this weird idea came to her. It struck her that what you should do when looking at people's faces (which was exactly what she did do all day long) was to look for what somebody else who loved that person might find there. Somebody ugly was not ugly to somebody. She didn't know why she thought of it or even where that thought came from, because it wasn't like anything she had thought before, but there it was, alive and kicking. What started out as a game to offset boredom turned into a gripping revelation that then made every person who walked by more a human being to be divined than a creature to be designated. It truly helped to pass the time.

———

Abilene was particularly interested in the man with the son in 667 at the end of the hall. She'd been watching him for days now as he tended to the boy. The critical point had come and gone but the days before must have been a nightmare for the man, who Abilene now knew as Jubal Pickett. The boy had been so hot with fever you could damn near feel the heat boiling out of his room. At one point the fever spiked, and the boy's entire body quivered with a fit. Right after that they sat him on the floor in a cold shower to drive the fever down. His father had stripped naked and got in to hold the boy and rock him gently while the cold spray rained down on the two of them. It must have been an hour he held his boy like that. Afterward, the boy dried, dressed in a fresh gown, and back

in bed, his father dried and dressed as well, they each fell
asleep, exhausted.

Abilene's shift was over just about that time, too. She went
down the hall to the boy's room to see if Mr. Pickett wanted
something from the cafeteria before she went home, coffee or
a bowl of soup, some black cherry Jell-O maybe. But the two
of them were fast asleep, the boy in his bed, his father in a chair
beside him. He sure is a pretty one, that boy, thought Abilene
as she watched him sleep. Movie-star pretty. It didn't appear
to Abilene like those looks came from his father's side, but
it was hard to tell given that the man had been under such a
strain. It's got to be the worst thing in the world to bury a child,
and the next worst thing is to worry that you'll have to. She
watched Mr. Pickett as he slept. God, he must be uncomfortable, all twisted up in that chair, she thought. He wasn't a bad-
looking man, a little on the short side, but, hell, so was Alan
Ladd. In fact, a lot of those movie stars were short: Cagney,
Raft, Richard Widmark, though she wasn't totally sure of him,
but Abilene was savvy enough to know you didn't judge a man
by a movie star. The man in the chair was a good man, and she
knew that. She could tell. Abilene knew she was being ridicu-
lous, given the circumstances, but one of the things that interested her about Mr. Pickett was that he never seemed to notice
her, not that she expected him to, under the circumstances, but
still. Abilene had been told more than once that she had a body
that would make a dead man weep, and the course of her life
had given her no reason to doubt it. One of the things Abilene
liked about her job was that she got to wear a tight white uniform. Abilene wondered sometimes if people thought she was

a nurse. Of course, she didn't have the little hat. Once, back home, she even got a proposition to do an auto parts calendar. Abilene thought about it, too, thought about herself splayed lengthwise over a black and silver Harley 1200, but then she came to the opinion that she didn't want her picture hanging in some grease monkey's crapper. She often wondered if that was a crossroad in her life.

Abilene stood there; she didn't know how long. She had lost complete track of the time. Jubal Pickett really does have a nice face all asleep and relaxed, she thought. Abilene turned back to look at Gideon again before she left the room and was startled to see the boy awake and staring at her. It was somewhat unnerving, she had to admit. He did not blink, and it seemed as if he had been watching her a good long while. Abilene shuddered a little. Her mother used to say, whenever such a shiver happened, that a ghost walked over her grave. "Hi. How you doin'?" whispered Abilene so as not to awaken the boy's father. The boy didn't answer. "Your name's Gideon, right?" Not a word, not a nod of the head. "Is there anything I can get you?" she asked, still in a whisper. Gideon just stared at her without uttering a word. She shuddered again and felt the ghost. "OK, well," she said, and forced a breezy tone on herself. "Ring the buzzer if you need anything." But still Abilene walked out of that room with an unsettled feeling.

Abilene was one cigarette into her coffee break with half an eye on Corinne working the register when she noticed Gideon Pickett's father standing at the door to the hospital cafeteria.

He looked around, squinting like a man staring into bright sunlight. When Pickett finally spotted Abilene, to her surprise he headed directly toward the table where she sat and stopped beside her. She noticed he had a little pep to his step now that his boy was out of danger and on the mend. He had a kid with one strong constitution, that's for sure.

"Excuse me, ma'am," said Pickett. He held a summer straw cowboy hat in his hand.

"Sit down," she said. "Have a cup of coffee."

"I believe I will," he said, "thank you," and went to fetch his cup.

"I don't know how anybody can drink that stuff when it's black," quipped Abilene as he came back and sat down opposite her, but she was smiling and didn't mean a thing negative by it. Abilene had always been good at breaking the ice.

"How do you take it?" he asked.

"Four sugars and lots of cream," she replied.

"Why don't you just order a banana split?" he asked.

"If you're talking hot fudge, I'm your girl," she said, again with a smile.

Then Jubal Pickett got deadly serious and said, "Uh, listen, Miss, um?"

"You can call me Abby," she said.

"Miss Abby—"

"Just Abby's OK, Mr. Pickett."

"I just wanted to thank you, um, Abby, for all the kindnesses you've shown me and my son while we been here."

"I'm surprised you knew I was in the room," she said.

"It dawned on me," he said. "I guess I can be kind of slow

sometimes," he said, mocking himself. "And Gideon always tells me."

"Gideon does?" she asked, perplexed, but stopped herself there.

"Believe me, when he wants something bad enough he lets me know it," said Jubal. "You know about teenagers, right?"

"I guess I do," she said.

"Moody," he explained.

"Right. Moody teenagers," she said. "It seems like I've just been one. Hey, I hear he's going to be all right now."

"Don't put anything beyond that boy once he decides to do it," said Pickett. "He's got a will of iron."

"He's a good-lookin' boy, too, that's for sure," she said. "Got a lot of his dad in him."

"Oh, yeah, I'm a handsome devil, if the light's out and your glasses is cracked," said Jubal.

"I don't wear glasses," said Abby, "and it's bright as day in here." Then, shifting the subject, she said, "Not much you love in life more than your boy, is there?"

"There's nothin'. Nothin'."

"Where's his mother?" she asked.

"Far away where she can't do damage," said Pickett.

"She's dead?" Abilene asked.

"That'll do," he replied.

"One of your favorite people," she said, and laughed.

"Up there with the Antichrist."

"But Mr. Jubal Pickett is not a man to bear grudges."

"Only one," he said, and laughed.

Something told Abilene she could place a bet on this man.

"I know this is gonna seem to come out of left field," said Jubal, "but I haven't sat down to eat since we got here, so why don't you help me celebrate? Let me buy you dinner. We'll find a fancy restaurant, eat a couple of thick steaks, fries, onion rings, ice cream . . ."

"Hold the ice cream," she said. "Gotta keep my girlish figure."

"Is that a yes?" he asked.

"Let's go one better," she suggested. "Come on over my place for a home-cooked meal. I got the stove, you get the steak, and let's cook us up a dinner we won't forget. We can stop off at the butcher on the way. Pick up a can of Crisco, too. Want me to call you Jubal or what?"

That night Abilene cooked Texas-style chicken-fried steak with cream gravy, mashed potatoes, and black-eyed peas (which, she informed him, were, in point of fact, beans and not peas). If Texas had a national dish, chicken-fried steak would be it. For starters she served up a batch of fried jalapeños, all of it washed down with cold cans of Mitchell's Premium Beer. Finally, for dessert there was French vanilla ice cream with Hershey's chocolate syrup. Where a man the size of Alan Ladd put all that food she did not know, but he damn near ate himself into a coma. By the time the night was over and the dishes put away, Abilene Breedlove had bored a hole through the skull of Jubal Pickett, crept inside his brain, and searched out all his dreams.

They were nice dreams, too, and she enjoyed listening to them. That one about treasure in the desert was a good one. He was a likable guy and a good talker. Abilene decided if Jubal was a cake, he'd be chocolate inside and out, her favorite combination, easy to indulge when she wasn't watching her weight. One of the things that tickled her about him was the way the man ate. Jubal could get more on a fork than any man alive. He'd spend time pushing the black-eyed peas to mix in with the butter and mashed potatoes. Then he'd take a glob, fix it to a piece of meat the same size, raise the fork with a steady hand, and smile—always that smile on his face when he looked at a fork-load of food—then his eyebrows would go up, every time, and he'd take that fork-load into his mouth like it was the finest thing of its kind on earth, and then he'd chew and chew with that same smile on his face. Jubal Pickett didn't bolt his food; he savored it, stretched out each of its flavors, smiled like a man having a great nap.

When he told Abilene about his plans he explained that he was, fundamentally, a practical man, and so all his decisions were based on sound reasoning. "Take where I'm going," he said, "Edom, Utah. You're sayin' to yourself, what's so special about a place nobody ever heard of? But I heard of it, and I got a good sense of these things. I said to myself if the treasure is at Edom, Utah, what am I doing in Natchez, Mississippi? Abby, see, a man knows when he's not movin'. He knows when he's stopped up, kind of constipated in the mind, so to speak. Stop long enough, and you're dead. Keep movin'. I only got a few words to live by, and that's one of them. I arrived at the point where I believed that to get money I had to be near money, but me 'n' Mississippi money had got to be strangers, and nothing was gonna happen unless I moved on. Trust me, Abby, it wasn't me and work that had the problem. I believe in hard work. I believe in prayer, too, but you've got to be near the work to do it, and if it ain't there, no amount of prayer's going to put it there. You move on to where it is.

"So, right now, if I was you, Miss Abilene Breedlove, sitting here across the table listening to all this razzmatazz from a perfect stranger, I'd be asking myself what a cracker from Mississippi knows about prospecting in Utah. Well, here's your answer: this cracker before you been reading up on mining, and he sent for an extension course on the geology of southern Utah from the state university up there at Logan. I learned so damn much somebody ought to give me a college degree," he said, laughed, and gave a whoop. "Some people might think I got a BS degree already, but let me tell you something I know to be true: most of these poor bastards are going to go home poorer than they were when they left. Know why? Either the sun's going to beat them, or some slick lowlife's going to swindle them. Know why? 'Cause they never educated theirselves. They didn't plan, but I did. I been cutting down on my water consumption ever since this idea took me because in the desert you got to learn how to do without it. And that's just one example. Plan for the worst, and never take no for an answer."

He claimed to be wise, but, in fact, Abilene saw him as a little boy, an innocent who didn't yet know he could not have everything he wanted. Jubal's enthusiasm was catching. Abilene didn't know anybody else like him: all things possible, every option on the table. Oh, yeah, OK, she did have to admit that RD, that son of a bitch, was enthusiastic in his own way, but who else did RD really love besides himself and dogfights? Jubal Pickett's real treasure was his son; this was clear as cold water. All things came from that.

If he could've twisted his big, dumb foot around backward, Jubal would have kicked himself in his own dumb ass. For starters, he cleaned out the cans of beer and ate every speck of food off the woman's table. After that, he wiped his plate with a wad of Wonderbread until it had a spit shine. He guessed he didn't know he was that hungry, but it had been days since he'd eaten a meal that counted for anything, plus the fact that everything she made was so damn tasty. Jubal figured when he wasn't eating he was talking, and even when he *was* eating, he couldn't seem to stifle his pipes. Blah blah blah. The thing is, he wanted to talk as much as he wanted to eat, maybe more. It had been so long since he'd had a conversation with a serious adult. But, really, all he could remember from dinner was the sound of his own voice blabbing through a mouth full of food. He guessed she got him to talk all right. Blah blah. However, what truly amazed Jubal was that this woman actually heard him, listened to him 'til he forgot the time and had to run all the way back to the hospital before the doors closed and kept him out for the night. Just as the night watchman was a key-twist away from setting the lock, Jubal made it back through the hospital's main door. He took the stairs two at a time to the sixth floor, so he was panting when he finally got back to his son's room.

One footstep across the threshold into Gideon's room and Jubal felt it: like stepping out from air-conditioning into the remorseless heat of the Sahara. Shadrach, Meshach, and Abednego!

Whoa! What's wrong here? Gideon was awake and staring at him. "Hey, kiddo, what's the matter? Uh-oh. I got it. Begrudge your old man two of God's great gifts, a good meal and a pretty lady? Even you ain't that coldhearted," said Jubal with a wink and a smile, and flopped back into the armchair where he usually sat and slept. By now, he expected the boy to smile back at him, to join in the joke, only Gideon didn't. "I apologize for being gone so long, pup, but I'm here to tell you that a man needs the company of females from time to time, and when he is denied it ain't natural. You're getting to the point where pretty soon we're going to have to tie you down, you'll see. Pretty soon it's going to be, 'Dad, can I have the pickup? Dad, can I have two bucks to take Betty Sue to the drive-in? Dad, I swear that scratch wasn't there when I parked.' Just wait. Make you write a hundred times, 'A stiff dick hath no conscience.' Come on, amigo. Ease up on the old guy. Hey, want to see a magic trick?" Jubal stood up, pulled a red bandanna from his pocket, and flourished it with a snap. "Watch close now. I'm a slippery son of a seersucker suit." Jubal showed Gideon both sides of the bandanna, as a magician would and then a bullfighter with his cape. He went on to show Gideon both sides of his hands and each of his armpits. "Nothing up my sleeve. Nothing up my ass. Uh-uh, can't smile. Do not S-M-I-L-E. Smile and the trick stops here. OK. All right. Like I said, nothing under my arms. Nothing up my ass. Watch out, buddy; I think I see a little piece of smile. Get rid of it." Jubal took the bandanna and covered his right hand with a proper flourish. "This is where you come in, pup. Pay attention. Sprinkle the bandanna with magic dust. What do you mean there ain't no magic dust here? Check your damn pajama pocket. Lemme see what you got there," said Jubal, checking Gideon's pajama pocket. "Nothing there. You're right. But I just happen to have some right here in my pants pocket. Had some of it wrapped in this old bandanna." Jubal took some "magic dust" from his jeans pocket and sprinkled it over the handkerchief. "OK. Say the magic words. Come on. Abracadabra. I can feel the magic! By God, I can feel the magic working. Tum-ta-ta-tum . . ." Jubal whisked the bandanna off his hand—"Voilà!"—and revealed his right middle finger punching straight up in the air. Gideon smiled and turned his head away. "Don't you laugh now. Uh-uh. Against the rules. Not allowed to laugh. Didn't know your old man was so full of tricks, did you, pup?" asked Jubal, and ruffled his son's hair. "Hey, you want your arrowheads and stuff? Where are they? Oh, yeah." Jubal reached down under the bed, retrieved a cigar box, and handed it to Gideon. "Here you go. I'm just gonna set here and read the paper." He sat back down again and shuffled the newspaper a little, but it wasn't long before Jubal Pickett fell fast asleep. The newspaper slipped off his lap, caught a little air, and fluttered to the floor.

———

It amazed him that his father could twist himself into that hospital room chair like he did until he got a fit. Didn't look like that chair could sit a midget. It was like packing a suitcase with too many clothes and then trying to close it. Stuff sticks out all over the place. His father slept on his right side with his knees tucked up to his chest. His feet dangled over the frayed edge of the brown leatherette seat. His right hand cushioned his head, and his left gripped the arm of the chair as if to keep himself from slipping to the floor like the newspaper had earlier slipped off his lap.

Gideon did not like being angry with his dad, so he was glad he didn't feel that way anymore. He watched his old man's eyeballs move behind closed lids and wondered what he was looking at. Gideon could tell by listening to the quality of Jubal's snore what kind of dream his father was having. A nice low purr meant it was something good; bursts of snorts, grunts, and hacks meant it was something bad. One night, back in Natchez, Gideon had been in bed listening to a radio station playing Hank Williams singing "I'll Never Get Out of this World Alive," which was his last hit before he actually did drop dead, though he really didn't actually drop dead like all-of-a-sudden for-what-seemed-like-no-good-reason dead. Whiskey killed him. That's when his dad told him, "Stay away from that stuff. Hank was only twenty-nine. Had the world at his feet, but it burned him out." Beer was OK as long as you didn't drink too much of it.

That same night his father's snorts got to sound like the playing card you attached to the wheel of your bike when you wanted it to whop against the spokes, and suddenly Gideon heard his father scream out in anger, "Get off me! Get off me! Get off of me!" Someone had broken into their house and attacked his father. Gideon grabbed his pocketknife and ran to his father's room to help him. What he saw was his father still sound asleep but struggling to push something only he could see off his face. He shook his father awake, and when Jubal finally came back to his senses and realized what happened, he began to laugh like he'd just been told the best joke in the history of the world. He tousled his son's hair. "You must've thought it was something awful going on, huh? Somebody hurting your old man?" he said, still tickled at what he had dreamed. "Want to know what it was? Swear to God, I was dreaming that a fat woman was trying to sit on my face. Swear. To. God. That's the truth. She was trying to sit on my face, and I was trying to push her off." Gideon smiled when he thought about all this. He felt safe now with his father asleep in the chair beside him, but he did not have a good feeling about that woman who was always stopping by his room.

She came by the next morning, too, a few minutes before the shift change when she needed to be at her station. This time Abilene walked in carrying a brown paper shopping bag. "Morning, gents," she said, and, taking a red and white checked gingham place mat from the bag, she snapped it in the air and smoothed it out on Gideon's bed table. Then she cranked the table to exactly the right height. "Growing boys ought to start the day with a good breakfast," she instructed as she took from the bag two fried-egg-and-bacon sandwiches on buttered toast. "Bet you're tired of hospital food, young man, and I already know that old man over on that chair there has an appetite." Abilene looked over at Jubal and winked as if he and she shared something. "One for each of you," she said, handing them the sandwiches. Next Abilene took out fresh sliced orange quarters wrapped in wax paper, a thermos of coffee, a handful of sugar packets, a quart bottle of milk, and three glazed doughnuts, and arranged them on the place mat. Jubal was dazzled by her performance. Gideon fixed her with an angry stare. Abilene didn't acknowledge either one of them. Instead, she picked up a doughnut in her hand and passed it under her nose in a parody of wine etiquette. "Mmm. Nice bouquet. I'm on a diet, gents, so all I'm allowed to eat is this one teeny doughnut," she said, biting down and savoring it. "Mmm, people, sooo good. Chow down!" She sat down on the bed, crossed her legs, and demolished the rest of that doughnut. Jubal thought he'd never seen anything so sexy in all his life. "How are you doing there, handsome?" she asked Gideon, and tousled his hair. He jerked his head away from her as if from an open flame. "They're gonna keep you in this hospital you act that way," said Jubal. Gideon's eyes snapped to his father's face. His mouth was tight. "You got a pretty woman sitting on your bed feeding you food and compliments, and you pull away? Son, you must be a damn sight sicker than we thought."

"I don't burn, and I don't bite, sweetheart," said Abilene. "Who do you think keeps them red Indians from coming in your room and taking your scalps when you and your daddy are both asleep at the same time? Didn't know that, did you? There's stuff you can learn, believe me."

Breakfast wasn't the last time that day that Abilene visited the Picketts in their hospital room, either. Early morning, during his rounds, Gideon's doctor said he saw no reason the boy couldn't be discharged the next day. He pronounced Gideon a good soldier, made him promise on a handshake to take it easy for two or three days and come in for a final checkup to make certain he was fit to travel.

"If you strike it rich in those uranium fields, you come back and treat me to a lobster dinner," the doctor said, shook Gideon's hand again, and left the room. Then it seemed like all of a sudden—whammo—Abilene appeared at the door with the makings of root beer floats with vanilla ice cream as a celebration. Gideon thought his father must have told her it was his favorite, or else how'd she know, and what the hell right did his father have to talk about him with her?

"Come on, Gideon, drink up. You know it's your favorite," encouraged his father, but Gideon made no move to pick up his float. He didn't even acknowledge that it was there. "You know what the best part about your being stubborn is? I get doubles. Drink it or sink it, Buster Brown. We're not talking about castor oil, son. We're talking about a root beer float. Don't tell me you ain't dying to jump into that glass with all your clothes on."

"If I may be so bold," Abilene said, placing herself between the two of them. "You know what the best thing about your boy is, Mr. Pickett? He's a young man with a mind of his own. He'll buck the crowd before he'll do what he don't think is right. That's the kind of man you want to vote for. Stick to your guns, son. You're a red-blooded American boy, and you don't tumble to anything you don't find true. You don't have to drink it if you don't want it, but I gotta tell you something that's a real live fact of my life right this very minute: what I need right now worse than anything else pure and simple is a cigarette, and I bet your daddy wants one, too. Please let me borrow him for fifteen minutes. A woman got accosted in the waiting room just a bit ago. In the telephone booth. Guy just reached in and tweaked her titty. Oh, boy, she screamed bloody murder! If that was me I'd've mashed my cigarette into the pervert's hand. But I say why tempt fate? Let me and your daddy just go have a quick smoke." She fluffed his pillow and fidgeted with the bed table. "I'll have him back here before you know it."

"I've got to pump out the bilge, anyway, Gideon," said his father. "Hold the fort 'til we get back." Jubal leaned over the bed and, in a confidential whisper, said, "You may be able to resist a pretty woman, but I can't." He pulled his head back and winked at his son. "I'm weak, son, and I'm a sinner. It's a constant struggle." Gideon didn't look their way as they walked out the door.

They sat at a table in the lounge and shared an ashtray. Each had coffee. He rolled her one and cupped her hand around his as he lit the cigarette for her. He used a matchbook from a place called the Palomino Lounge in Natchez, which got them talking about music and how they was both big fans, in particular, these days, the way Kitty Wells was singing "It Wasn't God Who Made Honky Tonk Angels" to the top of the country charts, the first woman there ever, kicking old Hank Thompson's ass on the way who was stuck lamenting his mistreatment at the hands of one of them so-called bad women he met in a barroom. Abilene and Jubal both believed he got what's coming to him, Hank did. Step aside, Hank. Make room.

My God, thought Jubal, how does that woman make smoking a cigarette look so damn delicious? Rare to find a woman who'd smoke a Lucky in the first place, let alone one who took the smoke in with such pleasure. She spit out a fleck of tobacco that had got on the tip of her tongue; Jubal thought that was tough. Also the way she licked a fleck from her lower lip. Tough. What he liked most was how she'd sometimes inhale and not blow the smoke back out, rather let it drift from her mouth and nose while she watched him. Sometimes, when she talked, she simply let the smoke come out and drift away. If he moved his head just a touch right or left, that put the ceiling light behind her head, and then he saw her through a haze as if she were an actress in a movie. When her face was looking that way the thought crossed through his mind that if he was drowning in the ocean and had the choice of grabbing a lifesaver or getting one last look at her face, he'd go for the face, no question about it. He also thought, when he saw the haze glowing around her head, that it looked like a damn halo.

"Brought you back a cold one, pup," said Jubal as he reentered his son's hospital room with a bottle of Coca-Cola. Gideon looked up from where he had been counting his collection of arrowheads and smiled when he saw his father, but the smile fell off his face when he saw that woman come in behind him like some fat circus elephant holding the elephant's tail in front of her in her trunk. Only this elephant wasn't big and fat, and she came and sat down on the bed beside him again. Her crisp white skirt pulled up over her knees just a little when she did. She took a comb from the bedside table and began to run it through his hair, but he pulled his head away and wouldn't let her touch him. "Hold still a minute," she said. "Really. Hold still. This is important." She leaned toward him with her finger outstretched. "Let me do this now, Mr. Pickett." She reached in and gently plucked something from a spot beneath his eye, then she examined it on the tip of her finger and showed it to him. "It's your eyelash. Now you get to make a wish. Go on. Make a wish. When you do, blow the eyelash off my finger, and that wish will be granted. Make a wish and give it a big blow."

At first, Gideon looked at her with disdain, then something occurred to him and Abilene caught it. "You got one, don't you? Got you a wish, right? I saw your eyes. OK. Make that wish and blow." Gideon closed his eyes and rocked a bit, then reared back and blew away the lash from the tip of Abilene's finger. "Voilà," she said, and held up an empty finger. She leaned in confidentially to Gideon and said in a tone that implied just the two of them, "Now, young man, you're probably thinking this magic stuff is just a bunch of bullroar. No way you're going to get your wish, right? Wrong. 'Cause I know what you wished for, and I'm the only one who can give that to you, right? We know what I'm talking about, don't we? You want me to go away. It's OK. That's your wish: go away and leave you here with your father. Well, Mr. Gideon Pickett, you're going to get your wish." Abilene stood up and went to the door. "Adios, gents," she said as she left the room and headed back to her station. "Wishes do come true." Father and son watched her go. Something had landed in their midst, and they weren't at all certain what it was.

"What?" asked Jubal. "You got something on your mind. What is it?" Jubal just knew by the expression on his son's face that the boy had a problem. "Speak now, or forever hold your peace. No? Hell, then, keep it to yourself. Right now I need to get a few nickels for phone calls. We got some pressing needs, like where're we going to park for the next three days. Wonder if we can stay on the hospital parking lot. That'd be easy. I'll find out. If not we're gonna have to find a trailer park someplace. Want anything? Chiclets? Baby Ruth? Good & Plenty? OK. One box Good & Plenty. I'll be back in a little bit."

It's like he was a different man was what Abilene thought when she watched Jubal Pickett walking up the hall from his son's room. No more head-down slope-shouldered shuffle steps. Uh-uh. He was taller. Seemed to her he had his heart back, and that was surely true. He looked at her and smiled, and she smiled back. "Getting some exercise?" she asked.

"You got any nickels?" he asked.

"Only wooden ones," she said. "Got a few of those. Try the gift shop downstairs."

"Hey, do you think the hospital will let us stay on the parking lot for the next three days?"

"I'll go you one better," she said.

"You know a trailer park?" he asked hopefully.

"I actually do," she said.

"Where we can sit 'til Gideon can travel?"

"It ain't nothin' but free for the next three days. Got your name on it," she said.

"Free?"

She nodded and said, "Better hop on it."

"You got a name and number? Will you write it out for me?" he asked, and she said she would, and she did, in a handwriting that looked like a parakeet walked across the paper. Abilene folded the piece of paper in half and handed it to Jubal, who put it in his shirt pocket. "I'll go make the call and get a look at this thing." He smiled and said, "Thanks."

"If you can't read my writing you holler," she said.

"I'm sure I'll manage," he replied. "See you in a little bit."

Abilene smiled at him as he left, and it occurred to Jubal, well, something occurred to him, though he could not grasp what it was, just a sense of something, really, and he had things to do, so it meant as much to him as a bird's shadow zipping by. After an hour had passed, however, Abilene began to wonder where he was. She had expected him back by now. She wondered, did she miss him when she got up to go potty?

You could learn a lot from arrowheads just by looking at them, whether they hadn't been broken yet, even how many times they had been broken and then chipped back into shape, whether one had been refashioned into an awl for punching holes in hides or made to strip the bark from branches destined to become arrows. Mostly they were named after where they were found, so, when they were found in an area far from where they were made, it meant that those tribes over there did business with tribes that quarried the stone somewhere else. So that was kind of like geography. The stone is flint or chert, both basically the same stone, except flint is black and chert is a bony color. Some had a little green or blue or pink color to them, and, if you held them up to the light, you could see clear through, the ones for birds anyway, because they were so tiny but not flimsy, nope, razor sharp with tiny chips along the edges that looked like fans or seashells. He loved to hold them in his hand and know that another hand, probably a lot hairier than his, had thousands of years ago also held them, worked them, pushed the point of the arrowhead into the pad of a forefinger to see how sharp it was, drew blood. You could buy arrowheads from stores and collectors but him and his father always hunted theirs. There was an old Indian mound hidden deep in the woods on their place in Natchez, so that's where they started. His father showed him what to look for. They'd also go to Indian mounds over to Louisiana and Tennessee, but now they were bound for southern Utah, so he'd have to learn how to see in a whole new place.

Gideon held an arrowhead up to the light.

He sure is a beautiful child, she thought to herself as she stood at the door watching him, but he was so involved with his box of stuff that he didn't know Abilene was there. She remembered thinking, from before, when he pulled his head

away from her hand, that his eyes were like two cups of coffee, black, no sugar: piercing, angry eyes but a beautiful child,
a face like an angel, one handsome devil on the way. Abilene
didn't think he got his looks from his daddy, though his daddy
was pleasant enough; absolutely nothing wrong with him but
no special spark. But she thought the boy's looks went way
back to a darker time in his family tree when a man's eyes had
to be a lot sharper, when we could still understand the things
that animals said because we were one of them. Just like in
cartoons. We all spoke to each other. That's what it must've
been like way back when. Like in the jungle, or Eden, maybe.
Probably. But she could never figure out when did we stop understanding each other. Abilene considered herself thoughtful
and informed. Every week she read at least a dozen magazines about all kinds of different stuff. Mostly she read them
in the library, but sometimes she got a soda in the drugstore
and looked over the rack. RD never got what the hell she was
always doing with her face buried in a goddamn magazine. He
liked his women stupid.

Yep, that Pickett boy certainly was a good-looking kid.

What must it have been like to finally, with a stone lashed to
a stick, be able to hold off a beast of prey, that terror of being
run down from behind by some carnivore bent on tearing
your flesh and devouring you, only now you can turn around
and face it, stick it, maybe even kill it? Jesus. What must it
have felt like the very instant a man creature finally got it
that he had the energy of the beast itself, the very instant a

sharp stone and a stout stick became a spear? The rush of pure power. The taste of fresh meat. Did the man creature feel what Gideon felt when, for his ninth birthday, his father gave him a brand-new jackknife, or, for his eleventh, when he got his first .22?

He remembered back in Natchez once his father left him standing at a construction site next to the drugstore while he went inside to get a tin of Prince Albert and a roll of Tums. He had his jackknife in his pocket, so he was probably around ten. The construction workers had all gone home for the day, but the heavy equipment was still there: a bulldozer and a steam shovel. His dad had said, "Take a look but don't touch nothin'," which was fine with him because he'd rather sift through the stones than play on the machinery, anyway. Maybe find an arrowhead. Never know. What was really fun was to look through piles of coal in the winter because you could usually find a plant fossil in one, ferns, mostly, guaran-damn-tee ya, as his father would always say. This was the sum-mertime, however. No coal anywhere. So he got himself into a game of Grenade Attack and launched stone after stone at an enemy bunker, a mound of dirt maybe twenty feet away. The enemy must die! Bombs away! Kamikaze! Kamikaze! Why he looked at the stone in his hand when he did, when he hadn't bothered to look at the dozens of stones he had already thrown, he couldn't tell you, but he saw that the one in his hand seemed to have a purpose to it, had a shape somebody intended to give it. It had a stone shaft that fit perfectly into the palm of his hand and a groove around the base. Maybe for a leather thong? Its head was shaped like a small hatchet, which Mr. Montanelli, the seventh-grade science teacher who was a friend of his father's and a neighbor, said it actually was. All of a piece, too. Chipped out of the same chunk of granite. Stone Age, no doubt about it. The blade part was too thick to cut anything but was nifty for conking an enemy on the head. He wondered if its owner had felt like he had when his uncle, who drove a jeep for General Patton in Europe, had actually, one Sunday afternoon, let him hold his military-issue Colt .45 in his own hand.

———

"I don't know whether to thank you or spank you," said Jubal.

"Let me help you make up your mind," answered Abilene. "My daddy didn't teach me much, but he did learn me to hook off the jab." She leaned across her desk and said in a tone of mock warning, "Let that be a warning to you, bub."

"You could've just told me," said Jubal as he stood there feeling like a dummy with her handwritten note in his hand.

"I could've, but that wouldn't have been as much fun," said Abilene. "Anyway, I figured you'd catch on before you walked out the door."

"I didn't even look at what you wrote until I started up the truck," said Jubal. "I'm driving and thinking something feels awful familiar about this."

Abilene laughed. "When did you figure it out?"

"When I got there and saw it was your house," he said.

"I was sure you'd get it because you'd just been there. That'll teach you to look where you're going." And she laughed again.

"I must've been so dazzled by your presence that I never even knew where I was," he said.

"You been saving that line for just the right time?" she asked.

"I'm better at blurting than saving," he said. "Ready to talk business?"

"How many days?" she asked.

"I'm saying three, but maybe we best throw in an extra day to hedge it," he said.

"Fine," she replied. "Three, four days parked in my driveway. Here's the deal: twenty-four-hour use of the facilities. You supply the food. I cook. You do the dishes. I only got two rules: don't pee in the shower, and remember to put the toilet seat down."

The news of their arrangements went down pretty well with Gideon. At least, he didn't fuss, which Jubal took to be a good sign. The boy was restless and ready for something new. His strong, young body had fought off a fearful attack, and his engines were once again revving.

"We'll stay put for a couple days 'til the doc checks your plumbing out," Jubal said to Gideon as they drove from the hospital to Abilene's house. "Once the doctor says go, we're gone. It's gonna be wham, bam, thank ya, ma'am."

Jubal could tell his son was in a pretty good mood. He was, too. Their good moods had rubbed off on each other. They'd weathered a crisis, and the adventure was back on. Father and son both accepted that, for this particular leg, anyway, a woman was on board. Jubal thought that years from now him and Gideon would look back on Abilene Breedlove and this part of their trip as a fond memory on their road to riches.

First off, it was home-cooked Mexican, a victory dinner to celebrate Gideon's first night out of the hospital. Abilene's second cousin learned her a chili recipe from south of the border, and she cooked it up special that evening for the Picketts. Even set the damn table. Would've used napkin rings but couldn't find any. Plus concocted a pitcher of atomic margaritas for the adults, although Gideon got to taste a little from a juice glass, and his father did let him drink a can of beer. All this was a big treat for the boys and not a little strange because, since the wife and mother walked out on them, they never sat down to eat anything, seeming, instead, to prefer standing at the kitchen counter with cereal or sandwiches, chugging milk from the bottle, eating ice cream from the carton with a couple of spoons or forks, depending on which was clean in the dish rack. It wasn't anything they ever really even thought about. Usually, they listened to the radio while they chewed, but that night Abilene played them the new Kitty Wells single on her Victrola. Then she played them this new guy, an acetate disk she lifted from her cousin's collection. Gideon perked up almost as soon as the record began to play.

"He's a white boy, out of Mississippi, too," explained Abilene. "But tell me that hillbilly don't have jungle in his blood."

Jubal agreed. "Sounds colored to me."

"Uh-uh," she said. "White as you are."

"He sound colored to you?" Jubal asked Gideon. Gideon shrugged.

"Watch out for this ol' boy," advised Abilene. "Somebody's gonna make billions on him. You hombres heard it here first."

The next morning Abilene put the percolator on and left the house early for work. Jubal and Gideon spent the night in the trailer and were still asleep. One of them was rattling the trailer's flimsy sheet metal walls with a snore like an outboard motor, and she suspected it wasn't the younger one, either. Abilene caught herself smiling and then felt a pang of pure sorrow as she realized how much she missed a man around the house. She'd rather not be by herself was the truth. She did not want to become a lonely old woman sitting in a rocking chair staring at the past, eating dog food from a can. Once when she was a little girl her mother dragged her to a convalescent home to see her great-aunt Gertie. Her mother always dragged her places she did not want to go, made her do things she hated with all her heart, like kiss her dead grandfather in his coffin. Abilene was only three, but she remembered being held over the corpse and lowered, held nearly upside down until her lips were just above his. "Go on," said her mother, "kiss him," and she knew in her heart that she wasn't getting down until she did. She knew even then that this was a test of wills, and she flat-out wouldn't until it came to her that her mother might get tired and drop her in the coffin, and then she made her lips thin as spaghetti so not much would touch anything dead.

Aunt Gertie used to be the live wire in the family. She knew all the popular songs of her day, and she taught Abilene to do the black bottom, a big dance back then. Her tragedy was that one of her cheeks was badly burned when X-rays were used to clear her acne, so she became a recluse, never married, never had children. There was only one bad thing about Aunt Gertie: as soon as Abilene walked through the door Gertie would plant a big fat wet one on her cheek—yuck—and Abilene couldn't wipe the saliva off until Aunt Gertie looked the other way. Those few seconds when Abilene had spit on her cheek was like boiling in a kettle in hell. Other than that, Aunt Gertie had been her favorite.

Now, at ninety, Aunt Gertie sat tied in a wicker wheelchair, held up by a sheet around her chest. Her teeth were in a glass of water on the bedside table, her cheeks sunk in like empty bags. Aunt Gertie's tongue lolled listlessly in and out of her mouth as if the thing had a mind of its own. Her eyes were fixed on the distance, on nothing in particular. The only thing the old woman was capable of doing was writing the same sentence over and over on a pad of paper, over and over, "Only a stone is all alone," over and over, "Only a stone is all alone," in a hand surprisingly certain. Abilene's mother made her kiss Aunt Gertie hello and good-bye even though the old woman was obviously vacant, and her cheek felt like moldy cheese. Abilene hated this memory—it spooked her—so she flushed it out of her system pretty quick. Before she even got to work she wasn't thinking about it anymore.

Now, as far as supper tonight was concerned, she'd stop by the Acme market on the way home and pick up the makings of sloppy joes. Coleslaw. Pickles. Chips. Kool-Aid would go good with that. Lemon meringue pie, maybe?

Work that day was pleasant. Abilene added Royal Crown Cola and beer to her shopping list. Connor, the proctologist, stopped by and flirted for a few. That was fun. Both of them knew it was a little harmless chitchat between two consenting adults, which is, of course, why they did it. Abilene thought he liked married life just fine, only he couldn't admit it. Then, later in the day, an orderly told her the little girl who looked like a werewolf was back upstairs, so Abilene went up on a break and took her the cherry Tootsie Roll Pop she'd been keeping in her pocketbook since the last time the child was there, just in case, you know? A really nice day; still, she was a little antsy and wanted her shift to end. Her mother, in a rare attack of clarity, used to tell her, "Don't wish your life away," and that was the only thing her mother told her that ever made any sense. Still. Two more hours.

Jubal spent most of the day outside tuning up the big V-8 engine on his truck. He also changed the oil and put in a new air filter, checked the spare, tightened the lug nuts with a wrench that spun like a propeller, tinkered with the timing. Jubal Pickett was a man who liked tools and equipment, kept them in spic 'n' span shape, and didn't mind getting dirty as part of the job. If Jubal was busy, he was happy, and today he felt like a million bucks. The only problem was that he couldn't stop running into the house to empty his bladder after all the alcohol that went into his system the night before. Abilene had made the point very clear that they were to come inside for their "private duties" and not to dare piddle outside in the bushes. "I don't care if it's a coal-black total eclipse of the sun, the moon, and every star in heaven," she said. "Step inside and relieve yourself in the proper way. Men and cats, both their pee stinks," she told them with real authority.

"Yes, ma'am," Jubal said.

"At ease, gentlemen," she told them, and laughed.

But Jubal didn't think it was so funny when he had to stagger back and forth from his trailer to her house so many times he lost count. He felt like a goddamn short-hop jitney.

One time, deep in the night, he stopped outside her bedroom on his way back from the john, but only for an instant. Her door was slightly ajar, and he stopped because he thought he heard her whimper like in some dream. For a second there Jubal thought he had stepped on a squeaky floorboard, and that squeak was what stopped him. With the second whimper, however, he actually stopped to listen. He hadn't heard a woman's private sounds in such a long time. Had he ever? he wondered. Jubal thought about waking her, but why would he? Plus he was afraid she'd rise up out of a deep sleep and shoot him for a burglar. Better let her alone. But he didn't move, not yet, stood there until suddenly he became ashamed of himself for being somewhere he shouldn't have been. The shame pushed Jubal out of there and shoved him back to his trailer.

She took one look around at the set dinner table and the neatness of the room and said to Jubal, "They gonna take your man card away you're so neat 'n' tidy. You worked on your truck, and you look like that?"

"Guilty," he replied.

Abilene had come home to a house that had a hum to it. She could hear the hillbilly singing about heartache from inside the living room and figured that must be where Junior was, because his old man was sweeping off the driveway. It made her feel mischievous. What is it about a man with a broom? she asked herself. Fred Astaire had his cane. Gene Kelly had his lamppost. This man had his push broom. When he saw her he smiled and pumped it in the air a few times like a conquering warrior with his spear.

"Come on in and let's have us a cold one," she called from the front walk. "Meet you inside. Gimme a minute to tinkle." She tossed the words over her shoulder as she opened the front door. Another thing of her mother's, Abilene remembered, was to say she had to pee so bad her back teeth were floating, only the old lady said *urinate*. Momma might've been disgusting, but she sure got it right there. Abilene dumped her packages on the nearest chair and beelined for the bathroom, only to find the door was closed and locked. She banged on the door with an open hand and shook the doorknob with the other. "Can a girl get in there?" she wailed as she hopped up and down in place. Abilene heard the snick of a bolt sliding back, then the door flew open and Gideon, red faced and mortified, tore out of there. She jumped aside to avoid being knocked down. Unable to even look at her, the boy rushed by and ran outside, nearly decking his father as he barreled through the front door.

"Hey!" said Jubal, but Gideon didn't stop until he was back inside the trailer.

"I swear to Christ," Jubal told Abilene when she came out of the bathroom, "every damn time I turn around today that boy's in the head, like he's got tapeworms or something." She found Jubal in the kitchen unloading the shopping bags.

"Sloppy joes all right?" she wanted to know.

"Hell, yeah," he said happily. "Weren't you talking about a cold one, young lady?"

She took a church key from the drawer, opened a can, and handed it to him as if it were a victory prize. He took it, toasted her, and chugged it to the bottom. Then he roared and crunched the empty sideways into his forehead.

"Bet you learned that in the navy," she said.

"Nope. Only had glass bottles then. I am a widely traveled and learned individual," he joked.

"So I'm finding out," she said.

By the time dinner was on the table, Jubal had managed to coax Gideon back inside to sit with them. Jubal knew his son was a food magnet disguised as a teenage boy, and he felt a slight pang of shame by playing on the boy's weakness: an appetite that spared nothing in its path. "He eats like his father," Abilene had remarked. What Jubal did was to go outside and simply stand by the trailer door while he described what's for dinner in a loud voice. Gideon perked up at the mention of fresh Vidalia onions cooked in with the chopped beef. Perked him up but didn't get him to move. The lemon meringue pie was what did that.

After dinner, Abilene put on a fresh pot of coffee while

Jubal and Gideon cleared off the table and set out plates for dessert. "Dessert forks, gentlemen," she said. Once everybody was on their second piece of pie, she stood up and rapped her spoon against the percolator. "Attention please, gents," she said, and got to her feet. "I made a discovery today that I hope gets your interest the way it did mine. Call it a whim or something, but, after work, I got this notion to go to this Christian bookstore I know called the Holy Book and check out something in the Bible. They got lots of Bibles, but the clerk recommended one used by both the Catholics and the Lutherans. OK. So listen here." She took a lengthy supermarket sales slip from her pocketbook and read from notes she had penciled on the back. "Right. Gideon. Judges, chapters six through eight. First time God spoke to him he was in hiding from the enemies of Israel. He kept his mouth shut and stayed put because he couldn't believe God was calling him to save his people. Gideon finally got it and raised an army of thirty-two thousand men, but God told him cut it down to three hundred so folks would know it was God's victory, not man's. Now, that might've been true, only Gideon was the one who whomped 'em in the flesh hands-on. For a long time he was quiet, too, but when the Lord asked him to rise up, he broke his silence and tore the Midianites a new asshole, if ya'll please excuse my French." She leaned down toward Gideon and said in a confidential stage whisper, "One of these days, young man, you're gonna open up, and then, Lord, watch out! Nothing gonna hold you back. You're gonna tame lions, son. Tigers. All kinds of whatnots. Good name your daddy gave you," she said. "Right on the money."

The lemon from the lemon meringue pie made him pucker. The white stuff from on top he kept in his mouth for a long time while it dissolved on his tongue because it was too good to swallow. After he scraped it clean with the edge of his fork, Gideon held the empty plate out for more. But instead of giving him more she was making noises to him.

"He ain't gonna talk to you, Abilene," said Jubal. "You get him to say something you'll be the first."

"All right, Gideon," she said. "I'll get you your third piece of pie, and you don't have to say one bit of 'please' and 'thank you' for it . . . this time." She handed Gideon his pie, a towering piece like the rest of them that you could barely get in your mouth if you opened it as wide as it went. *Pie* was a good word. You could pop your lips and almost get it.

They'd all moved to the small living room after dinner. "This place came furnished," Abilene apologized as she neatened up a pile of magazines on the coffee table, a thick slab of wood bound by iron straps at either end, originally used as a hatch cover from an old tramp steamer. "If it was mine to do with what I wanted, I'd throw it all out, except for maybe that coffee table, but I'd probably end up junking that, too, 'cause it really looks like it belongs in a dungeon, don't you think?" Jubal liked the workmanship but agreed it belonged someplace else. "Get more comfy stuff in here," she went on, "maybe a bunch of pillows, cheery colors, an Indian blanket, maybe, you know, make it somewhere you want to sit." Jubal and Abilene sat at each end of a dark green three-seater sofa with frayed seat cushions that looked like salvage from a cheap motel. Jubal's feet were on the coffee table. Abilene had taken off her uniform and now sat barefoot with her legs tucked under a lilac chenille robe. Gideon slouched in an overstuffed, rusty-colored chair with his legs over one frayed arm. He'd been playing the same achy song all day long, only now Abilene made him turn it down low because the adults wanted to talk, which was OK with him because he wanted to count his arrowheads, anyway.

"Show me whatcha got there," she said.

It took her three tries before Gideon realized Abilene was talking to him. "Hey, Mr. Gideon Pickett of Natchez"— she spelled it out letter by letter—"M-I-S-S-I-S-S-I-P-P-I!" Abilene snapped her fingers in the boy's face to get his attention. He winced. "Show me whatcha got in the box. I know they're arrowheads and whatnot, but you make believe you're a teacher and I'm a student who really wants to learn this stuff, because right now they look like just a bunch of stones to me. Like, for instance, what you've got in your hands. Them two."

"The big one's a spear point. Look at the heft of it. Chipped from a stone called chert. So's the small one. Chert," said Jubal.

"Chert?"

"C-H-E-R-T," he spelled.

"Chert," she said, liking the way it sounded. *Chert.*

"Had to be for something big, like a mammoth, maybe, or

a giant sloth—just imagine the surprise of the saber-toothed tiger when it realized that this puny, two-legged creature grew fangs, too—and the little one's an arrow, probably for rabbits and squirrels," said Jubal.

"Maybe he'd like to tell me himself," said Abilene.

"Trust me, ma'am, this is the closest you're gonna get."

"All right," she said, "then hear me out." She stood up, re-tied the knot in the sash of her lilac chenille robe, and com-manded their attention. "Hypothetical case. I move into this new house, and the man next to me, who come over here from Russia to escape communism and persecution and that evil bastard Stalin, my neighbor, this Russian, has this big hunk of chert right in the middle of his backyard. My kid—let's say I had a kid named Gideon—hear me out. If I had a kid I'd name him Gideon. Now, Gideon wants a piece of chert for his rock collection, so why not, I ask myself, go next door and ask our neighbor, who's got a lot of it, can we have a kid-sized chip off your chert? Hear me out—our neighbor, wanting to blend in and get along as such, says sure thing, comrade, and goes and gets it and gives it to my wide-eyed little boy. An act of true American generosity committed right here on American soil." At that instant, she drew herself up to full attention. "Gentle-men, that man from Russia was kind enough to give us the chert off his back. Drum rolls, please, drum rolls. Applause is allowed. What do you think, gentlemen? Do I belong on Ed Sullivan, or do I belong on Ed Sullivan?"

"Who needs Minnie Pearl when they got you?" howled Jubal, who genuinely thought Abilene was a stitch; however Abilene didn't consider that Minnie Pearl bullshit any kind of compliment. "Rosalind Russell deserves a mention here," she said. "Lana Turner."

"Lana ain't funny," said Jubal.

"Then Claudette Colbert," she commanded.

Jubal said, "May I have the envelope, please?"

Abilene rolled up a magazine, curtsied grandly, and used it like a microphone. "First, I'd like to thank all the little people, for without all the little people, I'd be a little people, too." Jubal felt like he was going to rupture he was laughing so hard, but nobody appreciated Abilene's routine more than Abilene herself. She threw back her head and yowled, tumbled onto the sofa, pumped her feet against the floor, and slapped her thighs.

Gideon thought the joke was just plain stupid, a lot like one of his father's.

"Gideon," Jubal called out breathlessly, "son. Help me. Make this woman stop being so funny. She's gonna laugh me clear out of the county."

"It's the law in this house says anybody eats dinner they got to laugh when the hostess tells a joke," said Abilene to Gideon. "Maybe you're just overcooked, you think? Let's see how cooked you are." She went over and poked his ribs with a finger. "Uh-uh, not done. Let's see if you're cooked here." She poked him again on the other side. Gideon seemed to enjoy it. She'd poke him, and he'd flinch out of the way. Poke and flinch. Poke and flinch. Poke and . . . Jubal saw the change come over him, saw the way fear took his son's eyes, and said gently, "Abilene. Abilene." She didn't hear him. She kept poking Gideon, thinking she'd be sure to get a laugh out of him.

"Abilene, leave him be. Abilene!" That one got through to her. She stepped back and shot him a curious look, but he already had his arms gently around his boy. "It's OK, Gideon, OK, son. Just let it go." The boy sucked air, sucked more. "It's OK, pup. Let it go. No big deal. It's OK. Let it go." She had only wanted to cheer him up, get him to join the party. Instead, she caused this . . . what? It was so painful to behold she wanted to turn away and press her hands hard to her ears, but instead Abilene forced herself to be still. Finally, his father's arms still around him, Gideon settled down.

"See," Jubal explained, "he can't laugh."

Jubal walked to the door with his son. "Time to turn in, anyway, right?" he said to Abilene. It was really a statement, not a question.

"What time's your appointment with the doctor?" she asked.

"Not 'til three o'clock," answered Jubal. "We get a clean bill of health, we're out of here."

"You be up for breakfast?" she asked.

"You bet," said Jubal. "I had a great time tonight. He did, too. I know this boy. If he don't want to be someplace or don't want to do something, he can make it nasty."

"Oatmeal and sunny-side-ups be all right?" asked Abilene.

"Coffee?"

"Cream and sugar."

"See you in the morning."

"Yeah."

She listened to their boots scrape along the poured concrete walk and clunk up the creaky metal steps of the trailer, then she made a mental note to run out the next morning while the coffee perked to pick up some bacon and a couple of fresh oranges at the grocery.

The thing she liked to do most in all the world was to take a long, hot bath before she climbed into bed for the night. Actually, it was really her second-favorite thing to do in all the world. Long ago she had come to grips with the fact that a woman's nature was given to her. She don't go out and shop for one until she finds a fit; she's got no choice but to follow her nature or damage her own mental health.

After the boys left, Abilene sat herself down in the rusty-colored armchair and thought hard about the evening. Bits and pieces of stuff, nothing that made much sense, like watching spaghetti boiling in a pot and trying to trace a single strand. Abilene could have sat there longer, but she knew she had a full day's work and an early start ahead of her. Also, her body began to ache. It surprised her. She knew you could get a headache from thinking too hard, but she didn't know it could beat up your body, too.

She got up, turned on the water in the tub, and went to her bedroom for a fresh flannel nightgown. Then she returned to the bathroom, fixed the tub the way she liked it, and settled into water as hot as she could stand. Abilene allowed the water to drain her strength while she smoked a Lucky, then soaped herself up and soaked for an hour more.

She emerged from the tub groggy, which was exactly what she'd been looking to do, patted herself dry, and rubbed a pink body lotion onto the skin of her arms and legs, abdomen, butt, everywhere there could ever be a wrinkle. Still, there were signs. Maybe nobody else could see them yet, but she could, and she feared she would wake up one morning and find out her face had ambushed her. A smart woman preserves her assets. She used coconut oil from a separate tube to moisten her cheeks and forehead. Now she was ready for her nightgown and next she'd be in bed. She really didn't want to think any more that day. Maybe her dreams would help sort things out. Abilene opened the door to her bedroom and wondered if a breeze had blown it shut. As a rule, Abilene always left the door open, a little bit, anyway. No big deal. Just her way. Unless, of course, she went to a motel, where she always kept the door closed. But that was obvious, wasn't it? What kind of dummy leaves their motel door open?

Gideon was already awake when he heard his father's footsteps on the metal treads of the trailer. It was four AM by the illuminated hands of the clock. The funny thing was that Gideon could sleep through his father's snoring, but the lack of all that same clatter woke him up. Jubal came in and the door snapped shut behind him. "You awake?" he asked Gideon. "Bad dreams, buddy?" It wasn't a bad dream but his thoughts that were keeping him awake. He turned over on his belly, knowing that his dad would sit down next to him and scratch his back. That always settled him down. He liked the way his father's calluses felt against his skin. His old man called it *scratchifying*. "No need to talk," he said, "you just go back to sleep." It wasn't much longer when Gideon did just that, but once his father was asleep, he couldn't hold back those thoughts anymore and jolted awake again.

It wasn't like he'd never been in a girl's bathroom. He had. Once. Back in Natchez when he was still in school. He was fifteen, soon to be sixteen, and a kid whose father farmed tobacco brought some sweetleaf to school. The two of them snuck down to the boiler room during recess and smoked it in a pipe the kid made out of a toilet paper roll and aluminum foil. It felt like Gideon left his mortal body and went somewhere he could sing. They smoked all he had. Gideon could have stayed there day and night. Except, suddenly, he had to eat, and he also had to "pump the old bilge," as his father always said. He floated out of the boiler room to an empty hallway. Everyone else had gone back to class. It was eerie walking through the empty halls alone. He could hear his footsteps. Gideon turned into the lavatory and had his fly zipped down before he realized something was just not right. The urinals weren't against the wall where they usually were. The urinals, in fact, were nowhere. There were no urinals! At all! Jesus Christ on a crutch! In his fog, Gideon had turned into the girls' lavatory. For an instant, he lost his bearings. No urinals. Where was the door? Which way to turn? Suppose he got caught? Get out of there! It was like a car that lost its brakes headed into an intersection. Would it make it on through without hitting anything? Could Gideon get out of there without anybody seeing him? He had to do it. He had to move. Now! Move! Another fraction of a second and Gideon was out the door and walking down the hall. He'd made it. No one had seen him. His heart was still thumping when he got back to the classroom. He was late but went to his seat without a reprimand or so much as a look from the teacher. She knew he would leave school in another few weeks, anyway, so why bother? As Gideon sat there in his own world, an interesting feeling overtook him, as if he had a secret, as if he were invisible and would stay that way as long as the secret stayed his.

So when Jubal and Gideon came to stay with Abilene, the boy had already been in a girls' lavatory, but this was a woman's bathroom. It was like falling into a crystal cave hidden deep within a magic mountain. Something happened here. Some thing *happened* here. Some mystery. A woman had taken off her clothes here. These were a woman's things: her lotions and lipsticks, eye shadow and rouge, the soap that cleaned her, the cloth that soaped her, the polished brass hook that held the lilac robe she tied around her waist. A woman had been naked in that same tub, a woman who wanted him to laugh. Candles were on its rim, white candles in small glasses, six of them. A pack of Luckies and a silver lighter sat within reach on a small stool. A woman had lay down naked in this tub and smoked a cigarette and was lit by these candles. He imagined her eyes made up like a 'Gyptian princess. He lit the candles with the silver lighter, lowered himself into her tub, sprayed her perfume in the air, closed his eyes . . .

Abilene hadn't slept well the night before, so she was glad when it was finally time to put on the coffee. It gave her something to do. She dressed for work and put on her face, not much, just a little touch of something here and there, and left for the grocery store. Apart from the oranges and bacon, Abilene decided to buy some chocolate milk mix that she thought the boy might like in his coffee. Oh, yeah, and fresh cream. Abilene walked the two blocks to the grocery store. On the way back, as she neared her front walk, she saw the two of them without their shirts doing push-ups with the toes of their boots hooked on the top step of the trailer. They matched each other push-up for push-up. Eighteen years separated them, but from the energy you'd never know it. Their bodies were so different, though. The father was about two inches shorter than the son, with a lower center of gravity, heavily muscled arms and back, and a barrel chest. It was a workingman's body, top-heavy and hammered into shape by tools and machinery. RD, who had never lifted a hammer in all his life, belonged to the point-and-tell school of home repair (he'd point to something, then tell somebody else to fix it). You could tell these two were father and son (they both had the same butt), but the boy had more willow to him, his body new and growing. His legs were more heavily muscled than his father's, and he didn't have so much body hair on him, either. She watched them pump out a dozen more, then called, "Breakfast! Half hour!" and went inside to cook it up. It made her smile when she saw that someone had already got started on the oatmeal.

Whatever time they had to chat had been taken up by Abilene's run to the grocery store. She had to skeedaddle, or else she'd be late for work. "Come by later and let me know what the doc said," she called as she haul-assed out the front door.

She wished she had someone to talk to. Corinne was out of the question since the pig came home. Abilene was still trying to trace that single strand of spaghetti in boiling water. She had to think this out. Through. Something was going on. Abilene considered dust motes in a beam of sunlight, remembered how impossible it was to grasp one. You tried to snatch it, and all of them spun away. Abilene thought of Jubal as a man who'd always put the toilet seat back down. He'd hold a door for you, too. Take out the garbage without being asked. Wash the ring out of the tub. Don't knock it, sister. There's worse in this life, I'm here to tell ya.

What was she talking about? Was there a chance here? Opportunity might be knocking. Was she really thinking about . . . about what exactly? Was this why she left Muskogee, what she was meant for? She knew she still looked just fine, but, face it, she wasn't a kid anymore. Yeah, but what about in the mornings? Would she look over from her side of the bed and be glad to see him there? She thought she could be good to him and for him if she set her mind to it, but that wasn't the same thing as really being happy when you woke up. Think about it, woman. You know how when you know something you just know it, that's all? You do. Like it's in stone. You might not know how you know it but you do know you know it. Like how much you could care for somebody. Some things you just know. If the spark ain't there you can't put it there, but maybe that spark was something she ought to learn to stay away from. Where had it gotten her so far?

Abilene was distracted by her thoughts all day long. She

found she liked having these boys around. She found herself hoping the doctor said to wait another day. Whoa, was that dumb or what? She needed more time. Well, too bad, hon', you ain't got more time. She caught herself talking to herself out loud. People kept asking her, "What?" Goddamn Corinne and that mess she called a marriage!

They stopped by her desk about four PM to tell her the doc's report was bon voyage. The trailer was packed. They were ready to take off and came to thank her for her generous hospitality, and, well, this was it, they guessed, time to say good-bye.

"Bullshit you will," she snapped.

"Miss Breedlove!" admonished the head nurse.

Abilene had come to a decision. She was not one to mull things over indefinitely. She did not take long to come to conclusions. She assessed the situation and came to them quickly. No looking back. It didn't work for Lot's wife, and it wouldn't work for her.

"Ma'am," she said to the head nurse, "I need five minutes. This concerns something of vital importance."

"Then take it to the waiting room, please. Five minutes," she said to Abilene, and to Gideon she said, "How are you doing, sport? You off to the badlands of Utah now? Take care of your daddy."

"Just listen. Don't say one thing. The only answer I want from you right now is a yes for dinner," she insisted. Abilene, Jubal, and Gideon had moved to the waiting room. "It's too late in the day to take off, anyway."

"We can make New Mexico before we stop again," Jubal told her.

"This ain't about New Mexico. We've got business, you and me."

"What's that?"

"After dinner."

"Why not now?"

"It's a tradition. State dinners. Big decisions. That's how nations are built. Also," she said, "I got a sneaky suspicion that this growing boy here could use a big plate of spaghetti and meatballs before he hits the road." She nudged Gideon. "Am I right, or am I right? Garlic bread. Lots of sauce. Third helpings. What's one more night between friends? Let me give you something to think about."

"What do you say, pup?" asked Jubal. "You got any opinion on the matter?" He looked at Gideon. Gideon looked at her. "I guess that settles it, Abby. You're on for dinner."

"Don't forget the fresh-perked in the morning before you hit the trail," she reminded him.

"Why don't you just come along as the cook on this expedition?" he teased.

"Because nobody asked me," she quipped. That stopped him. "Close your mouth and go by the grocer to get the meatballs. Sometimes he lets me have a bottle of his homemade vino if he's got extra. Tell him who it's for. Keep the meatballs warm in the oven, and boil a big pot of water. I'll be home directly from work."

———

Dinner was like a Quaker prayer meeting. No one said a word. She'd made sure there were three portions for Gideon, and it was a good thing. He wiped his plate and ate one of Abilene's meatballs as well. The three of them cleared the table and cleaned the kitchen, and, when there were only a couple more plates left in the sink, she asked Gideon if he wouldn't mind doing the final touch-ups while she and his daddy went outside and had a smoke.

"Just be a few minutes, youngblood," he heard his father say. Enough time to count all the dishes and put them in the right place.

———

Abilene had thought it over and over 'til she was clear as to her intentions. She'd rather be part of a great adventure and enjoy the ride than stand at a cash register all day. She could always do that. How was she so sure this was her next best move? Her options were limited. She accepted that. Now let's get on with it.

"Jubal?" she said, picked up her pocketbook, and walked outside. He followed her to the truck, where they both leaned against the fender while she took from her purse a crumpled pack of Luckies and a tin of Prince Albert. "Fresh can," she said as she handed him the tobacco. His wife had hated the damn stuff.

"So," he said as he rolled a cigarette and lit it with a wooden match he took from his pocket. She noticed how careful he was to get an even burn. "You got all my attention, young lady. What are you going to do with it?"

"I'm gonna give you your cake and let you eat it, too," she said. "It's not like there's much to discuss. This is basically a take-it-or-leave-it proposition."

"Let's have it," said Jubal.

"First thing in the morning I pull my savings from the bank, toss it in the pot, and the three of us take off for Utah. I lock the door behind me, and we go. This feels lucky to me, Jubal, and I don't mind a gamble. The way I look at it: you got the wood, I got the matches, let's make a fire. Are you following me?"

"Go slow," he said.

"I got the stove, you got the steak, let's cook dinner."

"Sounds like a proposal."

"A business proposal," she said. "I'm saying we could do good in business together, pool our resources, bring me in. Do I give a shit about giving people directions all day long? What's that gonna make out of my life? But you bring me on board and this bunch has got a whole lot of winning in their future. We can live together like kin until one of us chooses to quit the bargain, no hard feelings. No strings. I won't lie to you, Mr. Pickett, I don't know that I could love you but I could be true. Here's the best part: if you don't like the deal when we get there you can cut me loose, and I reserve the right to do the same. I'll make my way. At least I'll be someplace far away and new. So. In about five minutes I might want to eat my words. You might, too, so now's not the time to do anything but think. Don't say a thing. If one of us wakes up tomorrow morning with the fear of God in his heart, the deal's off. Now, I'm going to take my bath and go to bed early. If you decide to leave without me, don't slam the door behind you on the way out."

Abilene passed through the living room on the way to her bath. Jubal stayed outside to finish his smoke. Gideon sat in the rusty-colored armchair with his cigar box counting arrowheads, but he quickly hid something behind his back when he saw her. She didn't say anything to him, just smiled and tousled his hair. He still wasn't comfortable when she did stuff like that, but it wasn't as bad as before. He watched her until the bathroom door closed shut.

It was still a couple of hours before daylight when Jubal got up to go inside. As he passed Abilene's room he noticed a glow he hadn't seen when he passed it before. He went to the bathroom and washed carefully. On his way back, he stopped by her door and listened for her breathing. He couldn't hear her, but the glow on the wall flickered, and he realized that she must have a candle burning in her bedroom. Gently, Jubal pushed open the door. Abilene looked up from the magazine she was reading and smiled at him. Jubal thought she looked more beautiful than any woman he had ever seen. Abilene held the covers aside in order for him to get into bed beside her.

PART 5

In 1950, the population of Edom, Utah, was seven hundred and fifty-seven. Three years later, the population had ballooned by three thousand, all there cocksure positive that they were but a stick of dynamite away from good fortune. When Jubal, Abilene, and Gideon hit town in June of that same year, they made it three more. The trip from Port Arthur, Texas, might have been more tedious were it not for the fact that Abilene Breedlove was a woman who knew how to travel. She had a knack for turning the bleakest journey into a pure pleasure cruise. Most of what came through on the truck radio was static, so Abilene propped her new turquoise plastic portable import up on the dashboard. It wasn't much bigger than a Bible, yet the sound came through quite nicely despite the singing tires and steady growl of the big V-8. But Abilene had a rule that there were times when it had to be turned off, like when they ate. Which was another thing. For example, she insisted they stop at a grocery store for bologna, cheese, chips, and three bottles of cold orange soda, then she'd insist they find a shady spot off the side of the road, where Abilene would lay out a blanket and make a picnic for them. It was nice there, on the grass, under the trees, the three of them like that. Like always, Abilene came up with a good one at just the right time. "Anybody around here know the difference between mashed potatoes and pea soup?" she asked, apropos of absolutely nothing at all (she could shock you like that). Gideon looked at his father; Jubal shrugged. "Both of you give up?" she asked. Jubal put up his hands in an attitude of surrender. "The difference," she explained, "between mashed potatoes and pea soup is that anybody can mash potatoes." Abilene burst out laughing. "Boy, oh, boy, I really crack myself up!"

As far as Jubal was concerned, that was Abilene all over. She was just that kind of gal: sassy, saucy, smart, and full of surprises. What she had done that first night he'd come to her was to guide him softly and gently around the curves of her body, put him places he'd never been, whisper desire in his ear. Abilene told Jubal what he'd never heard. She made him feel like a naughty boy turned loose with ten fingers full of finger paint. That woman knew more ways to make the time go by than anybody else he'd ever met anywhere at all. In fact, if she could think it up in the first place, she'd pretty much just jump right in. As far as Abilene was concerned, Jubal took her like a rutting bull, not much artistry but, good golly, there was no doubting the man was there. He was as enthusiastic as a five-year-old tearing into a pile of Christmas presents. He was in perpetual motion. What Jubal lacked in imagination he made up for in energy, and he was hungry to learn. At one point he burst out laughing, first some giggles, then full-blown laughter just rippled out of him. "Tell me," she said. He couldn't, but she knew. He'd just found out what the fuss was all about. What she'd found out was that she could cover her end of the bargain.

The three of them spelled each other behind the wheel, so, except for groceries and pit stops, they kept that truck and trailer on the road. They made good time and no way was Abilene going to let them waste good money on restaurant meals and motels. Whichever ones weren't driving could sleep where they sat, and Abilene took it upon herself to keep their bellies filled with fine food. She quartered oranges to suck on, kept a supply of peanut butter and jelly sandwiches coming, found a pitcher and made them Kool-Aid. Once, when they stopped at a service station, Abilene bought Gideon a Baby Ruth. "Here y'go, handsome," she said, and winked as she handed him the candy bar. "Remember who your friends are." Sometimes she read them the newspaper—the headlines, anyway—so they could keep up.

Usually, Gideon sat in the middle, though sometimes she did, especially when he was driving. Wherever he sat, one of her hips always touched his. She didn't seem to be aware of it, but he was. Finally, at a Flying A filling station just across the New Mexico line, he moved from the cab to the bed of the truck so he could be by himself. He sat with his back against the rear window with the cigar box of arrowheads in his lap. The steady rush of wind was pleasure to him. Sometimes he lifted his hands up above the cab so he could feel the wind push at them. He liked the way the cuffs of his shirt flapped in the air when he unbuttoned them. Sometimes he just sat there and made like he was riding a comet.

Next time they stopped at a Sinclair station with a dinosaur on its sign: a green brontosaurus, all hump and tail and tiny head. Another sign, bold red letters painted on the window, advertised fresh coffee and homemade pie. "Apple pie's on me," said Jubal as he scampered toward the building. He'd been wanting pie and coffee for the past two hundred miles. Abilene, who had been driving, took her time climbing down from the cab and stretched herself out. Gideon stayed put where he was.

"No pie, handsome?" she asked him. "What could possibly be more pleasing right this second in the good old US of A than a thick chunk of apple pie à la mode stuck on the end of a fork about a half inch from your quivering, wide open, and wildly salivating mouth?" Abilene moved closer to Gideon and lowered her voice as if she were sharing a great confidence. "You and your daddy might be closer than two front teeth, but you and me, Gideon, we share a secret that he don't know about. You might even say we're talking the same language, you and me. Oh, yeah." Abilene's hands had been resting casually on the rim of the truck's bed, but they suddenly darted forward and snatched a magazine the boy had hidden under a sack behind his back. He grabbed for it, but Abilene had already danced out of reach. "Well, go to war, Miss Molly!" she exclaimed. "Help me read this, Gideon: *Flirt: A Fresh Magazine*." It was a girlie magazine: garter belts and dark-seamed fishnet stockings, push-up bras and Merry Widows, and a see-through nightie from the side, where the curve of the breast was visible while the nipple remained in shadow. The boy flushed. He found it hard to breathe. "Hey, hold on, kiddo," she went on. "We even got a how-to article: "How to Keep Your Honey Warm." Perfectly good topic. Ought to be a part of everybody's education. Maybe people'd stop killing each other." Gideon tried for the magazine again, and again she danced away. He slammed his open hand on the roof of the truck. "Will you look at that cover?" she continued. "That darling little kitten's pulling that good-looking lady's black lace panties down." Gideon lunged for the girlie magazine and this time nearly toppled over the side of the truck. "Your father treats you like a boy," she said as she moved away, "but I know you're ready to become a man. Hey, you don't have to be embarrassed with me. I respect a healthy urge." With a laugh, Abilene handed the magazine back to him—"Let me know how it ends, will ya?"—turned, and sauntered toward the coffee shop.

He wasn't worried that she'd tell his father. Even if she did, his father'd probably just laugh, probably want a look for himself. He always kept a pinup calendar on the kitchen wall, anyway, so it wasn't that. Gideon knew what he felt wasn't right. She'd stepped out of the magazine and given him a boner. He'd read a story—it had drawings—called "The Double D Avenger." It starred Dixie Davis and her twin 44s. Abilene wasn't that big, but she came to mind, anyway. It got him to wondering what Abilene really did look like. He thought of undoing her bra, the kind that hooked in front between the cups. She was smiling at him, but he knew that what he felt wasn't right. The box of arrowheads rested against his crotch. He clutched them and shut his eyes.

"Hey, you from Mississippi?" someone shouted. "Hey, you in the truck. Sleepin' Beauty. You from Mississippi?" Gideon opened his eyes. Three boys, older, bigger: one leaned against each side of the truck bed; a third, the biggest, stood with his hands on the tailgate. "You must be lost, Mississippi," he said. All three wore sweat-stained summer straws and scuffed cowboy boots. Their belt buckles were the biggest ones Gideon had ever seen, like shields to ward off bullets and death rays, bright silver shields with polished blue stones. "You lost, queer-bait?" the biggest one asked.

"I think he's a dummy, Bobby," said the boy on Gideon's left.

"Well," said Bobby, "one thing for sure: we got enough dummies around here. Don't need another dummy; do we, dummy? See what the dummy's got in the shoe box, Lloyd."

The one on Gideon's left reached for the cigar box. Gideon pulled away, but the boy on his right reached in, snatched the cigar box, and tossed it over to Lloyd.

"Touchdown Lloyd!" said Lloyd, but the smile left his face when Gideon leaped from the truck, drove him to the ground, and wrenched the box away, only to have Bobby kick it out of his hands. The arrowheads scattered. The boys kicked him but couldn't stop him. Gideon seemed impervious to their kicks as he crawled around to get his arrowheads back. Suddenly, he heard his father yell. "What the fuck? What the goddamn fuck?" Jubal roared, and ripped into the three boys. "Kick me, you little bastards!" he taunted as he tore the shirt off the back of one of them. "You're lucky I don't break your goddamn necks," he yelled. "You all right, son?" he asked Gideon as he helped him to his feet.

"What the hell you doin' puttin' your hands on my boys?" hollered a man who rushed over from the coffee shop.

"Teachin' them manners," said Jubal.

"I'm gonna teach you some manners of your own," threatened the man. Jubal took a tire iron from the bed of his pickup and whacked it against the rim.

"Come on. Teach me," taunted Jubal.

"He's crazy, Dad," warned Bobby, the biggest.

"I'm crazy, Dad," taunted Jubal, again slamming the metal rim of the bed with the tire iron. "Come and teach me somethin'!" But the man was smarter than that. He saw the look on Jubal's face and thought it wiser to step aside.

"Go to hell," the man said.

"Right," answered Jubal, and banged the truck bed one more time. The man retreated with his three boys. Jubal tossed the tire iron back into the bed of the pickup. It sounded like he'd bashed a galvanized garbage can. Abilene was there now, down on her hands and knees, helping Gideon gather up the arrowheads.

"How're you feelin'?" she asked. Gideon didn't answer.

"Your father's some kind of man, you know." Gideon took his cigar box and climbed back into the bed of the truck. "Want my portable radio?" she asked. Gideon didn't answer her, but she reached inside the cab and got it for him. "A Jap made it," she said.

Edom, Utah, in mid-June was so hot you could brew coffee on the manhole covers. Main Street was half a mile of cinder-block and wood-frame construction. The blistering sun ricocheted off the storefront windows back into the eyeballs of the unsuspecting passerby. There'd be a great white flash, and, for an instant, he'd be blind and blinking. That might be the instant in which a pilgrim got his wallet nicked by some opportunistic citizen—the MO, actually, of mostly everybody in town, Edom being a focal point for people looking in one way or another to fill their own pockets and empty somebody else's.

Edom was a one-horse town with a boomtown energy, and Abilene first felt that energy course through her when she drove Jubal's truck across the town line. It tingled up from the street, through the steering column, passed into her hands from the wheel, and made her palms hum. Her fingers waved in the current like anemone tentacles seeking to trap a fish. It wasn't quiet out there. There were a lot of people in the streets, every one of them looking like they had someplace to go, mostly men in work clothes and worn scuffed boots. Their pickup trucks looked like they did: dented and dusty. As soon as she saw them, Abilene knew she could find work here.

"Oh, daddy," she said to Jubal, "me and you are gonna strike it rich. Can't you just feel it?"

"Oh, yeah," replied Jubal, "I can feel it," though she wasn't absolutely convinced that he did. Maybe she was wrong. She'd bought the first newspaper she could when they finally crossed into Utah and stopped for gas. Abilene read Jubal the headlines while he checked the oil and scraped a hundred miles of bugs off the windshield. "Two Jews got executed at Sing Sing. Jubal, here's a fact for you: if you get the chair, there's a good chance your eyeballs will explode. Yuck. Friend of my uncle's was a prison guard and he told me. Hey, Jubal, listen to this and tell me we're not doing the right thing: It's an interview with one Charles P. Nickel, a prospector from Alabama who made history when he struck the largest single uranium deposit ever discovered. Says here he moved from a tarpaper shack into a five-bedroom moderne deluxe with two flush toilets in Edom, Utah. Alabama's somewhere next to Mississippi, right? Daddy, I'm telling you it's like a sign from God."

"Guess I know a good bet when I see one," said Jubal.

"Me, too, daddy," she replied, and brushed his thigh with the back of her hand. Right after, Abilene leaned in close and whispered into Jubal's ear, "Got her all fluffed out for you, honey," and gave his lobe a little nip. Jubal felt that little nip right down to the whorls of his toes. Then she spun the right amount and let him watch her walk toward the back of the truck, where Gideon sat rolling a cigarette from his own red tin of Prince Albert.

"Hey, Gideon, want a Chiclet?" she said, offering the boy the yellow packet of gum while taking one of the little square white tablets for herself.

Gideon shook his head and continued to roll the cigarette.

"Makes your mouth kissing sweet," she said, and popped in a second piece.

Watching Gideon, Abilene considered how Jubal made rolling a smoke look like something Houdini might have done, and how he'd handed that skill down to his son. Now, she'd given herself a good talking-to before she jumped both feet into this arrangement, and one of the big things she'd decided was that she'd be looking for every last inch of good she could find in the man—she vowed she would not nitpick the bad— and one of those nuggets was the way Jubal rolled a cigarette. Abilene got a real kick out of watching him do it. It's always the little things, right? He'd make a little trough out of a single sheet of cigarette paper, tap in a measure of tobacco from the red Prince Albert can that lived in his shirt pocket, smooth it out, and moisten the glued edge of the white paper with the pink tip of his tongue. Abilene liked that. Then, with a magician's hands, he rolled each end between his thumbs and forefingers, and voilà, a slender cigarette appeared at his fingertips. She wanted to clap every time he did that. Jubal was kind and had a playful way. Abilene really did like that about him.

"Don't you light that thing 'til we're clear of these gas pumps, you hear?" she called out to Gideon.

"Let me pay the man and get us the hell out of here," said Jubal as he slammed down the hood and gave it a little extra push.

Edom sat near the confluence of the Colorado and the Green rivers at the southern rim of the San Rafael Swell. In the old days, before the mania for uranium caused fortune hunters to pounce upon the town, there was nothing whatsoever to recommend it as a place to do more than put air in your tires. Someone suggested that its proper name should be Carbuncle Butte, and that moniker stuck, though not on the maps. The United States government insisted, and the United States government had its way. Edom remained the official name of the humble gateway to five hundred and twenty-eight square miles of fractured landscape that had pushed up from underneath like a blister, strained, then tore and broke apart, creating rift canyons eight hundred feet deep but two feet wide and pinnacles of stone that punched through the crust like needles. Other stones, tortured by the stress and force of tectonic ferment, sheared by erosion, took the shapes of goblins, trolls, and various assorted twisted creatures. Few people passed this way in those days. Those who could read the land naturally followed the paths of the creatures who went before. If they went in deep enough they likely came across mysteriously abandoned cliff dwellings in the nooks and crannies of impregnable stone walls. On a wide ledge beneath an overhang it was still possible to come upon an intact kiva, a sacred space in the shape of a circle built under the earth. One could always find shards of pottery and sometimes tools at these places. But an interest in archaeology was not what goaded these men. Greed did. There were riches out there, and the certainty of that drove men to look for them.

Even a dreamer must occasionally deal with the nuts and bolts of getting from A to Z or even B. What that meant right off was that Jubal had to find a place to park the truck and trailer, both in the immediate sense and in the larger picture as to where they would set up a permanent camp. The plan called for Abilene to get a job and live there while Jubal and Gideon went into the wilderness. Where exactly in the wilderness had yet to be determined, though Jubal was prepared for this. He knew for a fact that the main reason new businesses went bust their first year was because they didn't have enough money to see themselves through the hard times, but Jubal carried in his wallet a bank check payable only to him that represented the sum total of all his corporeal assets, enough to get them through famine and flood for the foreseeable future. "Let her ride," said Jubal, and tossed the dice. Abilene crossed her fingers and offered up a prayer. Gideon sorted through his arrowheads and organized them from the smallest to the largest.

Right off they had a stroke of luck that only furthered the proof that things were going their way. They didn't really need to pull into that gas station in the middle of Main Street, but Jubal figured there was still a full hunk of driving ahead and thought it best to top off the tank as the opportunity presented itself. So when Jubal told Abilene to turn right, she did, and pulled up to the high-test pump. It was Abilene's turn to clean the windshield. Gideon checked the air in the tires while Jubal struck up a conversation with the station attendant as the colored man filled the tank. He asked the man where was a good place to park his rig. "For when?" the attendant asked.

"For a while," answered Jubal.

"Here in town ain't much more than overnight parking, if you can find that, and then you got to leave first thing," said the attendant. "Every wash and draw for fifty miles got some rock hound in it. But you here for the scenery, right?"

"You're a shrewd judge of character," Jubal said.

"Just trying to stay one step ahead of the tax collector, boss," answered the man, and winked. "Check under the hood?"

"Might as well," said Jubal, and wandered away to roll a cigarette.

"Excuse me," a man's voice said from behind him. Jubal turned and realized he had seen the man before when they first pulled in. He had been tightening the nuts on the right rear wheel of his rusty pickup with a lug wrench. Jubal thought he'd seemed tired. Maybe because the man stooped as he spun the wrench. Maybe because the man looked more broke than his pickup.

"What can I do you for?" asked Jubal.

"Well," the man said, a sweat-stained gray fedora in his hand. "I couldn't help overhearing your situation. I was thinking I might could do you a favor." His wrists poked out of an old black suit jacket. The collar of his blue shirt was frayed, and he wore no tie. Jubal noticed the man bled from a scratch on his right hand. It wasn't much. The man ignored it. Jubal figured he got it fixing his truck.

"I'll take all the favors I can get," Jubal replied.

"Mind if I make one?" the man asked, referring to the can of Prince Albert. Jubal handed him the red tin and papers.

"Not at all," he said, but the man's hands shook so badly that the tobacco dribbled out of the rolling paper. Jubal took the tin back and rolled one for him.

"Bust a tire?" Jubal asked, and cupped his hands around

a match so the man could get a light. The man breathed the smoke in deeply. It settled him a bit.

"Spent my last dollar on a used one," said the man.

"You were talking about doing me a favor?" asked Jubal.

"Cost you a tank of gas and a box of groceries," said the man.

"What's your part of it?" asked Jubal.

"I got a place you can park your rig and set up camp," said the man.

"Why don't you want it?"

"We're broke. Going home."

"Never found a trace?"

"Claim's worthless. Toss in four bottles of orange pop, and you can have it," said the man.

"You got a place I can set up?" asked Jubal. The man nodded and inhaled another lungful.

"Got shade, water, privacy. Toss in the Prince Albert," the man said.

"This place better be the Taj goddamn Mahal, buddy," cracked Jubal. The man's weary expression didn't change.

"I'll fill up, then you follow me," he said as he pocketed Jubal's Prince Albert in his coat jacket. Jubal gave him the rolling papers, too. Abilene and Gideon, when Jubal told them, agreed it might be a deal.

They followed the man a good ten miles out of town on a paved, two-lane road before he turned east onto a single-lane gravel that cut across a large swath of barren, semiarid land pocked with boulders big and round as baby elephants but no clue how they got there. Gideon loved the sound of the gravel bits tossed up against the chassis by the tires. When he was much younger and heard the same noise on a back road in Mississippi, he believed that elves with very long fingernails were drumming them on the truck doors. Gideon didn't believe that anymore, but he still liked to hear the tat-tat-tat of the gravel and imagine the creatures of the road out there. Sandstone cliffs that had been distant were now closing in and appeared to be channeling them toward a mesa that loomed closer as the gravel road turned to dirt and the dirt road ran out and they were crossing wide open country on no road at all. Gideon felt like he was riding the wind. Roads took you someplace, but suppose you didn't want to go there, you know, where they wanted you to go? Like this out here, though, you could go anywhere you wanted.

The little caravan turned north and skirted the rough face of the mesa. Jubal thought it looked like some helluva rock, but Gideon saw it unroll like a scroll of cracks and crannies, ledges like split lips, gaps suggesting brute force and hidden places. Gideon braced himself against the pounding of the truck as it bounced along the uneven terrain. The tire iron rattled and banged against the tailgate. He knew his father'd be just flying if he didn't have to follow this other man, but maybe that was best because his tailbone was hurting as it was, and more bouncing would only make it worse. Right then his father followed the man through a slot in the rock wall barely wide enough to take their vehicles. A choke stone was jammed into the opening above their heads. He trailed his fingertips along the rock walls on both sides. Once through the narrow section of slot they picked up a dry wash and ground along its gravel bed until the wash widened and revealed a stand of cottonwoods and tamarisks. A badly battered house trailer stood in the shade of a cottonwood. It looked to be deserted. A large, natural stone basin, ten feet across, filled with water and very deep, sat at the end of the stand of trees. Slick red cliffs soared up just beyond the far edge of the pothole. Gideon thought they must've been a thousand feet high.

The man came to a stop beside his trailer, a junker if Jubal had ever seen one. The door opened. A thin and haggard woman stood there and stared out. She wore a threadbare brown dress, and, like her husband, bony wrists poked out of her long sleeves. A young girl stood up from behind a boulder. Her dress was too small and made for someone younger. Gideon figured her to be his age or close. He could see her nipples. They strained against the flimsy material of her dress.

"Help me hitch my trailer, and I'll get out of here," said the man to Jubal.

Jubal and Gideon gave the man a hand. Abilene acted funny and stayed in the cab of the truck.

"I got a Geiger counter, a pick, couple of shovels, other stuff. Toss in another box of groceries and it's all yours," offered the man.

Jubal was about to accept when Abilene hopped down from the truck and promptly squelched the deal. "No, thanks," she said to the man. "You take all your stuff. We'll get our own."

"Suit yourself," said the man, and tossed the pick and shovels into the back of his truck. "Somebody in town'll buy them," he said to no one in particular. "Mind throwing in another box of groceries, anyway?" he said. You could tell he hated to ask. Abilene nodded her head. Gideon handed the man a few extra dollars. "Glad to help," he said. Then the man waved "come on" to the woman and the girl. The woman got into the cab, and the girl climbed into the bed. She leaned her back against the rear window and kept her eyes on Gideon as they drove away.

"What was that all about?" asked Jubal. "We could've gotten that stuff cheap."

"Secondhand tools, secondhand luck," answered Abilene. "You want an orange soda?"

"Sounds good."

"Might be warm."

Jubal shrugged. "Still be good."

"I got some inside," she said, and went to get them. She came back out with three bottles of orange soda in her hands, joined father and son at the base of the cliff, and handed each a bottle.

"Gideon thinks there might be a cave up there," said Jubal.

"You'd have to be King Kong to climb that thing," she said when she saw the look of disdain on the boy's face. "What? You gonna climb it? Maybe. You're monkey enough. And you, Jubal Pickett, you've gone and got us beachfront property." She laughed and strolled to the edge of the pothole, kicked off her shoes, hiked up her skirt, and stepped in to her ankles.

"We got the walls of a palace around us," she said, and spread her arms out wide. Jubal stripped to his shorts and flopped in the water. He swam to the middle and called for Abilene to join him.

"I can't swim," she said.

"Uh-oh," he said with alarm.

"What?" she wanted to know.

"Oh, my God, it's got me by the foot," he screamed.

"Oh, God, Gideon! Gideon!" She looked to the boy for help, but he didn't budge. Jubal thrashed in the water. Something had him.

"Jesus, God, it's got me!" He went under. Abilene screamed and rushed forward but stopped when the water reached above her knees. She looked around helplessly, unable to move. "Gideon, your father! Jesus! What is wrong with you? Why don't you move?" she screamed.

Suddenly Jubal broke the surface and grabbed her by the waist. It was about the funniest thing he'd done all day. The man cracked himself up. He began to pull Abilene into deeper water.

"Now it's got *you,*" he laughed, but Abilene was in pure panic.

"Let me go! I'll drown. I can't swim. Let me go, goddamnit!" she yelled, and wrenched away. "Don't you ever do that to me again!" She scrambled out. "Do you hear me?"

"I-I was only joking," stammered Jubal.

"It ain't funny, goddamnit. You scared the living shit out of me."

Jubal splashed out and tried to put his arms around her.

"Don't you ever ever ever do that to me again," she hollered, and smacked him in the chest so hard he almost went down. "Get away from me! You do something like that to me again

I'll make you wish you never did! You will beg me for mercy, and, so help me God, you will not get it."

The three of them spent the hours to dinnertime in their own thoughts and doing whatever chores each needed to turn the wilderness into habitable living. As soon as Jubal and Gideon unhitched the trailer (which Abilene insisted be parked under a different tree than the last), she disappeared inside to do some arranging. Gideon set up an army surplus sleeping bag at the edge of the pothole where he'd sleep, and afterward wandered off to do some exploring. Jubal tinkered under the hood, then sat in the truck and got lost in the topo maps of the area. When Abilene poked her head outside to call the men to the dinner she'd cooked on the kerosene stove, she was alarmed to find Jubal sitting on the top step watching Gideon make his way up the cliff wall. The boy was ten, fifteen feet off the ground. "Good Christ, he's going to get himself killed," Abilene said.

"Climbs just like a goddamn orangutan, don't he?" said Jubal. "Hey, hotshot," he called out to Gideon, "come get dinner!"

I will never understand these creatures called men, thought Abilene, though, on the other hand, she understood them well enough. She crossed her fingers that the boy wouldn't fall and break his neck.

A little while later, when the men sat down to dinner, they found a table set with knives, napkins, and forks, with a vase of wildflowers in the middle. Abilene served up mashed potatoes, fried Spam, bread, butter, and a full pitcher of strawberry

Kool-Aid. Jubal offered up a prayer. "Good Lord, thank you for this bounty. Give us the luck to find what we're lookin' for and the good sense to know what to do with it. Amen."

Abilene chimed in, "Dig in, boys. I intend to make us a home right here in the wilderness."

After dinner, Jubal and Gideon cleared the table, and Gideon took the dishes down to the pothole to wash. "No climbing now," said his father. "It's getting dark, and you ain't a bat." Jubal chuckled at his own joke, but, the truth was, he'd felt a little uneasy since trading places with the guy he met at the gas station. He knew it was so and wished he didn't feel it, but that could be him one day. He felt troubled enough to want his son's company because it was a fact that just sitting next to his boy always settled him down. Sometimes, when Gideon was still at school, if Jubal got a speck unraveled, he'd sit on Gideon's bed and almost right away he'd feel right-side-up again. So he got up and went out to where Gideon was washing the dishes, didn't say a word to him, just sat there on a boulder nearby and rolled a cigarette, sat there and blew smoke rings. "Lemme see if I can get one of these things to go 'round a star," he said, inhaled deeply, set his lips, and puffed out smoke. It started small, then opened and grew until it circled the moon. "Damn," said Jubal, pleased with himself. "Guess I still got a few tricks left in my back pocket." He smoked his cigarette down as far as he could, then flipped the tiny butt into the pothole, where it sizzled out. Jubal tousled his son's hair and said, "Good night."

When Jubal got back to the trailer, Abilene was sitting at

the table in her lilac robe brushing her hair. He took a paper bag and a stubby pencil from the table drawer and sat down to make a list of all the gear and supplies they would need to get in the morning. Seemed like a truckload, and he wished she hadn't squelched the deal to buy all that equipment cheap.

"You a little bit nervous?" she asked, sensing his mood.

"I ain't that nervous," he said.

She was nearly purring now. "You are a little bit. I can tell."

"That's a lot of country out there," he conceded. Abilene got up, walked around to Jubal, and began massaging his shoulders.

"Money goes fast, I know," she said. "I'm going to look for work in the morning. I don't want you worrying about us tapping out the kitty. You got enough on your mind. People been climbing all over these rocks for a couple of years now. It's been picked over, some of it has, but only some of it. There's plenty more out there, and we're here to find it, you and me, we're in this thing together. Anyway, nothing we can do about it 'til morning, right?" She turned down the lantern to a soft warm glow. "Right?" she asked again.

"Right," he answered.

"Except," she said.

"What's that?" he asked.

"It's a chilly night, and you know what I forgot?" she asked.

"What's that?"

"My nightgown," she said, stood in front of him, and opened her lilac chenille robe. Abilene was stark wonderfully naked.

"Allow me to put your mind to rest, Jubal Pickett," she said. Jubal whooped, picked her up, and sat her on the table. She kissed him mightily. Her legs wrapped around his hips. He picked her up, and she clung to him as the two of them fell on the narrow bed together. "This is wilder than riding a bull in the rodeo," said Jubal.

"Do me a favor, buckaroo," she said. "Try to hang on for the whole eight seconds."

"Help me get these goddamn clothes off," he hollered. "I'm going for the record." She whooped and laughed and bounced her naked heels joyfully off his butt. Their shouts and laughter carried down to the pothole, where Gideon heard them. He pressed his palms over his ears, but a piece of him wanted to listen. A piece of him wanted to sneak back. That wouldn't be right. He felt his penis. It was alive. Not right. Not right. He wasn't thinking, did not want to think. Wanted . . . What? Gideon jumped up and went for the wall. He leaped and got a fingerhold, pulled himself up, and began to scale the cliff. There was the moonlight, and he had no fear of going forward, going away, going up. He didn't need the light; he climbed by feel. His fingers found the cracks, and the rest of him followed. He had no fear. All he wanted to do was climb. Not true. Not all. Climb, boy. Find a crack. Pull up. Climb. Pull up. Climb. Until he reached a ledge. Under an overhang. Pulled himself up and sat at the edge like an Indian. Gideon felt suspended between the earth at midnight and a sky spackled with stars. There was no wind. He saw forever. He took the red tin of Prince Albert from his breast pocket, rolled himself a cigarette, lit it, flicked the burning match into the air. It was so silent up there he believed he heard the flame go out before it reached the water. He inhaled deeply. Yeah. Better.

Jubal drove them into town first thing the next morning. He was determined to get a jump on the day. Abilene made oatmeal for breakfast, and Jubal attributed Gideon's sullen attitude to a teenage boy's natural annoyance at having to get up so early. When Abilene tousled his hair, he pulled away. When she asked, "If I sprinkle extra sugar on your oatmeal, will you be sweet?" Gideon just stared at the bowl. "Lord, Jubal," she said, "I guess I got my work cut out for me with this one." Then she walked over behind Gideon's chair, leaned down, and put her arms around him. "You're invited to the party, too, y'know. Give up now and save yourself some trouble. You're dealing with Wonder Woman, buddy. She got you surrounded." With that she gave him an extra squeeze, but Gideon did not budge. He sat stiff as a two-by-four. Jubal drank the dregs of his coffee and said, "Saddle up." On the road to town, they drove past a battered truck and trailer pulled off onto the opposite shoulder. It belonged to the family that had turned its campsite over to the Picketts. The man stood by a sign with the words FURNITURE 4 SALE. MINING TOOLS scrawled on the side of a torn piece of cardboard box. The woman squatted by an open fire with a coffeepot on it. Their daughter wasn't anywhere around, but they didn't seem concerned about that. Jubal couldn't help but stare at them.

"Uh-uh," Abilene said as she sensed his unease. It was an order. Just then a helicopter whomped over the road low enough for them to read the brash scarlet letters on its golden door: CHOSIN FEW AIR SERVICES. "Now, that'd be the way to travel," she said. Once in town Jubal lucked into a parking space pretty much right smack in front of the very store they planned to visit: the hardware store with a sign in its window, MINING SUPPLIES. As far as Jubal was concerned, it was an omen, a smack-you-between-the-eyes omen, so, once again, he felt on the right path. "I'll meet you back here for lunch," said Abilene when they had climbed down from the truck. She took a last look at her face in the side-view mirror. "Somebody ought to hire you just to look at you," said Jubal, and Abilene did look good, like a secretary, he thought, or a lady who sold china at a department store. "My seams straight?" she asked Jubal, then turned around so he could see for himself. Jubal felt himself harden. "Fine," he said. Truth was, she knew they were fine, but she wanted Jubal to take another peek at what he had, or, more to the point, what she had. She knew he liked to watch her walk. Most men did. Posture. That was the whole secret in a nutshell. You walk straight. You walk tall. You don't need to swing your big ass from side to side. No need to stick your butt out so far you could set a beer bottle on it. Straight but loose. Not suggestive but it drew your attention. Abilene's walk caught you like a smile. It was contagious. She felt good today.

"Wish me luck, boys," she said, kissed them each on the cheek, and walked away down the street. Jubal stayed transfixed until he caught a guy eyeing her as she passed by, looked around, and saw that other men watched her, too, and that was something he didn't know how he felt about it. Exactly. All in all, he preferred to think of himself as one lucky son of a bitch rather than think himself a damn fool.

Abilene, for her part, knew that she was locked and loaded to the best of her secret wiles and feminine abilities. She had an impression to make, and this woman was bound and determined to make it right. She had planned to wear a pair of those new seamless nylons, but once she got them on she looked like a bare-legged woman, and that meant one who was loose, common, and undignified, none of which being the impression she wanted to convey, so she took them off and put on a clean older pair, checked for runs, and made sure the seams were straight. She had hung up a full white slip and her yellow-going-on-gold dress the day they got in, so the wrinkles would fall out. The white slip and yellow dress made her feel like a sunny-side up, and she didn't care if it was a hundred and fifty degrees out there, a lady wore a full slip, and Abilene, goddamnit, was a lady. But the *prize de resistance* was her pointed brassiere with a pearl in each tip. Once, back in Port Arthur, while she was waiting one evening for her cousin to finish dressing, Abilene read in *Hollywood Confidential* that the crème de la crème of glamour du jour on the Strip wore pointed silk bras with real pearls sewn into the tips. Jane Russell admitted she was wearing one at the Brown Derby and emphasized that the pearls were real, and a famous casting director said absolutely do not come in for an audition without one. Abilene doubted the sanity of any man who got Jane Russell's bra off, then stopped and checked to make sure her pearl wasn't a fake, but still she had to have one for herself. Buying it was out of the question. Even if you had the money (a good four tanks' worth of gasoline), could you find one within a hundred miles of where she lived? Not hardly. But Abilene wasn't about to let a backwater burg stand in her way. She cut out a paper pattern from another magazine and asked her cousin could she use her sewing machine? She didn't doubt the answer would be yes, plus she had a great idea: she went to the Port Arthur Military Surplus and bought some old parachute silk to make the bra. Abilene snipped two pearls off her cousin's wedding dress where she didn't think anybody'd see them missing, and when she finished that bra she put it on, modeled in front of the mirror, and thought, Who could resist Abilene Breedlove? Now that she was in Edom she put the bra on under her yellow-going-on-gold dress, knowing full well that probably nobody else would wear a yellow dress for a job interview, but she wanted people to know they were getting a positive person with a cheerful outlook, and, anyway, she did not intend to work in a place where they wouldn't let a yellow dress through the door. Abilene had and would keep her standards.

The hardware store was packed floor to ceiling with gear: columns of coiled rope, stacks of five-gallon water cans, gleaming geologist's picks, cold chisels, cases of dynamite, Geiger counters. Jubal put his list on the counter and said to the clerk, "Guess we want just about two of everything." The clerk was a white-haired and leathery old bastard, with squinty eyes from too much time in the sun and a crotchety smirk on his weathered face. He took a look at Jubal's list and said, "Jesus H., another big dummy come to strike it rich." He hooted derisively.

"Who you calling a dummy?" asked Jubal.

"You," shot back the clerk, "and you better be glad I'm taking pity on you. Save you a lot of heartache, dummy." Jubal didn't like being talked to that way, especially with Gideon right there.

"You better be glad you're an old man," growled Jubal, just about ready to go over the counter at him, anyway.

"Why's that?" the old man taunted. "'Cause you'd bust me one? Go ahead. I been busted by better'n you."

"Your boss know you're rude to the customers?"

"My boss don't give a shit."

"Where is he?" demanded Jubal.

"Dentist. I'm filling in for him. Hear what I said? Dentist? Filling in? That's the kind of mind you're dealing with, buster," said the old man. "A steel trap."

"Who the hell are you?" Jubal wanted to know. The old man handed Jubal a business card that stated, CHARLES P. NICKEL, MILLIONAIRE.

"Charles P. Nickel, Bullshit Artist," said Jubal.

"Actually, it ought to say multimillionaire by now. I better get some new ones printed up," said Nickel. Gideon poked his father and pointed to a framed newspaper article that hung on the wall.

"Hold on, son," said Nickel, and took the article from the wall. "I'll give you a closer look," he said, and handed it to Gideon. "Your daddy might want to take a look at this, too." The framed article showed a picture of Charles P. Nickel standing in front of a pile of stones, leaning on a shovel with a stick of dynamite in his free hand. The caption stated, "Charlie Nickel, local prospector, strikes it rich."

"This really you?" asked Jubal.

"Who you think it is? Croesus? It ain't. I'm richer'n him."

"You really did it, huh?"

"Crawled all over these rocks for years. Found a little tin, found a little silver, found a little gold, found a shitload of carnotite."

"What's that?" asked Jubal.

"See what I mean, dummy? Carnotite's a yellow rock. Know what it's got inside it? You do, don't you, son?" he asked Gideon. Gideon nodded his head. "Go on. Tell your daddy."

"He don't talk."

"Why don't he?"

"Because he don't."

"Well, listen up and learn something: uranium's what's in it. Wheresoever you find it, you find riches that power the world."

"Well, Charlie Nickel, that's exactly what I'm intending to do," said Jubal.

"That's what everybody intends to do, and most of 'em go home without a pot to piss in."

"Appreciate the advice," said Jubal, then, referring to the list, he said, "Matches, candles, det cord, blasting caps, dyna-mite—"

"Where's your claim?" asked Charlie Nickel. Jubal stuck with his list.

"Blasting caps, dynamite—"

"Please tell me you got one." Nickel looked over at Gideon and raised his eyebrows. Gideon shook his head. "You ain't serious. No claim?"

"I'm gonna get one."

"How?"

"Awright, goddamnit! How?"

"Two ways. You either find one or buy one, and since you don't know the difference between a pile of tailings and a bag of peanuts, you better buy one."

"You wouldn't happen to have one in your back pocket you're willing to sell cheap?" asked Jubal sarcastically, and winked at his son to show him he was in control of the situation.

"I'm too smart for that. Once I found uranium, I sold my claim to a big company for a fat check and royalties. They put me on the board of directors, and now I just sit back and let the post office deliver my checks."

"Where can I buy a claim?" Jubal wanted to know.

"You might try one of those fellas in front of the courthouse," suggested Nickel. "You might also try putting your balls in a rattlesnake's mouth."

In fact, Jubal had seen what Charlie Nickel was talking about when he drove by the courthouse on his way to the hardware store. It reminded him of a bat cave—there was one nearby where he grew up in Mississippi—a bat cave at sunset when those airborne rats wheeled and shrieked their way out of the bowels of the earth, and bats, he thought then and thought this morning, got to be amongst the ugliest creatures in creation. What he saw in front of the courthouse came under the category of pretty ugly, as well: a pack of lawyers, most of them working out of the trunks of their cars, a couple from the tailgates of pickup trucks. There were signs saying FILE YOUR CLAIMS HERE and SHARES and BUY-INS AVAILABLE, signs like that.

You obviously had to go through these men to get to the court-house.

"They're vultures," said Jubal.

"The thing about vultures," Charlie Nickel said, "they do know where the meat is." Then he winked at Gideon, too. The boy looked down at his feet, a twitch of a smile on his lips.

Jubal knew to be cautious. When dealing with matters of property changing hands, he could horse-trade like his fore-bears, the river boatmen—give something, get something; give a little, try to get more, walk away, come back, kick the dirt, look to heaven, curse like hell, spit, nod, make the deal, and never ever let on that it made you in the least bit happy. Of course, Jubal was ready to concede that he knew the lay of the land back around Natchez a lot better than he knew the maze of desert canyons around southeast Utah, but he knew a valid deed when he saw one, and all legal rights therein and so forth and so on, and he had studied up best he could long-distance on the necessary geological formations that were needed on a claim to prove its promise. That carnotite business threw him, he had to admit, yeah, boy, but that was a mineral deposit, a whatchamacallum, a leach, a chemical reaction, not a geologi-cal feature. However, Jubal considered himself a judicious man and so realized that every new bit of information was a plus. He filed this one away with the other bits: carnotite, a yellow rock . . . Wasn't a doubt in his mind that Gideon had that one down cold.

By the process of elimination brought about by his patience, perspicacity, and powers of observation, Jubal finally decided he liked the look of one of them in particular, a distinguished gent with silver hair and a khaki suit, a button-down blue shirt, and a striped red and silver bow tie neatly done up even with it being June in the desert. The man had bearing to him and sat at a desk set up on the back of his pickup (this year's Ford Flathead V-8 without a ding in it; that said something for him), more like a judge than a lawyer, but Jubal and Gideon had been watching him for a while and seen how there was usually somebody waiting in line to talk to him, how he took his time before he took their money and seemed to have answers to their questions as well as customized advice for their next step.

"You've been checking me out for the past couple of hours, friend," said the lawyer from behind his desk. "Ready to do some business?" he asked.

"If you're ready to come down here or let us come up there, we might have something to talk about," said Jubal, proud to take a stand in front of his boy.

"Have a seat," the man said, and indicated the rim along the bed of the truck. Jubal vaulted up even with him, took the man's hand, gave and got names, and sat down. Gideon settled on the tailgate and rolled a cigarette. The lawyer took a fresh pack of Chesterfields from his shirt pocket, shook out a couple, and offered one to Jubal. Jubal took it. The man lit it for him with a silver Zippo emblazoned with the seal of a submariner in the United States Navy. Jubal informed him that he was navy as well, Pearl Harbor. "It's an honor," the lawyer said, sat up a little straighter, and shook Jubal's hand again. Then they commenced to talk business. Jubal turned to Gideon and said, "Listen up, son."

Diogenes Santweir, for that was the lawyer's name, spoke in a way that sounded like he hadn't said the exact same words scores of times. His voice was calm, professorial, reassuring. Jubal looked into his eyes, and Santweir looked right back. Jubal thought that was a good sign and listened carefully as Mr. Santweir detailed his services and went through his files to see if there was a match to be made. He didn't pressure Jubal at all, simply perused the options available to him, explaining the points his client didn't totally comprehend. To Jubal's credit, he listened carefully and learned a little bit more than he knew before he sat down. After a while, one claim piqued his interest, and he and Mr. Santweir began to talk a little more in earnest about the destination named Little Moqui Canyon. Plenty of ore had come out of the Moqui already, but it wasn't top-grade commercial ore. The problem was the miners needed to go deeper than their pockets. Even money placed a belt of high-grade ore down there, but they ran out of cash. They might've gotten to it but their drill snapped in two, and drill bits are costly. The original owners needed an investor with money, a strong back, and a fearsome will to win that uranium as bad as he ever wanted anything, and Jubal felt like he could be that man.

Santweir led the two of them into the courthouse to see the record of deed and its description, and also to examine the assay report. A clerk ushered them into an airless room filled with racks of oversize ledgers bound in canvas with corners reinforced by leather in which the transactions and boundary markers from Genesis day one were recorded. The clerk also rendered a certified copy of the assay report. Its raised seal and its contents matched that of the one Mr. Santweir had produced from his files. The possibilities were rich indeed. Some tonnage of low-grade ore had been taken, nothing earth shattering in itself; however, the most promising aspect of the current report showed the quality of the ore increasing as the depth at which it was mined increased as well. It might be a matter of inches. The good stuff was down there waiting for somebody with hard cash to win it. Mr. Santweir assumed Jubal Pickett had said cash and was assured he did. For a certain price, Jubal would be allowed to buy into the deal, his only obligation being that Diogenes Santweir get 25 percent of the take. Jubal thought that was fair, and, on their way back to Santweir's truck, he said he thought it might be possible to work something out. "I can have you boys breaking a sweat this afternoon," said Mr. Santweir. Jubal offered 25 percent of penny one after the investment paid back his buy-in at one thousand five hundred dollars. When they reached the truck the two men shook hands, and the lawyer climbed back up behind his desk and set about drawing up the necessary documents. Father and son sat on the tailgate and set about rolling cigarettes from their tins of Prince Albert. "Gentlemen?" called Mr. Santweir. Jubal and Gideon turned to see if he meant them, and the lawyer tossed them his Chesterfields. "Keep the pack," he said. Jubal winked at Gideon as if they'd won something big, gave the boy a cigarette, and took one for himself. Could be worse, he thought, him and his boy taking a smoke break, all the times that lay ahead.

What was intended to be a peaceful interlude was shattered by an automobile's insistent horn. It wouldn't let up. "Jesus Christ, will you pack it?" growled Jubal as he turned on the perpetrator. Jubal took the honking personally, which, as it turned out, he was right to do. There idled a fire-engine red, brand-new Cadillac Eldorado convertible, with 870 x 15 white-wall tires the span of a man's hand, and, behind the wheel, leaning on the horn, was Charlie Nickel. "Do you believe in divine provenance?" he hollered out to Jubal.

"Get the hell away from here, Charlie," ordered Santweir.

"Why do you want to separate these poor Christians from their hard-earned money, Diogenes?" asked Nickel. To Jubal he said, "Hand me those papers," and pointed to Santweir's desk. Santweir promptly slammed his hand down over the papers.

Jubal didn't like the way he moved so fast. "Let him see the papers," he said to Santweir.

"This is America, Diogenes," said Charlie Nickel. "Every citizen deserves a second opinion." Jubal took the papers and handed them to Charlie.

"You miserable old fart," yapped Santweir.

"You forgot to add 'filthy stinking rich' miserable old fart," chuckled Charlie, and took a look at both the deed and the assay report. "Little Moqui, huh? A good play, no doubt about it, but it played out two years ago. Somebody doctored the date on this document."

"Hell they did. This is a legal document," quarreled Sant-weir.

"You buy this," said Charlie to Jubal, "and you ain't got the brains God gave a banana."

"Bullroar," hollered Santweir. "That's a perfectly legal claim."

"Except," said Charlie, "I happen to know personally there ain't nothin' in there anymore. Listen, Jubal, I'll make you a deal."

"Charlie, goddamnit, stay out of my business," yelled Santweir.

"Ah, shut up, Diogenes," said Charlie.

"What's your deal?" Jubal asked.

"For five dollars I'll tell you all I know," said Charlie Nickel.

"If you got so much money," said Jubal, "why don't you just tell me for free?"

"Son," said Nickel, "this is America. Need I say more? Come on, Jubal, do your boy here a favor. Five bucks, I give you both a geology lesson."

"You like the idea, don't you?" Jubal asked Gideon. The boy didn't smile but he did nod, just a little; there it was. "Why me?" Jubal wanted to know.

"I like you and your boy. And I got nothin' better to do than spend my time and your money. Hop in." Gideon vaulted into the back seat. Charlie reached over to unlock the door for Jubal. "I owe you a beer, Diogenes," he yelled. To Jubal he said, "Scum. I'd send 'em all to Siberia."

Jubal admired the automobile. "This all yours?" he asked.

"Well, it ain't yours," said Charlie, gunned the engine, and laid a patch of thick, black rubber down the middle of Main Street. Before he stopped swerving and straightened out he had the radio on. Johnnie Ray sobbed out, "If your sweetheart sends a letter of good-bye . . . ." "Can't stand that guy," snarled

Charlie, and changed the station. "Damn fools pay him to cry like a baby, and the damn fool does it. Helluva way for a growed man to make his living."

―――――――――

The Eldorado purred at seventy-five. It sprinted over the two-lane blacktop like a great cat gaining on its prey, gathering speed, covering turf. This was Charlie Nickel's current version of reality, but, at that moment, Gideon Pickett and Charlie Nickel were in parallel worlds. Gideon felt like he was fired from a great gun, an artillery cannon. The wind tried to tear him off the big shell as it arced through space, but he hung on and rode high and wondered when the shell came down would it burrow deep into the earth before it blew the magic horde to smithereens and scattered its radiant pellets all over the ground like jelly beans. Jubal stewed and wondered if he'd just blown five bucks.

Edom was so small it was gone before you realized it was ever there. Maybe a mile the other side of town, Nickel steered the Eldorado off the paved highway onto a dirt road and followed it across the flats. He lined the Cadillac's hood ornament up on a distant mesa and made directly for it. They baked under the early afternoon sun but the top stayed down and nobody offered to put it up, so Jubal and Gideon accepted it as their condition. Charlie Nickel had a lot to say, and they were paying to listen to him. Gideon hung in close to grab the words he could before they got gobbled by the wind.

"Never wanted to do anything else but prospect. Even as a kid. Never could work for nobody but myself. Never will.

Been all over these canyons on foot, donkey, and jeep. When I got married, my wife said, 'Charlie, get a job!' One day I counted one hundred thousand dollars cash into the palm of her hand. Her mouth damn near dropped to the floor. She ain't said a word to me about gettin' a job ever since."

———

The mesa was called Frying Pan because it got so hot on top. Two thousand feet up closer to the sun. Its virtue was the view it afforded across a vast expanse of canyonland that spread out below like a web of capillaries. You could see the upturn of the swell, like the outermost layer of a bubble, and the tortured rock formations that had forced their way through its surface. Charlie parked the red Caddy at the mesa's edge, and the three of them got out. They were high above the wind. It was the most silence Jubal and Gideon had ever heard. At some point, out of that silence, Charlie Nickel commenced to talk.

"Smart men, dummies, all kinds get caught up in this fever, but a strike comes down to luck. Usually, the man with the most knowledge has the best luck. First lesson: everything out there'll either sting you, stick you, bite you, or burn you."

"We can handle it," said Jubal.

"Tell me what you're lookin' at," said Charlie Nickel.

"I'm lookin' at rocks," said Jubal.

"What kind of rocks, Einstein?" asked Charlie.

Jubal just stared dumbly out at them.

"Feelin' stupid? See, the old-timers was good at readin' the country. What they did was find a good play or structure and then work it. See them domes of rock way out there? They're called the Miscarriage Mountains 'cause they were almost but not quite born. Between there and here the whole kit 'n' caboodle's called the San Rafael Swell, and that's where your uranium is. Course, that's a good hundred square miles, so how're you gonna find it?"

"Geiger counter," offered Jubal limply.

"How y'gonna know where to put it? What color rock? Pay attention. You got two major formations out there—the Morrison and the Chinle. That's where most of the mining and prospecting takes place. The Morrison's got a whitish top and a sandy-red bottom. The Chinle's got a lot of yellow from all the carnotite in it. You want to look in the bottom of the Chinle but the top of the Morrison. You gettin' all this?" asked Charlie.

"No," answered Jubal. Had a touch of despair crept up on him?

"Ask me a question," said Nickel.

"How'd you finally find it?" asked Jubal.

"I witched it," answered Charlie.

"What?" yelped Jubal.

"Witched it."

"What you mean 'witched it'?" Jubal demanded. Nickel opened the trunk of his red Cadillac and took out a forked twig. He held it out in front of him by its prongs.

"Dowsed it. You know, like with water, a dowsing stick. You walk around until it quivers and points down."

"Piece of willow?"

"Yeah. Willow."

"You are truly full of shit," said Jubal.

"I wouldn't doubt it, but what I just told you was the God's honest truth," affirmed Charlie Nickel, and spit like he meant it. Then he went on. "Ore changes a man's soul," he said, "so the guy who looks for it ain't the same guy who gets it. No matter what, your life is gonna change. Those who love you will hate you; you'll love who you shouldn't. If you ever strike it rich you won't have a friend in the world, and if you don't strike it rich you'll suffer the abuse of yourself and others for the rest of your life. Take my advice: go home. You ought to listen to me, buster, but you won't."

Jubal stood on the edge of the world and stared out over that baking hell stitched with canyons like angry scars; and, right then and there, he suddenly felt like he didn't know a tectonic fault from a tonsillectomy. All the stuff he'd read and pictures he'd seen hadn't prepared him for this strew of treacherous rubble meaner than anything his mind had ever conjured up back in Mississippi. Winds would howl down those canyons. They'd play the rocks, blow through holes and crevices, and make all kinds of noise. It made his goddamn head spin. He made a mental note to pick up two extra compasses, the kind that pin to your shirt. Gideon walked over to his father and pointed to something in the distance. Two bighorn sheep. Out there on a ledge silhouetted against a patinated cliff. The air was so clear who could tell how far, but there they were, and, just below the two men, lazily riding the thermals, was a buzzard. Gideon felt happy. How many times did you ever get to see a bird from above? Jubal thought if he had his choice he'd be a buzzard because how the hell else could anything but a damn bird find its way out of that mess?

Abilene showed up back at the truck with three brown bags full of groceries, one in each arm and the third squeezed in between. It was later that afternoon as planned, and she was in a jaunty mood. When she spotted Jubal sitting on the running board with his head in his hands and a cigarette dangling dejectedly from his lips, she said, "Hey, hey, hey, is this Mr. Jubal Pickett, uranium baron, sittin' here waitin' for some funeral to get started?" Gideon was in the back of the truck listening to her turquoise plastic portable radio.

"I ain't no baron," said Jubal.

"Well, let me tell you something, mister," she said, "if you ain't, then I got no business standin' here 'cause I do not talk to strange men." It was a tone he hadn't heard before. She thrust the bags at him. "You gonna take these or what?" Jubal took the bags in his arms and carried them back to the bed of the truck. "Gideon," he said, and handed his son the bags. Before he could turn back to her she was right up on him. "I didn't come here to lose," she said. "Listen to me. You showed me a man who could dream the dream, buck the odds, turn himself into somethin'. Where's he at now? Stand up, bub. I got a bet riding on this, and I am not about to lose it."

"You don't just walk out into the desert and pick uranium up off the goddamn ground." Even he didn't like the way he sounded. Weak. Weak.

"I never thought it was gonna be easy, but I never thought you were gonna cave in on day one, either," said Abilene.

"I'm not caving in. Who said anything about caving in?"

"Thank you. That's what I want to hear."

"I never said I was caving in."

"Now you sound like a man I know. Be glad you got me, Jubal Pickett. I found myself a job, and I believe I have met our future. Let's go."

"Where?" he asked.

"The airport."

"Where's an airport?"

"I can't wait to show you, babe," she said. "Hold the door for a lady, will ya?" He did. He held the door for her, and she stepped up into the cab. One leg on the running board, one on the floor. He enjoyed the way Abilene's thighs parted as she slid across the seat. Especially nice was that portion of the bare inner thigh from the top of the stocking to the start of her panties. Jubal wished he could kiss it right now. Abilene knew this, which is why she lingered with them parted—just a little—as long as she did.

PART 6

Jack Savage had seen her sitting in the waiting room when he came out to greet another applicant, and he knew before he had ever said a word to her that he would give her the job. She had arrived early for her interview—a good sign, though it was not her punctuality that attracted him—and sat there composed and relaxed, not at all fidgety or stiff like the rest of the girls waiting there. Some touched up their makeup. One used Kleenex to wipe the lipstick off her front teeth. One filed her nails. One stuck her gum on the bottom of her seat. She thought nobody saw her, of course, but he had great peripheral vision and caught the move. Others read magazines or scoured the local paper circling more ads. He could see that each of them had that paper folded to the want ads, with his advertisement circled, but he didn't see one with her. That probably meant her fingertips would be the only ones not blackened by newsprint. Probably the chamber of commerce sent her over because he had posted a help wanted notice on their bulletin board. When he looked at her, she met his gaze. Her eyes were steady; her smile was polite. How many before he got to her? Too many, and none of them were going to get the job, but he had to go through the motions anyway. He couldn't just wave his hand and send everyone away except for her, but, damn, if he could have he would have.

For her part, she had an awfully good feeling about this job, didn't know why but felt right about it since she first saw the want ad posted earlier in the day. She asked the lady manning the desk if she'd let her use the phone to call and set up an appointment, which the good woman allowed her to do, and when told there was no transportation out there unless you drove in an automobile, she stuck out her thumb and hitched. Was she afraid somebody might try to take advantage of her? Not even a little bit. She was perfectly prepared to bite off anything some rude son of a bitch might shove in her direction. A perfectly nice older man in a Studebaker stake-bed picked her up and dropped her off right where she wanted. Of course, he felt obliged to tell her that he had a granddaughter who'd probably do something truly stupid like she just did—hitchhiking with all those crazy psychos out there—and he hoped somebody else's grandfather would do her the same kindness and pick his granddaughter up, too. "What goes around comes around, right?" he said. "I truly believe that," she answered, and she truly did. She had her working version of the cosmos, but she rarely thought about it beyond a certain point. She'd get notions, but then she'd get tired. Who had time for notions?

"Mr. Jubal Pickett, meet Mr. Jack Savage," said Abilene, smiling broadly as she introduced the two men. "And this is Gideon," she said with her arm around the boy's shoulders. "Shake the man's hand, Gideon." He didn't have to do what she said if he didn't want to. He did, though, shake, but he wouldn't look at the man. He thought Jack squeezed his hand too hard and smiled too much. He wondered if the man's gold tooth would glitter in the sun and figured, yes, why wouldn't it?

"Glad to meet you, Mr. Pickett," said Jack. "Mrs. Pickett's told me good things about you."

Jubal shot Abilene a look on that one. Mrs. Pickett?

"Call me Abby," she said to Jack Savage smoothly while she squeezed Jubal's arm. Jubal saw it, rightly, as a warning. She took him by the hand, grabbed Gideon's, and said, "Come on, boys, let me show you where Momma's gonna be workin'."

Jack had met them in the small waiting room where Abilene had first met him for her interview. He followed the Picketts and Abilene as she led the way outside to an adjacent building. As cinder block seemed to be the generic building block of Edom, the structure itself was cinder block, squat and square, bunkerlike, but the front was framed out with wood like the entrance to a mineshaft. Douglas fir was Jubal's guess, strong enough to support ceilings made of tons of rock. A sign advertised the place as THE HIDDEN SPLENDOR, A STAKE HOUSE, RARE CONDITIONED DINING. Jubal spotted the sign when he parked at the Quonset hut next door and wondered if anybody else besides himself had noticed that the words were spelled wrong.

Abilene, all smiles and bright energy, ushered them inside and held out her right arm as if she were showing off her new living room. "Gentlemen," she said to Jubal and Gideon, "you are looking at the new daytime hostess of the finest steakhouse in southeast Utah." She finished up with a little curtsy-bow. The Hidden Splendor had obviously tapped a vein in the community, because ever since day one the number of diners who went there grew exponentially, so much so that the owner, Jack Savage, added an extra shift and opened for breakfast, too, with staples of the mining country served hot, and plenty of 'em, specializing all day, every day in shit on a shingle, biscuits and gravy with chunks of deer liver, and slabs of blood-red meat two inches thick before noon with jalapeño pepper sauce if that's what the gent wanted. Nothing too fancy-pants, but a few steps up—red and white checked oilcloths on the tables, for example, oversize blue napkins, and a mahogany bar so's a man could belly up to luxury. This was a hardworking town. Let the folks know they're getting something a little special. Jack had promised Abilene that if she worked a full five-day work shift he'd see to it that she got two nights as well. The tips were better then, but she had to be willing to work seven days a week, which she said she'd gladly do. If the men were gonna do it, she was gonna do it, too. "You're a lucky man, Mr. Pickett," said Jack Savage, "married to a woman like that."

"Call me Jubal," said Pickett.

It hadn't taken long. No doubt about it, Abilene Breedlove could weave a web and wrap you up in her charms, if she wanted, and, before her interview was half over, Abilene had begun to make herself indispensable. She'd come up with this great idea: "This is a real hot moneymaker, Mr. Savage, I do not lie." When Jack asked her what it was, she asked him did she get the job? When he said yes, she told him: the house special, a drink she called the Hidden Splendor, kind of like a margarita except you added frozen lemonade plus a third of a bottle of beer to the mix. That was the secret ingredient. You'd never know it was there as long as you used a good American brew. Folks got ripped on it. Back in Oklahoma her people called it the Chain Saw Massacre. Abilene recommended swearing the bartender to secrecy, make him mix the brew in batches out back so the customers couldn't watch him and figure it out. Jack Savage said he'd see to it. "In fact," he said, "why don't you mix a batch right now and bring your family by to celebrate?"

"Sure," she said, "that'd be nice."

Later, while she was shopping for groceries (Vanda, one of the waitresses, had given her a ride in from the airport), Abilene's thoughts went to this man who called himself Jack Savage, her new boss. Let's be honest. By the time she reached the canned goods aisle Abilene realized that her mind had been filled with nothing else. It was like she had this balloon in her brain that kept getting bigger and bigger until everything was pushed out of it except an image of him. He was like a gypsy, she thought, a mysterious black-haired, blue-eyed gypsy with a smile she felt in the pit of her stomach. He made her think of a poem she'd been taught in high school: " . . . the highwayman came riding, riding, riding . . ." And he was very smart. And he listened to her. Something about the way that guy talked to you, something about it, he had this way of leaning in, made it seem like there was nothing else in this world right that minute more important than you. How the hell did he do that? She didn't even know the man, but it was weird because she kind of felt like she did. Know him. Abilene couldn't put a finger on any one thing in particular. She just knew she did. He had come to Edom after the war with a service buddy looking for an investment. They were survivors of the First Marine Division when Chinese troops swept over the border and surrounded them at the Chosin Reservoir. They fought their way out, and those who lived called themselves the Chosin Few. Jack had inherited his Lithuanian grandfather's fortune and decided that what the burgeoning place needed was an airport, so he bought significant acreage north of town, bulldozed out an airstrip, and built the Quonset hut for a waiting room and office. The fact that Jack had an airport and still no aircraft, let alone a license to fly one, was beside the point. He and his partner, Tommy Moon, learned to fly planes as well as helicopters, put one of each on their airstrip, and then built a sign on the roof of the Quonset hut touting the Chosin Few Air Service. A year into the business, Tommy died when his chopper clipped a power line and went down, and Jack had run the business himself since then. Abilene filled Jubal and Gideon in on the way over.

"There's something going on here, Jubal, I can feel it in the marrow of my bones. We set out to do something, and, goddamnit, gentlemen, I believe we're gonna do it."

She just about hired herself, didn't she? Put it right to him, didn't she? Do I have the job? Right to him! She was what she was, and she was bold about it. All the other women sat there in their proper suits looking, well, looking like business, proper, like they were supposed to. That yellow dress and those red heels. Made him think of a tequila sunrise. Orange juice and grenadine. Marine Corps colors. Scarlet and gold. She'd bring charm to the job, that's for sure, but if she kept on coming up with ideas like that Hidden Splendor, she'd help bring in the crowd, too. Before she left the restaurant, she made up a batch of Hidden Splendors from the well-stocked bar and put the pitcher in the refrigerator for all of them to have some when she got back. Which he wished she would. Soon. Jack had already sampled the Splendor, and what that one taste did was make him want more.

Midway through the second pitcher Jack insisted they have dinner with him right there and then at the Hidden Splendor. On the house. Thick sirloin steaks and French fried potatoes all the way around. He wouldn't take no for an answer, and nobody asked him to. They'd been sitting around a table in the restaurant when Jack told them that while they'd been sitting there a business proposition came together in his mind, something he thought might interest them. The Picketts had told him their hopes and plans by that time, and Jack had given their confidence great consideration. Now he asked their permission to run his proposition up the flagpole and see if it flew, and, of course, they said go ahead. Jack laid it out for them. Their situation was promising but perilous, to wit, their dealings with Diogenes Santweir. "That shark was zooming up to the surface to take a bite out of you. But something saved you. Charlie Nickel. He came along in his red Eldorado, some people might say, like a guardian angel. You might call that good fortune, but I'm not a superstitious man. What I figure is based on science. Stop and consider this: every single second since God said 'Let there be light' and the world began has brought us to this place and this table right here and right now. So let's talk about why. You've got muscle, and you've got heart, and that's two-thirds of the battle. You've also got a bankroll, which is more than most of these monkeys have, but you're going to go through that bankroll on a dead run and wind up more broke than an old horse . . . unless . . . you have a play that wins, which is difficult because most of the better possibilities are already tied up . . . except . . ."

Gideon heard bolts in a bucket, but he forced them aside and listened, couldn't make out the words but felt something begin he didn't like, in his stomach, which is where it always hurt first.

"Uh-oh," said Jubal. He hadn't intended to say it out loud. It just blurted out.

"You're right to be skeptical," said Jack. He was really very understanding. "I'd be worried if you weren't," he went on. "But, Jubal, I take you for a man of business and good sense. Hear me out. If sixty seconds go by and you don't want one other word of what I've got to say, you just tell me to stop, and we'll have cherry pie for dessert and say good night and good luck." Abilene admired his style. She didn't realize what her expression gave away, but Gideon did. He was watching her.

"Got your watch out, boss?" Jubal asked Gideon half in jest, but the boy didn't hear him. Jubal said again, "Listen up, buddy. Get your watch out." The command brought Gideon around. He took an old Bulova from the watch pocket of his dungarees—it had no band—and nodded.

"That's a boy who means business," remarked Jack. "If you're like the rest of us, young man, then you've got dreams, and I happen to know the personal telephone number of a lady who might be persuaded to make all your secret dreams come true. Ready, boy? You want to hear?"

"Give the man his say, honey," Abilene said to Jubal.

"You got sixty seconds," Jubal said to Jack.

"Go!" signaled Jack, and Gideon stared at the little hand of his Bulova as Jack began his pitch. "I was born into money, and I've made quite a bit of it."

"And you don't need ours," added Abilene.

"No, I do not. I'm not bragging. This is simply by way of information. I came here because the place seemed ripe for investment and made what turned out to be judicious moves. Now I'm looking to see what's next. Give me more time, kiddo?" Jack asked Gideon.

"Go ahead," said Jubal.

"Let me get right to the point," said Jack. "I've got a claim, and I've got a hunch. Of all the claims that come my way, and, trust me, they are legion, I believe this claim has promise. My grandmother, *v'shalom,* had a saying, 'It's the same soup only now you're hungry.' When a man is desperate he'll part with what he never would have parted with before. I'm proud to say that the money I tendered these poor, broke bastards helped them to go back home, but they left their dreams with me, most of them, like I said, worthless now, maybe worth something like Confederate money someday, so I've held on to them. But one of them, the one I got in mind, might be, I suspect, the fortune you're looking for." Jack leaned closer as if to take them even deeper into his confidence, although he was really leaning in so he could hear, having only the one good ear as he did, the silence in his right a souvenir from a grenade blast at Chosin. That was the same move Abilene found so endearing, the one she thought showed what a good listener he was. She was just not used to that in men, and she was a sucker for it.

"I feel it deep in my guts, and I'm ready to deal," he said, and then, "Are you, Jubal Pickett? Are you ready to deal?"

"I'm waiting for a reason to say yes," said Jubal, and winked at Gideon.

"Three words," replied Jack. "The Dark Angel."

"Tell us about her," said Abilene.

"How do you know it's a her?" asked Jubal.

"She's right," said Jack. "It's Lilith in the wilderness."

"Who?" Jubal wanted to know.

"A she-devil that roamed the wilderness and preyed on men who wandered there," explained Jack. "She shows up in Genesis."

"How'd she manage to find her way here?" asked Jubal.

"At this time and place on earth, where else but Edom would you go to find men so ready to be tempted?"

"And she's tempted you?"

"I'd say she's the topic of conversation, wouldn't you?" asked Jack.

"So what's the deal, gentlemen?" asked Abilene.

"As simple as we can make it," answered Savage.

"You with us, pup?" Jubal asked Gideon. The boy nodded. "Let's hear it," Jubal said.

"I'm looking at you and thinking to myself that this man is tougher than the others," said Jack. "More determined. I'm looking at him and playing a hunch. He's got something in him that will not die. He's got a family, too, with a strong young son and a devoted woman to keep the home fires burning, and he's not going to give up quick. He's not going to let a sun-scorched wilderness that might've cooked Lawrence of Arabia stop him. God bless you, you poor bastard, if you're the man to go out there and sweat in the world's meanest badlands, then I'd be proud to be in business with you. Just leave me out of the grunt work. I wouldn't be a damn bit of good to you out there."

"Why me?" asked Jubal.

Because I want to fuck your wife, you poor bastard, and I want to fuck her hard, and I want to fuck her a lot, is what Jack fought to keep from saying. Instead, he answered, "Why not? We're two men in the business of finding things, you and me, and today we happened to find each other, which I consider good fortune." Jesus, he could sling it! "What is it that we look for when we want to get into something? We look for signs. Indications. We commission charts and projections. We seek a confluence of talents and needs." Not one shred of shame. "But after all the deal points are hammered out and done, there's still what feels right or not. We're all risk takers, right, or else why are we here? Basically, you need to buy from someone. Well, here's someone right in front of you. Get Charlie Nickel to verify the deal. He's one of the few men in town that's got no reason to be dishonest."

"And the deal is?" asked Jubal.

The deal, you schmuck, is whatever it takes to get you out of town. Jack bit his tongue, or he would have said it flat out. Goddamn, that hurt! He tasted blood. Jack was shocked at how drawn he was to this woman, how from the instant he saw her in the waiting room at the airport, Jack's feelings went on autopilot. They'd broken free and gotten away from him. He couldn't rein them in. Jack listened to himself as he shamelessly pitched his heart out over a deal that meant nothing to him except insofar as it was designed to separate this woman from the man she walked in with.

"You give me a sum of cash. I stake the venture and give you an interest in the claim."

"What's the buy-in?" Jubal wanted to know.

"Two thousand five hundred dollars," answered Jack, though he was ready to throw it at them.

"Pricey," said Jubal.

"Two thousand five," considered Abilene. "To be paid off the top from dollar one?"

"Why not? If your Mr. Pickett here finds uranium, we'll all be rich as hell. If you don't find it? Well, we're no worse off, and you figure you learned a lot and you make a decision and you go on from there. You've got my blessing."

"We want your backing," said Abilene.

"Guaranteed. We'd be partners," answered Jack. "If you strike it rich, so do I."

"Fifty-fifty," said Jubal.

"Seventy-thirty," countered Jack. He had to go through the motions.

"Sixty-forty," said Jubal, then, before Jack could answer, Abilene chimed in with fifty-fifty. Savage saw something in her glance and shook on the deal. Even so, he cautioned the Picketts to check out the legality of the claim in the courthouse and suggested, once again, they might like to have their friend Charlie Nickel give the deal his once-over. Make absolutely certain it said what Jubal intended. Then, since it was going on sunset, Jack Savage suggested a little ride over the real estate. "See what you're getting yourself into. Have you back here for dessert."

———————

He never felt so free, the feeling it gave him as the helicopter soared above the massive sandstone formations of the canyon-lands just fathoms below. This must be what a mountain under the ocean looks like to a whale. Swimming over the top, then sounding down. It got him to wondering: When things die in the ocean, what happens to them? How did they disappear? What was it they became if it wasn't dust?

Gideon strained against his seat belt and pressed his fore-head to the canopy as he leaned as far as he could to look down at the ground. He never saw so much. Horizon to horizon. Endless. Like trying to imagine where God was. The little helicopter was no more than a moth in the sky. Gideon tried to imprint every crack and crevice down there onto his brain, tried to burn in that range of wilderness below: tracks, which, Jack explained, stayed forever; jeep trails that ended, simply stopped, in the middle of nowhere; fantastic creations of solid rock called chocolate drops, Chester and his family; needles; Gemini bridges; a maze so devilish it turned round and round on itself like a pinwheel that spit sparks. Lilith could be somewhere. Gideon saw their shadow on a sheer cliff wall as Jack swooped downward toward the valley floor. "There's where Charlie Nickel struck it rich," said Jack, and pointed out the test holes and tailings on the steep flank of a passing mountain. Gideon could see the narrow, winding jeep roads that switched back and forth along its ledges. Give him a screwdriver and a monkey wrench, he could take his father's truck apart and put it back together again; he figured he could do the same with a jeep if he had to.

"Now I'll show you the lady herself," said Jack as he skimmed across a flat of barren ground he called Desolation Valley. The terrain hooked right, and the chopper hooked right with it and entered a narrow side canyon with slickrock walls twenty stories high, so close together that Gideon felt as if he could touch them. Up ahead he could see where the walls flared and the canyon widened. At the far end stood the Dark Angel, a tall, severe monolith of ravaged shale. Gideon knew who she was before Jack Savage ever said a word. Her tip glowed red in the fire of the setting sun, like a wizard's wand, like a tusk dipped in blood. "Like a dick on a dog," cracked Jubal. Savage hovered above her and pointed out the boundaries of their claim: Dark Angel to Javelina Wash, east-west, and north-south from Finian's Arch to the pinnacles of Caligula. Jack dropped below the Angel's peak, descended slowly down her flank, and brought the chopper to rest at her feet. He cut the engine and leaned down to switch on a scintillometer wired to a case of storage batteries on the floor beside him. At first, the needle shuddered and seemed stuck in low, but it broke free and leaped into the hot zone, vibrating wildly. The soles of Gideon's feet went tickly.

"You know what that means?" asked Jack. "Somewhere below this ground is a slowly disintegrating hoard of rock. If you can find it, you'll be rich beyond your wildest dreams. Can you imagine what that's like? Five million? Ten? Fifteen? Fifty? Never for the rest of your life having to say or do any damn thing you don't want to do. Freedom! You're walking down the street and pass by a store window holding a brand-new Indian motorcycle with that big shift on the tank standing up proud as a battle flag. My God, Jubal, you really want that bike, and what do you know? You can have it! You can have that motorcycle, buddy. You can have damn near anything. We all can."

Amen, thought Abilene. Millions would solve her two biggest problems: room and board. She'd take a roof over her head and three hots a day. That was her practical side coming out, but she did, too, have her dreams. Jubal could have his motorcycle. If she was rich with all her own money she'd start her day with breakfast in bed—a hot-fudge sundae served in a silver bowl with a silver spoon. That was just for starters, and Jack would be the one to bring it to her.

"What is it, son?" Jack asked Gideon, who stood there staring at him. "Does he want to say something?" Jack asked Jubal. Gideon held a baseball-shaped rock in his hand.

"You got a toolbox in that rig?" Jubal asked Jack. Jack said he did. "You mind letting the boy have a look?" asked Jubal. Jack took a tool kit out from under the pilot's seat and handed it to Gideon. They all stood around the boy as he chose a hacksaw, a hammer, and a chisel, squatted down with his baseball-shaped rock, and began to saw it through. He sawed with precision and persistence, and then he worked the chisel through it and around it, sawed and worked the chisel, sawed and worked the chisel, until a final blow broke it through into two pieces, almost equal halves. Gideon showed the two halves of the geode to his father. Even in its unpolished state, the raw stone danced with color.

"Does anyone need a better omen than that?" Jack asked.

Abilene agreed. "It's a sign," she said. Then, because it was nearly dark and they needed what little light there was to fly, Jack hustled them aboard and lifted off. He suggested ice cream to go with the cherry pie when they got back, but Abilene said this called for champagne, only there wasn't any in Edom, a fact that Abilene said better be corrected to give the place an air of celebration. Jack agreed that she was exactly right and made a note on a little spiral pad he carried in his back pocket. His handwriting, Abilene noticed, was real squiggly, like he'd dipped a piece of cotton thread in India ink and wiggled it across the paper. Otherwise, you really didn't notice much he was minus the trigger finger on his right hand. He'd lost it to frostbite at Chosin.

That night Jubal was inspired, driven less by artistry than the raw power of the rut. Abilene flipped over on her knees and thrust her ass high in the air. He grabbed her hips. She reached back and worked him inside her. Jubal bucked her and fucked her, one hand playing with her titties and the other strumming her pussy. "Oh, God!" she cried when she came. "What did you do to me?"

Later, in the dark, she whispered in his ear, and the words bored into his brain like weevils. "Make me rich, daddy, and I swear to you I will keep this cock as hard as you want, whenever you want, for as long as you want." She said the words slowly, savoring them as if they were hard candies. She flicked her tongue softly in his ear, and she teased his lobe with tiny bites. He got hard again, and she whispered, "I'm your good luck piece, daddy. You get to wear me close, rub me like a magic lamp."

Gideon sat against the right rear tire with his knees hugged to his chest and a blanket wrapped loosely around his head and shoulders. He had to be there. He knew he shouldn't have been, but he couldn't help himself. He'd always wondered why the colored boys back in Mississippi called it the blind pig, but now, looking at his father, backlit by a sickle moon as he pissed from the top step of the trailer, Gideon saw what they meant. He watched his father pitch his arc high so his stream went far, watched as he leaned back and pitched it farther. "Oh, yeah," sighed Jubal with relief. Then, with a little whoop of victory, he pitched it even farther. Gideon didn't think he should look, and so he turned away, but when a coyote yipped from across the wash and he heard his father answer it, he couldn't help but turn back. Jubal stood there stark naked, his hands on his hips and his head thrown back so that his nose pointed up at the sky. "Aiyiyiyiyiyi." His voice uncoiled across the wash like concertina wire. The coyote came back with one that shredded the air, and Jubal began to chuckle.

"Told him go kiss my ass. You been here the whole time?" he asked Gideon. The boy started with surprise. He hadn't known his father had seen him. Whole time meaning what? What did he mean? "I feel like we come to the Promised Land. Do you?" said Jubal as he sat down on the top step, hunched over, elbows on knees, and settled in for a good talk. "Got your Prince Albert on you?" asked Jubal. Gideon took the tin from his shirt pocket and handed it over with the papers. He didn't look at him though. He didn't want to look at him. This was new, this feeling that he was embarrassed by his father's nakedness. The boy rarely sought Jubal's arms anymore, but he always knew they were there for when he wanted. Now he'd just as soon huddle down in the wheel well. He knew he couldn't hug his father anymore. It wouldn't be right. But it was a scary feeling because where else could he go? Hmm? Where else?

Jubal talked as he rolled one. "When you was real little, still in the crib 'n' all, I'd put you in at night; you'd stick your tiny paw out through the slats and wouldn't go to sleep unless I held it. I kind of miss it, too, but you had to let go sometime, and I had to let you. I love you more than anything else in this whole world. Don't even begin to doubt it. Now, I won't lie to you, either: Abilene swept over me like prairie fire over a ditch. I ain't saying it's true love, and I know she ain't your momma, but she ain't intended to be your momma, plus the fact may I remind you who your momma really was and see if you're so sure you want her back. If you do, we ain't thinking about the same woman. As far as that one back there is concerned," he said, indicating the trailer, "heaven can't be much better than this, with the emphasis on the *can't*. I pray to God that you're lucky enough to have one of your own someday, but, for the time being, look at the bright side: you got me all to yourself for two whole weeks, or as long as we got water, and God knows how long after that. For the foreseeable future, you'll be up to your armpits in Daddy; but, eventually, you're gonna have to make your peace with her. I need you thinking clearly. Son, I confess, I got my limitations but you ain't one of them. You see things out there. Me, I pick up a rock, and you know what I got in my hand? That's right. A rock. You pick up a rock, and you know what you got in your hand? A treasure. Gideon, it's my butt 'n' your brains. It behooves me to say it but it's true. We got a whole adventure out here before us, just you 'n' me. I know damn well you're excited about that. You're gonna be my right hand, my eyes, and my ears. I'm countin' on you to make us rich. Now, about that off chance we don't find anything? It won't be as much fun, but, hell, we would've looked for it, wouldn't we? Now, would we go back to Mississippi? Who knows? I like it that there's things we don't know, don't you?"

Gideon shrugged. Jubal hunkered down and put his arm around his son's shoulders. His penis dangled above the dirt. The boy shuddered and clutched his blanket tightly around him. "You'd think I'd be shivering, too, wouldn't you?" his father went on. "But, I'll tell you what, pissing outside makes a man feel good. Able to leap tall buildings at a single bound." Jubal pulled Gideon closer. Gideon had to hold himself tight to keep from tearing away. Jubal went on. "One thing I do know that never will change: you're my precious blood. You can't know, 'til you have a child of your own, what kind of love that is. It makes everything else—all these rocks, every damn thing—seem puny. I love you, boy. I love you more than my own life." Jubal's face shone with perfect peace. Gideon wished his old man would go back inside and leave him alone.

———

Usually, when the three of them drove in the truck together, usually she sat in the middle with both feet on the floor, knees together. Put a carpenter's level across her knees, and the bubble wouldn't budge from absolute zero. One or the other of the Picketts would be driving. Her hips touched them both, like the three of them were bound together. This morning she sat with her right leg crossed over her left and leaned into his father behind the steering wheel and consequently away from Gideon. No part of her touched him this morning.

Thinking was not permissible.

He didn't have the words, anyway.

"What's got you so talky this morning?" she asked him, and ruffled his hair. He pulled away and plastered himself against the door like a spitball, and then he stayed there sullen as mud all the way to town.

When they had all separated the night before, Jack said he'd have two copies of the contract typed and ready in the morning. Charlie Nickel would be there to verify the claim, but Abilene said first of all breakfast was on her—"We're going in there with our bellies full," she said. "Let's not seem hungry to the man"—so before they did anything at all, she had Jubal drive to the BonTon–Breakfast All Day in the middle of town, where she planned to buy them all the grub they could eat. The problem came when Jubal tried to get Gideon to vacate the truck and come inside. "You know most fathers would whack their kids for this kind of insubordination," Jubal said to Gideon, who sat sullenly behind the wheel locked inside the cab of the truck. The boy's hands gripped the wheel; he stared straight ahead. He might as well have had his head in a deep-sea diver's helmet for all he gave any indication that he heard one word his father said. Jubal had watched him do this before. Well as Jubal knew that boy, sometimes he went places in his mind where Jubal just could not go. A ton of iron would slam down like a portcullis, and Jubal would be left to watch it rust. No way was that boy going to budge. Dynamite wouldn't do it, so Jubal gave up and left him there while he and Abilene went inside the BonTon–Breakfast All Day, where they each of them ordered the Sunrise Special—six strips of bacon, four sausage links, and two eggs sunny-side up like clown eyes on a thick piece of ham, sides of home fries with red peppers and onions, and bottomless cups of coffee for the table, or, in this case, the curved banquette, one of four along the wall with frayed red leatherette seats. Jubal just loved to watch this woman eat. She could get more on a fork than a Chinese acrobat. She'd get this smile of delight, and her eyes would go all wide, and that mouth of hers would just about unhinge to take in all that food. Then she'd slowly chew every last bit of flavor out of it, and when she finally swallowed, her eyes closed and a state of serenity passed across her face.

Midway through his third cup of joe, Jubal felt his bowels grumble and excused himself to scoot to the toilet. Must've been all the excitement. Abilene remained at the banquette picking the peppers out of the last of her home fries. What was left was mostly crispy nuggets, none very big, crumbs mostly. She wet the tip of her index finger in her mouth and rolled it from side to side in the crumbs as if she were getting inked for a fingerprint. Then she put her finger back in her mouth and licked it off. Abilene thought of something that made her smile, roll her finger in the crumbs once more, close her eyes, and lick it clean all over again. When she opened her eyes this time she saw that he was still standing there on the sidewalk side of the plate-glass window, partially hidden by the Sunrise Special poster advertisement. That nearly new, summer straw cowboy hat was the dead giveaway, especially since he'd nervously lifted it and run his hand through his hair before he set the summer straw back down again. She caught him looking, grabbed his eyes with hers, and locked on. She held up a menu and beckoned the boy to the table with it. He stared at her dumbly. She picked up a fork and made eating motions, then pointed it and cocked her head for him to come on inside and sit down. Finally, he did, kind of slid through the door sideways and approached the banquette steadily but slowly, as if he didn't want to budge but had no choice. He reached the table as she loaded up a plate of food with generous portions from his father's and her own and held the bait out to him. One thing Abilene knew how to do was get the attention of a teenage boy. She laid the plate of food on the table in front of him, took a napkin, and stuffed it in the neck of his shirt as he sat down. "Go on, boy," said Abilene, "eat," and, while he ate, she ordered him a cup of hot chocolate with whipped cream because she had come to know that was his favorite thing. When the waitress brought the hot chocolate, Abilene took it from her and set it down in front of Gideon herself. She nicked off a dash of whipped cream with the tip of her spoon, flicked her tongue out, and got it like a fly. "I remind you of a frog or something?" she asked him and giggled. "It's been said by some that I'm a princess in disguise. Want some for yourself?" she asked as she held up her empty spoon. Gideon took his own spoon, scooped up a wad of whipped cream, and hoovered it. Abilene smiled. "We all got our part to play," she said. "I don't expect to be your momma, but if I'm gonna dote on your daddy, I damn sure am gonna dote on you, too, whether you like it or not. Know what my blood type is? Go on. Guess. Won't guess? Can't guess? OK, I'll tell you: B positive. Get it? God's truth. B positive." She nicked another smidgeon of whipped cream from his plate and licked her spoon clean.

After breakfast, Jubal, Abilene, and Gideon drove to the bank, where Gideon stayed in the truck and polished his geode while Abilene and his father went inside and got a safe-deposit box with two keys. They each took one and agreed that the Dark Angel contract would go into the box for safekeeping. They agreed that it was best not to take any chances. After Jubal and Abilene fin-

ished up at the bank, Jubal drove them all back to the offices of the
Chosin Few, where Charlie Nickel gave his blessing to the Dark
Angel Development Company as a good deal all the way around.
"There's room in this town for a couple more millionaires," was
what Charlie said. No trumpet blasts or drum rolls accompanied
the signing, but when he crossed the second T on *Pickett,* Jubal felt
like the gates to his future sprang wide open and fortune lay just
beyond. His plan was to get out there as soon as they could, turn
around and go back to town with Gideon to pick up two weeks'
worth of food and supplies, pack the truck, and leave as early as
possible that same day. Daylight savings and a full moon reflect-
ing off the naked sandstone would provide hours of extra light.
Abilene wanted to go to town with them, but Jack had a list of
things he needed to run over with her—he was real anxious to get
started—so she stayed behind for her first full day at work. There
was just one more thing to do. "Hand me your fancy pen," she
said to Jack. He did, and she signed "Abilene Breedlove Pickett"
with a flourish on the line indicated in the contract.

By six PM Jubal and Gideon had the truck gassed up and ready
to travel. They could make three hours before dark. Charlie Nickel
was there with Abilene and Jack outside the Hidden Splendor to
see the boys off. It was at his suggestion that Jubal released some
of the air from the truck tires. Better traction in sand that way.
"Remember, boy," he said to Gideon with a twinkle, "you want
to look in the bottom of the Chinle but the top of the Morrison."
Gideon looked at him and smiled. "I'll take half of that smile," said
Abilene, and gave Gideon's ear a little tug. Jack had a tectonic map
spread out on the hood of the truck. Jubal looked on as he traced
the route with his finger. "It's about a hundred miles from here to

the claims. Here's Finian's Arch. There's the Dark Angel. Pick up the dry riverbed almost directly north of here and follow it west. Once you spot the Dark Angel just make a beeline for her. You've got everything you need? Ore samples, dynamite, iodine . . . ?"

"Got it all," said Jubal.

"See you in two weeks, then," said Jack. "Good luck." Both men shook hands.

"You take good care of your father," Abilene said to Gideon, who seemed to nod, but when Jack went to shake Gideon's hand, too, the boy just stood there and stared at him. "I don't like you having bad manners, son. This man might just be your lucky day," said Jubal. "Go on. Shake." Gideon did what his father bid him, but it was palpable how much he hated doing it. What the boy wanted to do was to get out of there, and he had the feeling that this man wanted them out of there just as bad as he did. He turned away, got behind the wheel of the truck, thumbed the starter, then slid over so his father could drive. Jubal got in beside him. "Don't mix up the top and bottom, son. Mind your daddy," said Charlie, and waved again. Jubal gunned it and hollered out the window, "Tell Mr. Rockefeller Jubal Pickett says, 'Move over!'" He ground into first and lurched off into the desert. "Dr. Livingstone, I presume?" said Jubal in a phony Brit accent. Gideon smiled. He really loved it when his father used funny words.

A few miles down, his father took a hard turn off the main road into desert and headed for the heart of the canyonlands. The force of the turn caused Gideon to slide across the seat toward him. "That's a special move," his father said, and winked, "designed to get the ladies closer. Might come in handy some day you take a young lady to the drive-in or whatnot. I'm imparting wisdom here, youngblood." Jubal chuckled. Gideon smiled. "I see it. I see it. Don't break your face," Jubal said, and poked his son in the ribs. Gideon slid back to his side of the seat and relaxed against the door. All was right with his world. He was where he ought to be.

What Gideon knew in his heart of hearts was that he needed to be strong. If he was strong, his own strength would radiate out and keep his father safe. He would act like a shield to protect his father from harm, to deflect evil or meteorites or enraged tigers and poison darts. This was why he practiced keeping his pain in a very small place. Even when he had that appendix time, he wrapped himself around it and kept it in a very small place. This was very important to Gideon, to protect his father if they came for him, "they" being Nazis, Japs, the gooks with bloody fangs he saw in war comics and Freedom's War trading cards, and aliens, beings that tortured people in the most worst ways. If they came for his father and his father hid and Gideon knew where his father was, they'd torture him to find out, and he had to be able to withstand the worst torture in order to save his father's life. He wondered if he could withstand the pain it would take to keep his father's hiding place a secret. Everything. He would take everything. It could happen. He loved the man that deeply.

———

It didn't take Abilene long to figure out that everything Jack wanted her to do could have waited. There was none of it urgent, nothing that couldn't have been done some other time, you pick it, any hour during the day and some of the night even, so what this is all about is me, became Abilene's conclusion. If there was anything she claimed to be expert in, it was chemistry between the sexes. I believe I have piqued this ol' boy's interest was what she thought, except Jack wasn't anything like a good old boy, which was what made him interesting. He seemed to be a man comfortable around tools and workmen, but he wasn't one of them. There was something different about him, something elegant, and he had class, and he had smarts. She found that attractive. A few years ago she'd gone to the movies at the local bijou (she didn't just go to drive-ins) and seen a picture starring Peter Lawford and June Allyson as college students. *Good News* was its name. Now, she liked June, but June was a touch too prissy for Abilene. Jack was more like Peter Lawford in that he probably didn't, for one thing, spit like all the guys she knew back home. Always spitting something, and chewing tobacco was the worst. The problem was that Peter Lawford didn't look like any football player she'd ever seen. He looked more like the kind of guy who did the quarterback's homework for him. She could see him with a tennis racket in his hand but not a football, uh-uh. OK, so Jack Savage didn't look like a football player either, but what he looked like was that he could play one in the movies. Now, who could play Jack Savage in the movie? She settled on Tyrone Power. Right. He'd be good. Maybe him.

Uh-oh. Something was not going as planned, or maybe it was, the plan being out of her hands. She'd give God that much but she'd like a little clarity, please! All our lives has brought us here to this place in this time, she pondered, him, me, them. We're here to find out why we're here was her understanding of the Situation with a capital "S." She tagged Jack a man who liked wine, not the treacly, syrupy stuff that burned the paint off walls, not the straight shot with a beer back, but the French kind from a château. He had appraised her as she imagined he would a fine bottle of wine, something to savor, not toss back. Something was going on. He'd been looking at her in the waiting room long before she acknowledged him with her polite smile and dipped her head just a little bit once in his direction. His eyes swept the room, came back, and stayed on her. She knew that much if she knew anything. Something else she knew, too: he was always touching her, not in any way meant to threaten or persuade but "protective," that might be the word, a light pressure in the middle of her back to guide her where he wanted her to go, a touch of a finger to her forearm to emphasize a point. He listened to what she said and didn't interrupt her sentences. She sensed he did not regard her purely as a piece of ass, and she bet that his family used tablecloths. Also, his teeth, the best she'd seen, straight and white. Dazzling. At one point, their hips touched, and she felt an actual arc of electricity pass between them, whether from her to him or him to her she could not tell and did not know. She'd never felt such a thing before. Something was going on, and she didn't know if she or anyone else was capable of stopping it.

Later that day she counted out the down payment in fifties on a red '46 Ford Club Coupe over to the Atomic Auto Yard. It was in pretty fair shape for a car seven years old, kind of sporty, had a few miles on her but plenty more to go. "Like me," she said to herself and laughed. Jack had advanced Abilene the cash for the down payment and went with her to check out the stock. Also, as he knew everybody in town, wasn't anybody going to try to cheat this lady. Abilene got herself a pretty fair buy, not one speck of rust, clean interior. Yessir! She couldn't wait to take Miss Ruby Watch Out home after work for a shakedown (the name just came to her in her mind), really burn that baby in across the desert flats, but when she got back, after a couple of quick stops in town, Jack told her that Vanda called in and said her mother was sick, could Abilene take her shift and stay 'til closing? "Her mother's dead," said Abilene.

"Then she's even sicker than I thought," said Jack.

"Better start cross-checking your facts, boss," said Abilene. "I'm good at picking up discrepancies. One of those little critters tries to sneak by I pounce like a cat."

"I'd better be careful," said Jack.

"You heard it here first," Abilene replied. "Better call Vanda back, too. I gotta get home before dark, my first time driving it, you know?"

"How about if I follow you home, help you find the place in the dark?" asked Jack.

"How 'bout if you do not?" said Abilene.

"Somebody told me I was the boss. That means I've got to look after my employees, make sure their health and welfare is in order," said Jack.

"You are the boss. I know I work for you, Mr. Savage, but you're gonna have to work for me, too. That's the rules. Some little boy should've learned that in first-day civics class . . . boss."

"You're gonna make this hard for me, aren't you?" asked Jack.

"As hard as I can."

"You're terrible," he said, laughing.

"Wicked when I want," she said with a little giggle. Her giggle made him think of those Christmas tree lights where the tiny bubbles kept rising through a tinted glass tube. "Got to skedaddle, boss. See you early in the mañana." Then she floored it, laid rubber, and streaked away down the blacktop, only to scream to a stop twenty yards later, slam it into reverse, and back up to where Jack stood.

"You got guts standing there with a crazy woman at the wheel," she shouted out the window.

"You forget something?" he asked as if she hadn't fazed him.

"Yeah. Forgot to ask your opinion. Hold on a sec'." Abilene tugged on the emergency brake, got out of the car, and opened the trunk. She took out two boxes, each a bit larger than a board game box. "I bought these at the craft shop. They're the latest thing in home decoration. Paint-by-numbers kits? Maybe you can help me decide which one of these to keep. This one's *Whistler's Mother* by a artist of the same name, and this one's *The Seduction of Venus* by a unknown master. The saleslady said to return whichever one I didn't want. Got any preferences?"

How is it that somebody can literally take your breath away, reach way down deep inside your throat and yank it out like distributor wires from under the hood of a car? His knees had buckled—God's honest truth, they had buckled—when she'd smiled at him, right away, right there in the goddamn waiting room, for Christ's sake! She had surfaced from nowhere and taken a chunk right out of him. Now all he could think to do was to stand there like a dunce in the middle of the street and watch her as she tooled away. She tapped out a little beep-beepdabeep on the horn and waved good-bye without turning around. Jack's father would have thought her a shiksa goddess. His mother would have called her *nafka,* whore. He wasn't sure whether the struggle was on or already over.

She watched him in her rearview mirror until he became too small to see, a speck, then not even that . . . She knew he would not stay that small, an anonymous speck in the distance.

"You've got yourself some possibilities, old girl," she said to herself. "Let's us think this thing through."

Abilene knew her power, and she knew she'd have that power until her tits began to sag. Right now they were still perky, especially when she stood up straight, which is what she reminded herself to do. Walk with a book on your head. Stand up straight. She was under no illusions. If she'd been a hag Jubal would never have taken her. And if she was a hag what was happening right now wouldn't be. Period. She was not just a casual flirt. OK, well, she was, but she knew when it meant something and when it didn't, which was most of the time. But not now. How she assessed the situation that was going on was to be cool, calm, and collected while she listed the facts as she knew them. Jubal Pickett: a man of dreams. Jack Savage: a man of means. She'd hitched a ride with one man and connected with another, and where was the wrong in that? She hadn't violated any covenants because there had been none. She'd pitched in and done her part, gone from there to here with a smile on her face, but that didn't mean she was home, not yet she wasn't. She'd trusted RD Thompson, a mistake she swore never to make again. He screwed her out of her fair share because her name wasn't on a piece of paper. So being with RD had taught her what to look out for next time. Which might be now. Look for a decent return on a long-term investment, and get it in writing. What would it be like, she wondered, to never have to worry about money ever again as long as she lived? All those things out in the world that she'd love to have! They made her breathless. She'd long since chucked the notion of Mr. Perfect. Too many honky-tonk nights had taught her different. She told herself she'd have to look at this strictly for investment purposes, though it didn't hurt a bit that Jack Savage was the most exotic man she'd ever met.

PART 7

That night she sat on a large, flat rock by the pool wrapped in an oval of light thrown by a red kerosene lantern. Outside the oval the darkness was complete. Her paint-by-numbers kit was at her feet; the panel she was painting sat on her lap. She was on the blue, and she liked that. She heard the whop-whopawhop of rotary blades long before she saw the chopper itself, but to look at her would not reveal that she heard or saw a thing. She sat there studying her painting, the brush with the tiny tip poised in her hand. When she saw the helicopter clear the ridge, its lights now searching the ground, she smiled to herself, but she never did look up. Even when Jack set the chopper down near the trailer about fifty yards away, even when he walked toward her, his shoes crunching on the dry ground, even then she did not acknowledge him. He stopped behind her and stood there for a few seconds watching over her shoulder.

"You were just out walking the dog and decided to drop by?" she asked.

"Actually, I brought you a present," he replied.

"Kind of a housewarming thing?" she asked. "Look at this," she said, holding up *The Seduction of Venus*. "I'm almost finished with the blue. Then I get to start with the flesh tones." She put the painting down in her lap again and stretched her arms out high and wide. "Gosh, I'm stiff. Imagine laying on your back for—how many years did that fellow take to paint the pope's ceiling?"

"You're not afraid to be way out here all by yourself, are you?" asked Jack.

"My guess is it's safer than town," answered Abilene.

"Still," he said, drew a .45 Colt military-issue from his belt, and held it out by its barrel. "Just in case."

She smiled and drew a .25-caliber pearl-handled semi from her apron pocket. "Just in case," she repeated.

"That's a lady's gun," he scoffed.

"Well, I'm a lady, or hadn't you noticed? No kick to speak of from this thing, but she'll put a neat little hole no bigger than a thumbtack smack in the middle of your forehead— *one's* forehead, nothing personal. Anyway, let's get back to your question: am I afraid to be out here by myself? What you really mean is: am I lonely and do I want your company?"

"That's kind of blunt," he said.

"Isn't it sort of more to the point?"

"You're an interesting woman."

"Men always say that when . . ."

"What?"

"When they want something," she replied, replaced the .25 in her apron pocket, and began painting again.

"Do they?" asked Jack.

"That's what Momma told me," said Abilene.

"What do women say when they want something?"

"They don't."

"Want something?"

"Say," she replied.

"Then how's a man to know?" asked Jack.

"He's got to be smart. He's got to know the risks a girl takes and convince her it's worth it. Do you pay this much attention to all your employees, Mr. Savage?"

"No."

"Why me? I'm just a simple country girl," said Abilene.

"Somehow I don't see you putting up okra," he said. Abilene laughed. "That boy's not yours?"

"No, but I'm trying to be a mother to him in my fashion. Me and his father, we share a lust for adventure and have similar ambitions," she replied.

"Jubal's not your husband." More a statement than a question.

"No," she said. "I was just trying that on. I wanted you to think I was a respectable woman. Tell me something, Mr. Savage, how much do you think those claims are really worth?"

"Could be a fortune," answered Jack.

"Could also be worth considerably less, though," she said.

"Depends on how industrious he is and, I admit, how lucky, but I didn't bullshit either one of you on that."

"No," she replied, "no, I believe you've been fairly forth-right, and very, very smart."

"How's that?"

"You fly planes, move people and supplies in and out. You run the best slop chute in this town, but you don't bust your ass on rocks. You get someone else to do it for you."

"Like I said, I don't see you putting up okra," countered Jack.

"Jubal may be the engine, but I'm the high-octane in this operation, his lucky charm."

"You sound like a businesswoman," he said.

"Given the opportunity. See, I believe I make a goddamn good partner, Mr. Savage," she said. "I believe that if a person goes into business with me, that person benefits from the bargain."

"You think you'd like to go into business with me?" asked Jack.

"I am in business with you, Mr. Savage."

"But you'd be negotiating a new deal."

"It's nearly dark. You'd better go," she said.

Jack started for the helicopter, then turned and asked her, "Walk with me?"

She shook her head and said, "You don't need me to help find your way. I don't know if I can resist you, Jack Savage, but I sure better try."

"Then we've both got our work cut out for us. See you to-morrow," Jack said, and walked away.

"Bright and early," she called after him, though Abilene never turned around. She held the painting at arm's length and appraised it as Jack revved up his engine and disappeared over the far ridge deep into the darkness. The whopwhopawhop of his rotary blades continued for some seconds even after the helicopter could no longer be seen, and then, gradually, once again, the silence descended, thick and full. Abilene felt satisfied with her work. She smiled as she packed up her things, and, by the light of her lantern, she walked back to the trailer. Now it was time to sleep.

To behold the full moon at night in a cloudless sky over the desert is to know why people worshipped her, but what impressed him most about this endless wilderness was its silence. It was absolute. There was nothing to hear. Not even his own voice. And what would he hear then, if he did hear his own voice? But there never was a voice, so how did he talk to himself, and, if he didn't talk to himself, whose voice was that?

Talkatalkatalkatalkatalkatalkatalk. That's what people did.

He liked it out here, just him and his father, liked sitting here staring out across the campfire while the old man slept. It was so simple. They each had an army surplus sleeping bag, though Gideon wasn't anywhere near tired. Jubal admitted it: he was whipped. The truck had worn shock absorbers to begin with, so after hours of a brutal ride, his father took to bitching and moaning every time they hit anything bigger than a baseball. He claimed it was like taking body slams from Gorgeous George, claimed he was going to be passing blood for a week. The first night they stopped three hours in, still not yet in sight of the Angel but long since swallowed up by the rough country as they passed through. The rocks flowed and folded like custard, rolled in on themselves and swept up into petrified dunes, dropped into terraced faults, a layer cake of shale, sandstone, and limestone. He counted six different colors of rocks during the day, only now, at night, with this moon, there was only one, plus its shadow, the color of a silverfish. If he wanted to, right this second, he could get up and walk one minute into the formations beyond the campfire's small circle, and then not a person in the world, not even his father, would know where he was. Even he wouldn't know, would he? But that might not be so bad. "Walk downhill and keep walking 'til you come to it," was his father's can't-fail advice on finding your way back from anywhere. "Just 'cause you lost the trail don't mean it's the end of the trail" was also something he was fond of saying.

Gideon slept little that night, yet now, at sunrise, he felt light, alert, nowhere near groggy. He watched in awe as the sun inched up and, foot by foot, color by color, lit the earth. No more silverfish. No more shadows. Coffee'd be a good thing right now. He stoked up the campfire, dropped two handfuls of coarse grounds in a pot of water, added some eggshells and a little salt, and put the pot on the fire. Then he sat back on his haunches and waited for it to boil.

He heard it before he saw it, a whine like a puppy's. There

was a coyote pup out there maybe ten feet away. Gideon stayed on his haunches but shifted from behind the fire so the pup would have a clear lane in; then, because the pup had more curiosity than brains, the little thing worked its way forward step by cautious step. Gideon held out his hand, and what a wonder if that pup didn't come within sniffing distance! Gideon stopped breathing. He and this wild thing were about to touch when an ugly snarl came at him from his blind side, a snarl cut short by the blast of a shotgun. Jubal was still in his sleeping bag, but the old ten-gauge double he slept with was out and aimed to fire the second load if needed. It wasn't. Jubal's shot hit the beast in the neck and the ten-gauge damn near tore her head off. "She thought you were gonna hurt her pup," said Jubal. "Now who's gonna take care of you?" he asked the pup, which had retreated back a few yards. "The rest of the pack will eat the poor little thing," Jubal explained to Gideon. "Or else a hawk or a lion's gonna get it, or else it'll starve 'cause ain't nobody to feed it." With that he fired the second load. What was left was carcass. "At least," said Jubal, "that was quick."

Midway through the day the Picketts reached the dry riverbed and turned west. They had never seen a place so barren, what you call remote. Apart from a thin strip of ugly scrub that ran down the center of the riverbed, there was nothing alive that they could see. "It's a marvel stuff finds a way to live," said Jubal as he navigated a bone-jarring slew of boulders. A few yards later he plowed straight through a tangle of juniper that must have washed down at some point. "You drinking plenty of water?" he asked Gideon. Gideon showed him the canteen, took a swallow, and handed it over to his father. "Here's mud in your eye," Jubal said. A few yards after that Jubal announced that he had to get out of the sun for a while. It was that fierce. The brakes squealed a little when he brought the V-8 to a stop, so, as he crawled under the truck to get away from the sun, Jubal made a mental note to have them looked at when they got back.

The thing about his father that always amazed Gideon was that the man could sleep anywhere, anytime, on a moment's notice. Less. The other thing was that he could wake up just as fast. No sooner had they gotten underneath the truck than Jubal put his hat over his face and went out. Gideon didn't feel like sleeping, so he laced his fingers behind his head and just lay back. He heard a low rumble of thunder from way up-canyon somewhere, far from them, another world. As it rolled away, he heard an insect buzzing in the heat. Everything in the desert will either bite you, scratch you, sting you, or stick you, that's what Charlie Nickel had said, and it sure seemed like the truth. Bite you, scratch you, sting you, stick you. You could get stung in Mississippi. You could also get bit and scratched in Mississippi. But he didn't think you could get stuck in Mississippi, not as a rule, anyway; maybe people who grew roses.

Later, when the rain came down, Gideon realized he, too, must have fallen asleep because the thud of drops on the hood and fenders brought him back from wherever it was he'd been. There weren't too many drops—it was over fast—but the ones there were seemed the size of marbles and hit with a concussive plop. Maybe it lasted a few seconds. Not much. Gideon thought of quail hunting with his father's friends. Every once in a while somebody shot almost straight up. Then the birdshot rained down on everybody else. The little pellets felt just like raindrops, and nobody ever got hurt, just laughed. The other thing was the sun stayed out the entire time.

The first thing he felt was when it got wet under his crotch. He was horrified he pissed himself like he always did as a little kid. Always pissing himself. But then he felt it get damp under his shoulder blades and realized moisture was seeping from below ground, percolating up and moistening the sand beneath him, which then shifted and pulled him downward, just a fraction, but still. He felt himself sink and saw the tire sink and scurried out from underneath that truck like a spider. The truck was actually sinking, the tires already more than an inch down when he sprinted around to the other side and grabbed his father's outstretched arm, pulled the man with all his might, pulled him and woke him up. The boy banged on the door then grabbed his father's arm and pulled again—"Jesus Christ, I'm comin'!" yelled Jubal and scurried out from underneath the truck just as it sank another inch. The two men stood aside and watched a sump hole seep up and suck in the truck, which then settled down even further, stopping only when the hubcaps were submerged. "That would've been real unpleasant," said Jubal. "Put on my tombstone, 'Stuck in the muck with a face full of truck.' Beer's on me, but first we're gonna have to winch her out."

They took the cable from the winch and wrapped it around a boulder shaped like an anvil, if you were to look at it a certain way. Gideon took the hook, stretched out as far as he could over the sump hole to prevent getting stuck, and latched on to the front bumper. He signaled his father to start the motor on the winch. As the front end began to clear, the sump opened up, and the rear end sank to the axle; but when the rear end finally pulled free, the hole closed up behind it with a rush, and, while father and son watched dumbfounded, the water seeped back down into the ground and disappeared. The sun had never once gone in. Jubal took off his hat and scratched his head. "Son of a bitch," he muttered.

Except for the dimple in the front bumper made by the winch hook, the truck proved itself a rugged traveler. Gideon packed up the winch while Jubal gave the load a once-over, tugging here and there at the ropes. "Nobody claimed it'd be easy, right, pup?" said Jubal, and clapped his son on the back. "You ready to saddle up?" he asked. The boy gave him a thumbs-up. "You drive," said Jubal. "I think I'd like to just sit back and ponder my good fortune." Then he climbed into the shotgun seat, tipped his hat down over his eyes, folded his arms across his chest, and settled in against the door. Gideon knew his father trusted him, and that was good.

He saw it first. He'd followed the riverbed where it turned north for about a mile, then it turned west again, curved around, and there she was: the Dark Angel, stark as a gun sight aligned on the sun. His father sensed it. He came out from underneath his hat like he'd just won a bet on a horse.

"You see her, Gideon? You see her? She's my dream girl. She's my lucky lady. Ain't she worth suffering for? Don't be shy, son, say hello. Ask the lady for a dance." That got a smile out of him. "On my way, sugar. Keep it warm for me! Come on, boy, let's go get us some!"

PART 8

It seemed to Abilene that everybody in Edom (women as
well as men) all dressed in the same basic outfit—some
kind of dungarees, steel-toed boots, and a cotton work shirt
with a sweat ring around the collar. But this was not Abilene's
style, and she was not about to "when in Rome, etc.," especially when she was pretty sure she had practically the only
glamorous job in town. She was going to do what she could to
help pack the Splendor, and part of that meant looking good
for a clientele she rightly pegged as PHBB (Prospectors Horny
Beyond Belief). Going up to do some shopping in Salt Lake
was out of the question, but Edom did have a Sears catalog
store. People from all over did their shopping at Sears catalog stores—she had, too, back in Oklahoma—and, since she'd
been blessed with the same size for years, Abilene knew they'd
pretty much have what she needed, probably they would, but

she wanted to go on the fancy side just a little bit, the cock-tail dress collection, nothing cutting-edge but fashionable (she was going for allure, not shock value), with a fitted waist to show how trim her own was and a flared skirt that swirled as she turned and swayed gently as she walked. She thought maybe one with a flared skirt and a second one a sheath, but she decided on both dresses being flared because that fashion made her legs look better, then, at the last minute, decided she needed a sheath as well and ordered one in chocolate. Variety, she thought, variety. The sheath would make her seem more sedate and sophisticated, and that wouldn't be a bad thing, ei-ther. Variety. The item she thought was a little risky but she had to have at least two of anyway was something called a fas-cinator—dainty concoctions of feathers built on a gold comb and worn in the hair, graceful little whimsies popular in royal circles in London at the time. She decided on three because she couldn't decide on two—a black one, of course; an emerald that picked up the hazel in her eyes, and a lilac, so demure. The new clothes would arrive within five business days. In the meantime, Abilene had brought a couple of outfits with her that would do, the gold dress she wore to her interview with Jack being one of them.

Abilene was in a fine mood all the rest of that day. Charlie Nickel stopped by for dinner and thought there was something about her. He just couldn't put a word to it.

"How-de-do, missus," said Charlie, and removed his Stetson. "You got the tip, I got the table," she answered, and held his chair while he settled in.

"Be my pleasure," he said.

"Tell me something," she said as she unfolded his napkin and fit it around his neck. "What's it like having all that money?"

"It's more damn fun than anything in the whole world. How do you like being a rockhound widow?"

"I'm vowed to keep the home fires burning," she answered.

"We also serve who sit at home and wait," he said in an important voice.

"Don't go highfalutin on me, Charlie. It's my plan to be rich as you someday."

"It ain't a race, and, anyway," the old man chuckled, "I already won."

The afternoon of their second day at the Angel, his father taught him all about setting an explosive charge. It didn't occur to the boy to wonder where Jubal learned how. His father knew lots of stuff, so why question this one? Gideon watched and listened carefully because he wanted his father to entrust him with a job as important as this. A slot canyon was a smaller canyon off to one side or the other, sometimes visible only through a crack in a vertical wall. You wanted to be real careful because these were the ones that twisted back and around on themselves. You don't know what you're doing you could get real lost real fast, and then you'd die. They found one not too far from the Angel herself. A boulder into which someone had drilled a hole almost deep enough to take a charge blocked its entrance. Why it was never blown remained a mystery to Jubal, but he took it as a good sign that someone else besides himself thought the place showed promise, so he went about finishing the job while Gideon watched. First of all, he deepened the hole. The deeper the charge, the greater the damage. Gideon spelled his father, and the work went quickly. He liked the heft of the sledgehammer, and he never felt so powerful as when the hammer hit the drill dead center. When Jubal judged the hole deep enough, he said, "Now you want to time your det cord." He cut off a two-foot strip of detonation cord, got out his pocket watch, scratched a wooden match, and lit one end. Ten seconds later it fizzled out. "Now we know," his father said, cut off a six-foot length, inserted one end into a firing cap, crimped the neck, fit the firing cap into the stick of dynamite, and pushed the primed charge as far down the hole in the boulder as possible. Get it set up like that, then light the det cord and walk away. The "walk away" part, that was important. You didn't run. You never ran. You could get hurt, trip over something, get all blowed up.

Gideon knelt down behind another boulder ten yards away, watched as his father lit the fuse and walked back to join him as calmly as if he were bringing hot dogs back to their seats at the ballpark. Thirty seconds after Jubal lit it, the charge went off. It split the boulder and made it possible for a man to squeeze through into the canyon beyond. "You be the first," Jubal said to Gideon. He took two fifty-yard coils of rope, spliced them together with a fancy knot he learned in the navy, tied one end around his son's waist and the other around his own. "Take a look around," Jubal said to Gideon, "see what you see." Gideon squeezed through into the canyon. Almost immediately it opened up like a funnel, then branched out and became another canyon with a sandstone arch across its midpoint. There the rope went taut, but Gideon could see where the canyon branched out into two more canyons, right and left, beyond the arch. It stood like the gateway to another world. The walls of the side canyons were vermilion, russet, amber. Gideon didn't have words for them, but the colors glowed in the golden light of late afternoon. He wanted a closer look, wanted to press his cheek against the glittering wall set back from but framed by the arch, seeded with red garnets and silvery white mica schist. He untied the rope from around his waist and retied it around a small boulder, tied his red Hercules bandanna around the rope so he could see it flutter from a distance, walked the fifty yards or so to the arch, and stepped through. A few yards beyond the arch Gideon looked back to see where he'd been and gasped at how different it looked from when he walked through it. His focus had been on the arch ahead, and so he had taken no note of the gray-brown walls on either side that curved around like the hull of an ark. Boulders were strewn about the canyon floor like a handful of peas. Random. No point; no design. He'd turned expecting to see something that wasn't there, and he knew as sure as he knew anything that had he kept moving forward so absentmindedly he might never have gotten out of there alive. He took it as a lesson learned: keep looking back. With a jolt he also realized that he was no longer tied to his father. His father thought he had him safe but all the man had was a stone, and that made Gideon feel like a liar, and he didn't want to be that to his father. Would his father ever do that to him? Untie the rope he thought was keeping him safe? Leave his son to wander away and die alone? Gideon fought an urge to run, but he remembered what his father had said and forced himself to walk. He never took his eyes off the fluttering red bandanna as he picked his way to where he tied the rope around his waist and followed the length of it back to where he knew his father waited. He'd want to know what Gideon had seen, carnotite maybe, a streak of yellow in a gray stone wall. That would mean right off the bat they'd found a good play, but Gideon hadn't seen any.

"Hey, pilgrim," Jubal said when he saw his son coming, "what'd you do, lay down and take a nap?" Gideon was confused. "You were gone so long I thought you booked a hotel room in there, maybe had a couple of babes," said Jubal, and laughed at his own joke. Gideon thought he'd only been gone a few minutes, but Jubal said not hardly, more like a couple of hours. He untied the ropes from around Gideon's waist and then his own, coiled the length of rope over his shoulder, and said, "A cold beer would go pretty good right now, wouldn't it?" He knew his son would appreciate that. "One day you'll be old enough to say, 'Hey, Dad, let's go hoist a chilly!' and we'll be able to just drop everything and do it. Put up our feet. Put a little Patsy Cline on the Victrola. Hang on to that, pup, will you?" he asked as he handed Gideon the coil of rope. The boy slung it over his shoulder, proudly, like an epaulet. "Let's go cook dinner," said his father. "We got beans, more beans, and even more beans after that. Take your pick," he said with a wink and a chuckle.

He loved driving that jeep. It was squat and uncomfortable, but all you had to do was point it and it could go anywhere.

When he first arrived in Edom, Jack had acquired a vintage World War Two Willys jeep from the widow of an old prospector who had driven that same model for General Patton. It had been deteriorating in a ramshackle shed and wasn't much more than a tin can on bad rubber, but it stoked something in Jack and he had to have it. "Just tow it away," replied the widow when Jack asked if she'd sell it. He did and rebuilt it from the shocks up, painted the body red with CHOSIN FEW lettered on the doors in gold. Sometimes you just do something for the simple thrill it gives you, and driving that jeep never ceased to be a thrill. He felt like he was sitting on a roller skate and loved the feeling of wind all around him. So that afternoon he'd suggested to Abilene that they take a ride. It was between lunch and dinner, the slowest part of the day. She had work to do, of course, but when the boss calls, you answer. Any fool knew that, and here she was sitting next to him now laughing and whooping every time they hit a bump, and meaning it. Abilene had an appetite for the thrill herself. She didn't know where she was or where she was headed, and she didn't care. Just floor it and take her away.

The jeep fishtailed down a gravelly slope before Jack brought it to rest on a flat, gray-black rock floor as vast as five football fields. Red rock cliffs lined the rock floor and loomed over it. Abilene jumped from the jeep and ran with abandon, her arms flung out to her sides. Laughing, she twirled round and around, making herself dizzy, like a child. "Whoa," she said, staggered, and lost her balance. Jack caught her, but she sprinted away and spun again until she could barely stand, then plopped down onto her back, her arms outstretched, her legs wide apart, like a kid in a field of grass. "If this was the beach," she said, "I could make a sand angel." Abilene brought her arms up and down, up and down, her legs open and shut.

"It was the beach," said Jack.

"Say what?" she asked.

"I'll show you," he said, and searched along the ground until he found what he wanted—two stones, a flat chunk of gray-black and an oval one. Jack sat Indian fashion beside her and held out the flat one first. "Look." He pointed out tiny, pale-white shapes in the dark stone. "That's a little seashell in there, a prehistoric organism."

"You're kidding," she said. "Uh-uh. There it is. I see it!" Jack showed her the oval one.

"That's a fossilized clam," he said.

"You're kidding," she said.

"Two hundred million years ago this place was all underwater," Jack explained.

"Stop it."

"It's the truth."

"You mean," she exclaimed, "that I am standing on the bottom of the sea?"

"You could say that," said Jack.

"Oh, my God in heaven," she shrieked, "isn't that something? I am standing on the bottom of the sea! Jesus Christ, the bottom of the sea!" She was having a joy attack, and the joy she felt was genuine, contagious. Jack caught it, too. It transformed her. She became childlike, open, never more beautiful. Jack tried to kiss her, but she pulled away and said, "I'm not ready for that."

He blurted out, "I'm crazy about you."

"How crazy are you?" she asked. "You're a businessman, a type not usually known for going off the deep end."

"Well," he said, "I'm off it now."

"Are you crazy enough to dance on the edge? Are you crazy like Jubal?" Abilene wanted to know.

"What do you mean, like Jubal?" he asked.

"That man took me on the adventure of his lifetime," she said. "I know what you want, Jack Savage. I'm just in the dark about how badly you want it."

"So badly I save the man a partnership."

"How rich are you, Jack?" she asked.

"I'm not a Rockefeller, but if Jubal doesn't find uranium, I'll be just fine," answered Jack.

"But will I be just fine? That's my big question."

"What's your big answer?"

"You," she said.

He moved toward her and said, "I was hoping you'd say that."

She stepped back away from him. "Learn something right away, Jack Savage," she said. "I'm only easy when it don't count."

"What do you want?" he asked.

"To win."

"Then why not trade up?"

"No guarantees."

"My best intentions."

"The road to hell."

"I mean it," said Jack.

"I want it all, Jack Savage. I want to give it. I want to get it. Don't get involved with me if you're looking to get away easy."

"I'm looking for a run on my investment," he said.

"I want you to be as crazy for me as I am for you. If I'm with you, and I find you with anybody else, I will track you down and put a bullet in your head."

"You're serious," he said.

"You'll be the first to know."

"What do I get if I'm good?" he wanted to know.

"The woman you dream about. She'll look good and provide your increase, but she'll want you body and soul. You ready for that?" she asked.

"What about Jubal?"

"Somehow, sometime," she said, "we'll get him to go away. But we were talking about you."

"You're different than I thought you'd be," he said.

"Of course I am, precious. People always are once they get to know each other. Let me see you smile." Jack suddenly felt self-conscious. He smiled shyly.

"Look how shy you are! I can see what you must've looked like as a little boy. Sweet. Will you be sweet to me, Jack Savage?"

"Yes."

"Promise?"

"Yes, yes, yes."

"Did you bring me out here so you could fuck me, Mr. Savage?" He hesitated. She'd shocked him, though he'd never wanted a woman more. "Do not lie," she said.

"Yes."

"Say it: I brought you . . ."

"I brought you out here . . ."

"So . . ."

"So I could fuck you."

"I like it when you tell me what you want."

"I wanted to fuck you the first time I saw you."

"Then do it, Mr. Savage. Give me your cock. I want your cock right now." She held her arms open wide and beckoned him toward her. Good sex was not something Abilene ordinarily had trouble finding. But this was unexpected. The intensity of it. The raw energy of it. The absolute and total abandon of it. There. On the ocean floor. Naked as the stones. Take me now, Lord! Jesus God almighty! It could not get any better than this.

And yet it did. Sex ruled the days that followed. Abilene and Jack were no more in control of what they did and when they did it than they were of the weather. Once, when they only had a minute, literally sixty seconds, only time to enter her once, which he did, one thrust, instantly they both came together, at which point they cracked each other up with their laughter. The pleasure they got from each other was boundless. One morning he suggested they take the chopper to Salt Lake. He had some business with the bank there, but for all the time it took she wondered why he hadn't just done the thing by mail. When he suggested they grab a bite before heading back, and she thought that was a good idea, he said he knew someplace, hailed a taxi, and asked the driver to take them to the Grand Hotel in the middle of Salt Lake City. The doorman smiled and greeted them as if he meant it, held the door for them, and tipped his hat as they walked through. Abilene felt so like a lady. Her body felt as if it were sheathed in silk. They crossed the lobby, but instead of taking a right and going up the stairs toward the restaurant on the hotel's promenade, Jack steered Abilene to the elevator and pressed the button. When the elevator man opened the door, Jack ushered Abilene on board and requested the fifteenth floor. He rested against the rear wall of the elevator as it climbed the floors, and when she leaned back against him she felt him hard, and she shivered with excitement. When the elevator reached the fifteenth floor, he took her arm to help her, and that touch nearly set her off. She no longer wondered where she was being taken, for she had given herself over to simply being taken there. He guided her down the hall to a room, unlocked the door, and held it for her as she walked through.

A small table was set with silver and linen, champagne on ice, fat strawberries, portions of exotic cheeses, crackers from Belgium. Beyond the table, on the bed, sat a gift box with a beautiful ribbon. She looked at him and smiled, then she took the box and without opening it disappeared into the bathroom. He could barely breathe and lost his breath altogether when she opened the door and emerged dressed in the silver-blue negligee he had bought for her. She asked him to sit on the edge of the bed, and then she undressed him and flung herself on him. The two of them clung to each other, rolled around, and moaned and screamed until a harsh knocking came at the door demanding to know if anyone was sick in there, security demanding that the door be opened. So Jack had to get up. He wrapped a towel around himself and opened the door to see a burly hotel security guard standing there with a wizened, bitter-lipped old lady glaring daggers from behind his fat ass. Jack regarded them with disgust. "There's nobody sick in here, and you know it," he growled, adjusted his towel, and shut the door in their faces. That afternoon had to go down in history as the best couple of hours in Abilene's entire life. Jack's, too. They knew the gods had smiled on them, and they celebrated their good fortune as often as seven times a day. She called him her gypsy lover, and when she said she wished she were a virgin for him she meant it.

———

Two weeks of busting rocks under the pounding sun and who knew for sure what they had? Work this hard would break the spirit of a man if that man weren't as hopeful as Jubal Pickett. The Angel exacted fourteen days of hard labor from these two, fourteen days of struggling up the debris of talus slopes, hacking through juniper stands, clambering along vertiginous ledges, days in which they were parched, burned, blinded, bruised, and battered. Foot by foot they probed with the Geiger counter. Whenever the instrument chattered, they took ore samples with a geologist's hammer and put the specimens in a gunnysack. They set charges and pulverized rocks, and, at the end of each grueling day, they ate beans and stared into the fire, except for the time with the rattlesnake, which was, by the way, thick as a welder's forearm.

Gideon had watched mesmerized as it crossed in front of him, a beautiful creature, he thought, four feet long, and lucky to see it when the heat made it slow. He counted its rattles and knew that most people thought you could tell a rattlesnake's age that way, but Gideon knew different, because rattlesnakes sometimes molted three times a year, and each molt meant another rattle. Sometimes you killed one, cut her open, and saw all her babies still alive and wriggly inside. People claimed that's proof they swallowed their young to protect them from danger, but his father explained what kind of horseshit that notion was because any damn fool knew that baby snakes were hatched right inside their mother's body, crawled out of the eggs, and then crawled out of her.

"It's like you been hypnotized," said Jubal. His voice startled Gideon, who had been so intent on the snake he hadn't noticed his father come up beside him. Jubal stood there leaning on a shovel, watching the snake with his son. "I never get tired of staring at them either," he said, then he slashed out with the shovel and severed the snake's head. The move was so sudden it took Gideon by surprise, though it meant no more to Jubal than slapping a fly. He bent over to lift the headless snake by its tail. "Make a nice belt," he said. Jubal took out his pocketknife, gutted, skinned, and filleted the thing, and two minutes later had chunks of it skewered and cooking on the fire. "Dress up the beans a little," he said as he mixed in the chunks of meat and sprinkled some salt and hot sauce into his concoction. Jubal stirred the pot one more time then ladled out a plate so full it almost creaked and handed his creation to Gideon with a flourish. "What's a fancy French restaurant got on us, anyway?" he asked as he loaded up a plate for himself.

Fancy French eating or not, both father and son were ready for a real meal once they got back to Edom. Jubal declared he was going to cook them up a batch of steaks thick as Bibles, rare and juicy (long as they didn't talk back on their way down). Gideon conjured up a ice-cold orange soda. The number one thing they did was drop their sack of samples at the assay office. The next thing they did was swing by the Hidden Splendor and pick up Abilene. Jack was there, too, but what could he say when Jubal asked if she could go home a little bit early? Vanda was on the premises, after all, and they all knew she could fill in. Abilene had given Jubal a hug like she meant it, groin to groin. Jack hated him for it. He hated them both. Gideon did, too, except he really didn't hate his father, but Jack really did hate it when Jubal lustfully slapped Abilene on the butt and led her toward the door with a "My chariot awaits you, *mon chérie,*" said in a faux French accent. Then he gave Jack a little man-to-man nudge: "I'm gonna get her to give me a bath," he said, winked, and followed Abilene out to his truck singing like a country-western star, "I got the hungries for your lovin', and I'm waitin' in your welfare line."

Gideon sat Indian fashion on his ledge high up the wall. He chipped methodically away at an arrowhead and ignored the sight of his father and that woman at the pothole below. It looked like a pool to him, but his father always called it a pothole. He couldn't hear a thing, and that was fine. The wind mostly muted the chipping sound, too.

As far as his father was concerned, this was it, this was heaven. Jubal sat buck naked in the pool with a cold can of beer while Abilene soaped up his back. "What am I drawing?" she asked as she traced a heart in the white film with her finger.

"Give me a clue," said Jubal.

"It's shaped like a heart," she said.

"Got to be a heart," he said.

"You win the prize," said Abilene.

"What's the prize?"

"Me," she said as she traced the letters "JS" inside the heart.

Jubal whooped with joy and dove into the pool. Some of the splash got on Abilene; she shied away from it as if from a nasty smell. She couldn't help it. It genuinely scared her. To sink into a warm bath and soak was one thing. Up to your neck in suds. Flicking water with your toes. But once up in Oologah Lake on a family vacation when Abilene was a little kid was another matter. She accidentally went over one side of her daddy's bass boat while he was busy horsing a smallmouth on the other. By the time her old man realized she was no longer on board and dove off to find her, her small body had become entangled in lake weed, its tentacles pulling her downward, and she knew then that she was going to die. The thought pierced her heart like an icicle. She couldn't scream because she was underwater. She couldn't kick free, and the terror made her lose control of her bowels. She was passing over, and she didn't want to, didn't want to, didn't want to, and was nearly gone when her father ripped her free and carried her back to the surface, where she gulped air barking like a seal.

———————

By the time Jubal surfaced, all the soap had washed off his body. They heard the motor engine before they saw it. Abilene knew right away who it was. What did that man think he was doing? This is all wrong. Where is your self-control? Gideon could see the red jeep from his vantage point. But Jubal wondered about it until he saw Jack wave as he parked the jeep near the trailer and walked down to join them, a bottle of wine in each hand.

"Hey, partner," yelled Jubal as he climbed out of the pool and stood there stark naked and dripping wet.

"I'm here to celebrate," said Jack, although he was clearly uncomfortable with the sight of Jubal naked.

"Celebrate what?" Jubal wanted to know.

"The future," answered Jack.

Two hours later, Jubal (now in his boxer shorts), Abilene, and Jack were still sitting around the small table in the trailer, all of them drunk, but none as drunk as Jubal. Abilene's *Seduction of Venus* hung from the wall. Gideon opted to eat his dinner alone down to the pool. "I want to make a toast," said Jubal as he staggered to his feet. "I want to make a toast to my own angel—the Venus of Serenity Wash. She said, 'Jubal, you got dreams, but if you don't get your ass in gear, dreams is what you're going to die with.'"

"Amen," said Abilene.

"So here's to Abilene Breedlove, her brains and body, may

they go down in history," Jubal said, and fell back into his seat, whereupon he immediately leaned forward, arms on the table, and locked eyes with Jack Savage. "Now see, Jack," he said, "I'm wondering. You're a man with looks. I'm a man with a face like a dirty plate. You tell me: how'd I get so lucky?"

"Enjoy yourself while you can," answered Jack. Abilene registered alarm.

"Shh," she cautioned.

"Hm?" asked Jubal.

Abilene covered quickly. "Bad luck to talk about it," she said.

"'Scuse me," said Jubal as he staggered out the door. "I gotta pee. Be right back. Everybody behave." It wasn't until she heard him urinating off the steps outside that Abilene broke the silence. "He pees like a horse, don't he?" she said to Jack. "Hey," she said when she noticed Jack's expression, "I never expected you to be so jealous."

"I'm not jealous," Jack protested.

"Then why'd you invite yourself to the party?" she teased. "Hey, I think it's sweet. Just don't let Jubal catch on."

"I'd like to kill him."

"You don't mean that, darlin'. It's the alcohol talking. For now he's got a certain priority."

"What do I get?" asked Jack.

"Everything he don't," she replied. Jack made a move toward Abilene, but she pushed him away. "He's right outside the door," she cautioned at just about the same time as Jubal staggered back through. "Hey, partner," he said, and passed out. Abilene grabbed him and held him up. "Help me get him in bed, will you?" she said to Jack. He took Jubal's head, Abilene took his feet, and together they carried Jubal, still unconscious, to the bed. Abilene drew a curtain between the sleeping area and the kitchen. "Don't try anything, Jack. The man can wake on a dime." She surveyed the mess from dinner. "When I'm rich I'm going to eat off nothin' but paper plates and plastic utensils, so I can throw everything away and not have to wash a damn one."

"You'd probably want china," he said.

"Oh, yeah? You gonna give it to me?"

"I might," he said, and tried to kiss her. Abilene laughed and resisted at first, then she gave in and kissed him back, then she pulled away again.

"Better leave," she said.

"He's out cold," said Jack.

"I'm told people in a coma still hear what's going on. The boy's out there, too. Go home now. Scat!"

Abilene held the door for Jack to exit, followed him out to the top step, and watched as he walked to his jeep. Before he'd gone too far he stopped and turned around, walked back to Abilene, and placed a hand gently on her foot. "No," she said as she pulled her foot away. "Gideon." She indicated where the boy was camped out down by the pool. "Go on. I'll see you tomorrow." She stood there and watched until his taillights disappeared, then a thought took her and she walked down the steps of the trailer over to where Gideon lay asleep in his bag. He looked that way, like he was asleep. Out. Kaput. Good night. "Hey," she whispered, "Gideon. You up?" He didn't move. "You ought to be in the movies, boy," she said. "I can't tell whether you're alive or dead."

———

They all met up again first thing the next morning at the assayer's office. Charlie Nickel, too. Jubal figured Jack had told him. The news was not all bad. The assay clerk confirmed that they were dealing with ore, no doubt about that, but his opinion was that it was just this side of commercial grade. "Close but no cigar" was what he said, except for sample number seven, a gray-brown stone with a pale greenish streak. Sample number seven he said was promising, though he couldn't tell whether they were an inch away or a county. However, he suggested it might be worth it to take a closer look. That word "promising" rang in Jubal's head like a bell, the kind of bell that starts horse races, the kind of bell that makes a dog drool. From the instant he heard the word, Jubal was busting out of his skin to get back to the claim. He kept singing, "I can smell the money, smell the money . . ." He snapped his fingers and danced a little jig as he sang: "Smell the money, oh, Lordy, smell the money . . ." Charlie suggested a drill might be what they wanted at this point. As soon as they could get a drill rig and reload the truck, Jubal wanted back out there. In fact, said Charlie, he had one, his good luck drill, the one he was using when he made the strike. He'd saved it for sentimental reasons but would be willing to rent it to them at the going rate, to which all the members of the Dark Angel Mineral Development Corporation said yes, each figuring good luck had to be worth something. When they got to the storage yard where

Charlie Nickel kept his equipment in impeccable condition—
the parts and accessories for the drill rig were each wrapped in
oilcloth and packed neatly in wooden containers—he showed
them the actual core sample itself, a cylinder one foot long
with the circumference of a cucumber, the very one that made
Charlie a wealthy man. Jubal tingled when he touched it, and
within hours he and Gideon had the truck loaded for another
two weeks working the claim.

Abilene fussed a lot about being left alone, being a rock
hound widow, having to worry, being out of touch, but she
knew Jubal as a man of firm determination who would not let
them down, and she pledged to keep it fluffed for him. Jubal's
knees went weak to hear Abilene say it, but he wished she'd
kept her voice down. He thought he saw Jack wince on that
one. He had. The expression registered. Gideon saw it, too.
"Take good care of your father, Gideon," she said to the boy,
and kissed him on the cheek so suddenly he hadn't time to turn
away. "Ha!" she said triumphantly. "Gotcha!" Gideon wiped
his cheek. "Too late," she said, and laughed. "Now you know
what fast is."

PART 9

Three hours later, Jubal and Gideon were camped out near the wash they almost went down in, and Abilene was astride Jack in his bedroom, her back slightly arched so that her breasts were high and her stomach flat, with her silver-blue negligee draped around her waist like icing on a wedding cake. She knew Jack liked to watch, and she enjoyed moving herself any way she desired, her hands back on his calves giving her purchase, rising and falling, swaying gently like a devout in prayer. No words you could discern came from her lips. She spoke in tongues.

"You must be a witch," he said. She laughed and moved her hips. "What are you doing to me?" he said.

"I'm casting a spell," she answered, and moved again. His head thrashed about the pillow. "How 'bout this?" He groaned from deep in his throat. "Or this?"

"Oh, my God," he said, "I know you're a witch," and flopped

his arms out to the sides as if he were knocked cold. Abilene remained sitting on him, though now she tucked her knees up under her chin. She took his hand and held it against her belly so he could feel himself way up inside her.

"You are," he said, "an amazing woman. I—"

"Shhh."

"What?"

"Don't say anything you'll be sorry for," she cautioned.

"I can't get enough of you," he said.

"You're my sweet daddy lode, and I love you for it," Abilene said with a winsome smile.

"You mean that?"

She thought he sounded like a little boy.

"I don't dissemble, boss," she replied.

"I'd do anything for you, you know that."

"I'd like to think so."

"I can't stand the thought of him touching you," he said.

"Then don't think it," she said. "Doesn't do you any good. I signed on with the Picketts, and that's a real true fact of life. Do you see the winds of change around here? I don't."

"What are you suggesting?" he wanted to know.

"A lady's not supposed to suggest anything," said Abilene.

"Then how does a lady get what she wants?"

"I think you know," she said, and made the sound of the wind with her mouth.

Jubal and Gideon were each of them pretty fair mechanics, but still they had to spend most of the first day back at the Angel putting the old drill in working order, so they weren't able to take a whack at sample number seven until the next morning. There was no longer any moon to speak of, no clouds, black on black, stars like billions of lightning bugs tossed against a gargantuan spiderweb. Jubal and Gideon. Father and son. The way it was best. His father was no slacker. He pulled his weight, that's for sure, and he did know his way around tools. They'd let the campfire burn down low so they could feel the stars all around them. Mostly it was quiet except for when his father started to chuckle to himself—something had struck him funny—and Gideon knew it wouldn't be more than a minute before his father told him what it was. Right on cue, Jubal chuckled again and said, "Guess how many penises a koala bear has? True fact. Guess how many?" He was all bursting to tell. "Give up yet?" Jubal asked. Gideon smiled, which Jubal took to be affirmative and blurted out, "Two! A koala bear has two penises. Abilene told me. She's a pistol, that woman. I meant to ask her whether the female has two pookies, too." He couldn't help but laugh out loud again. "Sense of humor in a female covers up a multitude of sorrows," said Jubal, feeling very much like a sage.

———

Next morning they were on the rig early. The spindly derrick seemed like a Tinkertoy in the vast canyon. Gideon filled the motor with diesel fuel while Jubal fit the drill bit. He told Gideon to "fire this thing up" and eased the revolving drill down until it began to slowly grind its way through the bedrock. Sharp chips and dust spewed from the deflector as the drill ground deeper. It would be slow going. At best they could expect to drill maybe three and a half feet per hour, maybe thirty feet in an eight-hour day. Anything more than that meant they had to acquire a much larger rig, which also meant the cost of the crew that came with it.

By the time Jubal and Gideon packed it in for the day, they had gone down nearly thirty feet. Every five feet or so they reversed the rig and removed the core sample, and then ran it by the Geiger counter, but there was never an indication that they were near any kind of treasure whatsoever.

Jack sat with his feet up on his desk and stared through the window at the landing strip. Abilene was out there, caught in the downwash of a helicopter that had just lifted off with documents to be delivered to Salt Lake. She had turned her back on the wash, but still it messed with her hair and whipped up the hem of her dress. She held her hair in place with both hands as she walked back to the office, but the wind continued to play with the hem of her dress, the blue one, and revealed snippets of white slip like miniature whitecaps. He wondered if she knew he could see her. He was getting hard. Is that what she wanted? He shifted in his seat and freed his penis from a wrinkle in his jockey shorts. He began to open the middle drawer of his desk but thought better of it and waited for her to knock on the door, which he knew she would. A minute later, given time to cross the tarmac and come back inside, she did, and poked her head through the door without waiting for an answer.

"I'm going to grab a bite for lunch," she said. "Want me to bring you something?"

"Not hungry," he said.

"Penny for your thoughts."

"They're worth more than that," he said.

"I'm not surprised a bit," said Abilene. That smile. He felt himself harden even more.

"Come here," he said.

She shook her head. "We've got to start exercising some self-discipline, boss. Jubal'll be back any day now."

"Come here," said Jack, "and lock the door behind you."

"Then promise me we'll start exercising it soon," she said.

"I promise," he said.

"You'd promise anything just to get me over there, wouldn't you?"

"I would. Yeah."

She smiled and locked the door behind her. "How do you want me?" she asked.

Later, he sat behind his desk in the dark. It was late, a night with no moon. He knew she'd be waiting for him at his house, probably already in his bed, there for him when he got home. But he had to think and he had to think hard, and he wouldn't have been able to do that if Abilene were anywhere in range. She was available to him even while she slept. He woke up one night still aching for her. She was asleep beside him. She purred. He oiled himself up with a lotion they kept by the bed, and carefully, so as not to startle her, bearing his weight on his arms, he eased himself over her, gently shifted her body, and slid himself inside her. Abilene never opened her eyes, but a little smile came to her face, and she clung to him and moaned softly with pleasure. Every time they made love it seemed impossible that it could get any better, but the next time always eclipsed the last time, while sex itself eclipsed everything. Their pleasure was so intense as to be excruciating. Each time it sent them into a deep sleep, what Jack told her the French called *la petite mort,* "the little death."

Jack opened the middle drawer of his desk and stared at the .45-caliber pistol sitting there, the one he had learned to use in the service. He fought the urge to pick it up because he believed that if he touched it he would use it. When Jack was satisfied that not every last drop of sense had been drained out of him, he felt some relief and shut the drawer.

Gideon loved it when darkness came because with it came the silence again. Days were filled with the grinding of the drill, the clanking of its chains and hoists, the relentless pounding of the diesel engine. As soon as the engine was cut, the silence poured into the void like thunder roiling into a vacuum caused by lightning. Then Gideon could relax and let the wilderness cradle him.

They'd been working really hard, Gideon and his father, although Jubal liberally sprinkled short breaks throughout the long days, breaks for water and salt tablets, lunch, smokes, or just about whenever he thought a break might be needed. Every hour or so they shut down the rig and reversed the hollow bit so they could bring another core sample to the surface. Then they'd pass a Geiger counter over the foot-long cylinder of sandstone to check its radioactivity. When nothing registered, they'd put the core sample in its place in a row of samples stored neatly beside the rig, crank up the engine again, and lower the drill back into the borehole, where it continued its slow but persistent dig through what seemed to be an endless substratum of sedimentary rock.

They were nearly two hundred feet down when suddenly the old drill, which heretofore had worked slowly but without a problem, began to shriek and belch smoke. It sounded like bats in a blender. Jubal raced to shut it down, but Gideon was there first and brought the rig to a stop. When they finally wrangled the chain to the surface they immediately saw that the bit had snapped off.

"Shit 'n' shinola," groused Jubal. "Be better off if we had a A-bomb to bust through all this stuff. However, not only do we not have a A-bomb, we ain't got a second drill bit, either. Son, I believe this calls for a command decision. We got a couple days' more food and water, but it looks like we're going to have to pack it in early for resupply."

Since it was growing darker, Jubal decided they'd load up and leave in the morning. He'd chopped the head off a second rattler earlier in the day, so he said, "We'll have my signature dish for supper tonight, Beans 'n' Rattler à la Pickett"—said in his phony French accent—"roll us some smokes, and relax in creature comfort under God's heavenly stars. Be nice if we had a little bacon, too. Maybe a beer. Definitely a beer."

They did what they always did after dinner: rolled smokes, leaned back against a rock, and stared at the stars. It was pure, moonless black out there, so it seemed like they could see every star ever born. Must've spotted a dozen shooting stars, too, the both of them, every corner of the sky. When his father inhaled, the red ash from his cigarette lit some of his face, and Gideon assumed it was the same for his own face, his nostrils, some of his mouth. Apparently something had struck his old man funny because he chuckled to himself and next said out of nowhere, "I know what you're thinking, pup, and I'm right there with you." Jubal chuckled again, but the truth was Gideon hadn't been thinking anything at all, so he didn't have a clue as to what his father was laughing about. It could've been anything. "Somebody I can't remember once told me something I'll never forget," said Jubal. " 'Life is a tragedy filled with joy,' and I believe that." Gideon didn't know about that tragedy part, but he couldn't think of anything better than hunting for buried treasure during the day and smoking under the night sky before dropping off to sleep. A cold beer maybe.

Way out on the horizon one of the stars seemed to break free of the assembly. It appeared to drop down below the multitude and head straight for the Angel. Noise followed—the distant whop-whop of rotary blades, louder as the chopper closed the distance. It sounded to Gideon like each turn of the blade was an angry slap. The slaps became a racket as the helicopter circled overhead. Gideon clapped his hands over his ears, but the racket had already penetrated his skull and stayed there long after the chopper settled down in a puddle of light and cut its engines. "Hey, partner," Jubal called out as Jack climbed down from the cockpit. "You come out here to count your money?"

"Not quite, but I did come out here to count yours," replied Jack.

"Meaning what?" asked Jubal as Jack entered the ring of soft light thrown by the campfire.

"You came here to make a fortune," said Jack as he took an envelope from the inside pocket of his flight jacket and handed it to Jubal. "Here it is." Jubal opened the envelope and took out a five-hundred-dollar bill. "There's fifty of them in there," said Jack. "A fortune."

"How'd I get so lucky?" Jubal wanted to know.

"Some people," said Jack, "everything they touch turns to gold. You won't do any better digging here."

"I must be kind of slow," said Jubal.

"What do you mean?"

"I think I must've missed something, Jack. Partner. Don't I have to do something for this money? Speak slowly. Lemme get this."

"Where's Gideon?"

"Why?"

"This business is better off just between us."

"You see him anywhere? Neither do I. He goes his own way. Show me what else you got in your pocket."

"You and Gideon pack up and go back to Mississippi. On your way out of town, I'll have another twenty-five thousand for you. You two will go home rich men."

"Didn't you leave somebody out?" asked Jubal.

"Fifty thousand dollars," said Jack.

"When did she go on sale?" Jubal wanted to know.

"I'm glad to see you're taking it so lightly," said Jack.

"I'm not taking it that lightly, Jack, not that lightly. You're giving me news here. You're giving me a headline. Must be a story to go along with it." He took a burning stick from the campfire and impaled a scorpion that had been crawling on his sleeping bag. He held it over the fire and watched it crackle and smoke.

"We've been seeing each other," said Jack.

"What's that mean, 'seeing each other, see-ing'?" hissed Jubal.

"We're grown-ups, Jubal. What do you think it means?" asked Jack.

"Like with your clothes off? See-ing? Each other? With your clothes off?"

Jubal flicked the burning scorpion in Jack's direction.

"This doesn't have to be hard," said Jack as he shifted his weight away from the flaming insect.

"How do you know my heart ain't breaking?" asked Jubal. "How do you know I ain't out of my mind with grief?"

"She brought you luck. She brought you riches. Now let her go," replied Jack evenly. He took the contract from his pocket, showed Jubal what it was, and tossed it on the fire. "That leaves you with the only copy. I don't care what you do with it," he said.

"She must've fucked you every which-a-way. She do that thing with her tongue where she—"

"That's all I have to say." Jack cut him off and turned back toward the helicopter.

"Mind if I add my two cents?" asked Jubal.

Jack held out his hands to signify "Say what you want" and

continued walking. Jubal took his tire iron from the bed of his truck.

"Talk to this, you thieving son of a bitch," he hollered as he winged the iron toward Jack. It whirred over his head like a propeller and missed him by a breath. Jack hit the ground, pulled the .45 from his jacket pocket, and turned on Jubal, who faced him without a hint of fear.

"Didn't they teach you in the marines not to point a gun at somebody unless you're gonna shoot him?" taunted Jubal as he advanced on Jack. Jack fired but Jubal was still standing there.

"Missed me, you piece of shit," jeered Jubal. "Know why you missed me, scumbag? You missed me because you're scared. A scared man can't do shit. How 'bout I give you a better target?" taunted Jubal as he advanced on Jack. Jack fired a second time, but an instant before he did, Jubal leaped out of the way and grabbed for the ten-gauge hidden by the sleeping bag. Jack's third shot took him on his right side where the man's neck met his shoulder and dropped Jubal with a look of impatience on his face more than anything else. He was still scrambling for his gun when Jack shot him again. This time Jubal flopped backward and lay still.

Jack stood back for a few seconds to see if Jubal would move, and, when he didn't, Jack crept forward, step by step, as if afraid he'd wake Jubal up. He peered closely at Jubal's face, curious. He'd never seen the face of someone he'd killed before. Jubal's eyes were closed, but, other than that, he bore no expression of pain or shock. "He got himself killed," Jack told himself, and started to straighten up when he was hit from behind and ridden to the ground. Gideon had leaped from a boulder above him, wrapped his arms and legs around Jack, sunk his teeth into Jack's neck, and driven him down. Pain like that obliterates everything else, like red-hot rivets screaming through your veins. You go blind, and the air ripped from your guts sounds like the shriek of a stuck pig. You'll do anything to get rid of it, lash out, slash out, kick, roll . . . Jack's .45 had fallen out of reach, but he was able to grab Jubal's shotgun and struck out with it over and over against the boy's head, so much so that you'd think he'd pulped it, and still Gideon wouldn't turn loose. Jack knew death. He knew eternity. He knew hell. This anguish forever? God, no! God, no! Jack bellowed furiously, summoned all his might, and slammed the stock into Gideon's forehead. Another second, he thought, I will be dead, I will be dead, but this time the boy went limp, and Jack wriggled out from under him like a fish fighting to get back to the water. He gulped air and shook his head to get his sight back. He kept the shotgun in his right hand but retrieved the .45 as soon as he could find it. The boy was beginning to move again. "Stay still," yelled Jack, but the boy didn't stay still, wouldn't stay still; he tried to stagger to his feet. "Don't stand up," yelled Jack. "Goddamn you, don't move!" And then the boy was on his feet again. He fought through the beating he had taken and got to his feet. His head was a mess. He lurched forward. Jack pulled the trigger, but the .45 misfired. What guided Gideon was pure fury. Jack knew he would have to kill him, switched the ten-gauge to his good, left hand, and fired. The shot took the boy full in his right hip and slammed him back against the boulder. Jack didn't know what kept him on his feet and fired again, but this time Gideon twisted away, fell backward, and disappeared over the edge of the precipice that bordered the campsite. Jack could hear him falling, and then he couldn't hear him anymore. That was it. Nothing more. Jack ejected the jammed round from his .45 and emptied the remaining rounds into the darkness where he supposed the boy had fallen. The rounds ricocheted off the rocks, and the ricochets echoed back and forth from one canyon wall to another until they played out and the silence seeped back in.

PART 10

He had no sense of how far he had fallen or even when he stopped, but when he did, Gideon looked up and saw Jack's silhouette way above him walking back and forth along the lip of the drop-off. Gideon spit the twigs, dirt, and bits of stone from his mouth, felt the fire in his hip for the first time, and passed out again. Jack moved back from the edge into light from the campfire. He hadn't come out here to kill these two, hadn't wanted to, but things got out of control, Jubal and his boy, crazier than shit. Now what? Breathe. Think. It was a serious job for one man, but he managed to dismantle the drill and derrick and toss it in the bed of Jubal's pickup along with the sleeping bags and dirty pots, anything that showed the men had been there. Then he took a five-gallon can of gasoline and emptied it in that same bed. He carried a second can to the passenger side of the cab, sloshed some of it on the floor and seat, and left the open can on the floor. He saw the keys were in the ignition and that pleased him because it made his job easier. Jack got behind the wheel and hit the starter. The truck shuddered but didn't start. Jack hit the starter again. This time the truck whined yet still refused to start. Jack hit the starter a third time, then a fourth, and then he smelled gas so he knew he had flooded the damn thing and there was nothing to do but to wait and do it again. Piece of crap truck, he thought. Goddamn Jubal would have a truck that was too damn stubborn to start! And that's when he saw him again. When he cursed him. Jack looked out the passenger-side door and saw Jubal crawling toward him. 'Goddamn the man, thought Jack, doesn't he know he's dead? You cut a chicken's head off in a garbage can and then slam the lid on and the chicken keeps beating its wings, fighting for . . . what? It was dead. But here came the man crawling on his belly. Jack could see the smear of blood and guts on the ground where the man had passed. He took a handful of bullets from his pocket and reloaded the .45. It was almost funny except it shook him, too, like watching a torn and bleeding corpse come to life. Jubal crawled slowly as a zombie but Jack had no doubt Jubal was coming for him. He waited until Jubal reached the running board. When Jubal did and grabbed hold and pulled himself up to where Jack could see his eyes, Jack shot him again, took the top right off Jubal's head, saw death in those eyes and fired point-blank.

Jack climbed down from the cab, walked around to Jubal's side, and took the corpse under the arms. Jubal was a strong man but not a big one, so Jack was able to muscle his dead weight onto the passenger seat and slam the door on him. The hell with the starter, thought Jack as he removed a chock of wood holding the right front wheel in place. On his way around to remove the left-hand chock, Jack tossed a match into the truck bed and suddenly the whole back of the truck was in flames, heat so searing Jack had to duck away. Once the left-hand chock was removed, Jack took hold of the steering wheel with his right hand and pushed with his legs and left hand. The truck moved forward smoothly toward the edge. It picked up speed. Jack jumped out of the way and was stunned to find himself yanked back, the sleeve of his jacket hooked by the door handle. At that moment, more than anything in this world, Jack Savage wished to be someplace else, anyplace else, but the pickup rolled over the edge of the mesa out into space, and it yanked Jack out with it like a five-pound fish on a ten-pound line. Gideon heard a scream and looked up to see the flaming pickup with Jack attached as it arced and fell through the air, hit the rock floor below, and exploded like an atom bomb.

He had retreated to a place of survival where nothing else mattered but the will to move, not the pain, not the sorrow, only the will to take another step. He might as well have been dead for all he was conscious of anything at all until a sharp pain drove through his hip. His eyes snapped open and he saw a bird with a bit of meat in its beak, and he knew the meat was a part of him, had been pecked from his hip. He wanted it back and grabbed for the bird, but the creature leaped off the ledge and sailed safely away. The bird thought he was dead and brought him back to life. He didn't know what time it was or which day, only that he was on a ledge baking in the sun and something had tried to eat him, something that stank. He had to move or he would die there, and Gideon wasn't ready for that, not death, no, not death. He didn't think why he had to move, only just knew that he had to do it. Where was he? On a rock ledge. Where? On the face of a cliff. Climb. He hadn't the strength to go up, had only one good leg, really, so the only way was down. Which was what he had to do. Climb down. He would have to bear the pain in his hip because he hadn't the strength to pull himself up. He could not tell how far it was to the bottom, and it didn't matter because no matter how far it was he had to get there. So he began his descent to the canyon floor, his good foot searching for the small cracks and ledges that made descent possible, but truly the only thing that made descent possible at all was that there was no other choice. It had to be possible. Or nothing.

There was no sense of time, barely a sense of movement as the descent was so slow, digit by digit, muscle by muscle. Ignore the pain. If you looked at him from a distance, invisible on the cliff face, a spot on a wall, he seemed to be clinging to the stone like some creature with suction cups for hands. He barely moved, and yet he did move, banished pain and thought and moved as he could. Each time he moved he thought, I will not die. Each time he moved he thought, I will get out of here, even when the sandstone crumbled and his foot slipped. Panic grabbed his heart with an icy fist and twisted, froze him in place. No, he said to himself, no, move, just move. Movement is your prayer. Movement is your guide. Movement is your only salvation.

The sun came and went and came again. Gideon clung to the cliff in darkness, moved when the first rays seeped into the canyon, moved as the light crept up and down the wall, spent another night on a ledge barely wide enough to hold his body. That was the morning he awoke and saw himself within jumping distance of the ground. He was tempted to just let go but he forced himself to lie on his back and slide the rest of the distance down. The slide shredded the remnants of his shirt. Dirt and pebbles worked into the wound in his hip but he reached the ground and collapsed there with his back against the wall. He was down, his back burned from the sun, his throat parched, his body aching and screaming for water. He had to have water, and he had to have sleep. Exhaustion won and he slept, but when he awoke the need for water shoved almost every other thought out of his mind, every thought in fact except for water and the other one.

Get up! Get to your feet, goddamnit! Get up! Get up! Move!

He pressed his back against the rock wall, strained, and pushed himself up using his one good leg. He could put very little pressure on the hip that took the shot, enough to barely limp at all, but as he did move he discovered he *could* move. The pain was little worse than if he stayed still. He was a strong boy who had taken a beating. He could move. He would move. He sucked in his breath, pushed off the rock face, and stepped out on the good leg first. The bad leg followed, its foot dragging a shallow trough in the sand, and that is what it would take and would be.

Tell yourself to move, Gideon. Tell yourself to move.

His father had always taught him, "You get lost, you head downhill. Find water and follow it." Water had once run through where he was walking but nothing ran there now. The rubble of a dead streambed was what he followed, but he came to no water and the sun wouldn't go away. His head throbbed and his back had already begun to blister. The rays of the sun were without remorse and tried to drop him to his hands and knees, but the boy fought back, one foot followed by the other. A covey of quail exploded out of a willow thicket. Suddenly the air was filled with something besides the sun. The birds scattered in all directions, but he knew they'd come back if he waited long enough and was still. They had to have water, too. They would show him. He crawled into the sparse shade of the thicket to wait. He could not lie on his back because it burned too much, so he stayed on his stomach and endured what he could not stop. That's all there was: endurance.

He smelled them first—must and urine—then heard their little grunts and squeals and focused on that until one of the pigs, a javelina, snorted and sniffed his way in Gideon's direction and stopped with his snout against the wound in Gideon's hip. The boy struck out and sent it squealing from the thicket. Others squealed, too, though he couldn't see them, only heard them clattering across the rocks as they ran. Where? Did they know a way out? He pushed himself forward until his head cleared the thicket and his eyes were able to focus on a muddy hole not much larger around than a tractor tire, with a smattering of water in it. There was that fish in Africa his father had told him about. When water was scarce, he said, damn things use their fins to crawl from one hole to another, and that's what he felt like—a fish crawling toward water. His arms were fins. They would take him there, and they did. He made no effort to push the scum on top of the pool aside but instead slid head-first right into it. It was only a few inches deep, so, at first, the boy took in as much mud as he did water. The only thing that mattered was that it be wet.

Gideon did not remember closing his eyes or turning over, but when he opened them his head rested against the rim of the pond and his back was in the muddy water. His hair was matted with dried mud, a grayish-brown-colored mud. His face was smeared with it. But he had slept and was the better for it. He came to his hands and knees in the water and was able to see where the tracks of pigs led to and from the pond. A small deer nibbled on some white, trumpet-shaped flowers a few feet from the pool, and it occurred to him that they must taste good. White as sweet cream. The deer watched him crawl from the watering hole and start for the flowers before it shied away. White as sweet cream. Except it wasn't. It was bitter. He swallowed it all, and there weren't any good parts, like on a honeysuckle, but he was still starving so he ate some dirt, crawled back into the watering hole, and rested until nausea set in as suddenly as a spiked fever. Tremors took him. He began to shiver violently. The dry heaves hit. He retched and retched but nothing came up. His father would've told him to get up and walk it off like you would a horse that foundered, but the water sucked him back. It felt like Jell-O and made sucking sounds. He fought to stand up. It seemed to be hardening and growing wider. He stood in the middle. Get out, stupid! You're too dumb to die here. It was that choice again: no choice. Move! He pushed his feet through the muck and stumbled out, picked up the javelina tracks, and followed them through the willow thicket where they headed down a rocky slope.

At the base of the slope stood an ocotillo plant. Its long, slender arms stirred with the breeze of his passing. He didn't know why but they reminded him of how a lady played a harp. Such things from strings! The arms began to writhe and vibrate and throb with bright light. The ocotillo was alive! Gideon put up his hands to block the light but the long limbs of the cactus burst into flames of green, blue, and yellow, and he could no longer look away. Rays of light penetrated his palms, and rainbows danced on his face. The shockwave that rippled out when the plant exploded wracked his body and added to his pain. It almost toppled him, and he knew he had to push it away, to clothe himself in asbestos in the midst of all the burning so he could continue to move his legs. He knew the pain was there but he would not feel it. Would. Not. Feel. It. Until convulsions overwhelmed the boy and threw him to the ground again. The pain fought to reach him, but at the instant he thought it would take and incinerate him into tiny particles of bone, each particle pulsing with unbearable heat—the fierce red tips of one million matches—the pain vanished. Vanished. Went where smoke went. Left him limp and depleted and lying in the dirt. That was the instant the world became marvelously still. He lay there and felt the earth breathe gently beneath him. His own heart slowed to the same pace, and he rested.

The next time he opened his eyes he was walking. He didn't wonder where. He was moving. Downhill. He remembered seeing a story in one of his father's magazines where Turkish soldiers tortured their female captives by strapping a copper pot containing a rat to their naked bellies. Then they lit a fire on the pot and cheered as the rat gnawed through the woman's belly to escape. Gideon was so hungry his stomach hurt that bad. His body would not die on him if he had food. Don't eat flowers, boy. Red berries maybe. No, not red berries either. Not dirt either. Light and dark were trading places. Don't eat flowers. He found himself thinking about the pain again, how it worked its way back, seeped in, a whole basement full. He beat on his legs to make them move. By now blisters on both feet had burst, and the rough weave of his socks rasped the skin and kept it raw and angry. Focus. Focus. Walk. Move. Move! One foot. Then the next. One foot. Then the next. Oh, God, it's a hellish hurt! But God said move. Don't think. Don't stop. One foot. The next. God said that.

He never stopped to wonder why the ground was glowing, but the light had become a soft layer of copper haze that held low to the earth. He waded through it as he would wade through water. The air crackled like cellophane as he pushed it aside. He didn't acknowledge it. The air had the aroma of a fuse that blew. He didn't acknowledge it. The desert sun was merciless and sapped the strength from his body as he skirted the rim of a crater left by a huge explosion. The twisted, still smoking wreckage of a truck lay at the crater's core. Black birds swarmed over the crumpled cab and pecked at fragments of burned meat. He passed an arm on the ground encased in a leather sleeve. One of the birds sat on a head torn from its neck and held an eyeball in its beak. It watched him. He never looked its way. Stones tossed up on the crater's rim were still as warm as loaves of fresh baked bread, but the thought of warm bread made him weep. Pebbles the size of small cookies lay strewn about. The ground was still breathing, and each pebble shone like a well-set jewel. They seemed alive. Like jumpy toads. Pebbles glittering and hopping like jumpy toads. A rumble of thunder could be heard somewhere. It muttered like his father when he was angry. Keep moving, boy. The thunder muttered again. Keep moving, boy. He scooped up some pretty pebbles, put one in his mouth to quench his thirst, and put the others in his pocket, then trod on down-canyon until it bisected a smaller canyon where water once flowed. He walked through tamarisk trees and pickleweed, by ancient mud banks encrusted with alkali, white as plaster. Thunder muttered again from somewhere down-canyon, closer this time, a little more insistent. "Hey, boy," it warned. Lightning exploded over the canyon like artillery fire. Darkness closed over the gorge. It was an instant was all, but now he felt the ground beneath his feet grow soggy. He wanted to move more quickly but it became even harder to walk. Another bolt of lightning shook the ground and rattled everything around

him, like how when you lived in Chicago trains came by and
rattled the windows, dishes; sometimes even the doorknocker
shuddered. His father had been there. Water, only an inch or
two, but still, there it was, and it began to accumulate around
his feet. He would lie down and wait out the storm. It would
be good. He was so tired. An ironwood tree was wedged between the canyon walls some seven feet or so above the ground.
Gideon homed in on it while the thunder muttered and the
lightning flashed, could just make a lower branch by stretching to his fullest, and pulled himself up to the trunk of the tree
just as the rain broke and battered the gorge with drops the
size of buckshot. He shimmied up to the ironwood's crown
and clung to the trunk while the warm rain drenched his back
and gave his burns some relief. A second or so. That was his
relief. A second or so before a roar like a volcanic explosion
caromed off the walls of the canyon and an angry tongue of
bloodred water came surging around the bend and bore down
on that ironwood tree. A panicky host of small gray birds fled
before it. Javelinas were caught by the current and shrieked as
they drowned. Gideon crawled deeper into the crown and hung
on as the flood smashed over him. The raging water tried to
pry him loose and carry him away, but he wouldn't let go. The
tree began to bob and sway like the needle of a compass, and
the next surge of the flood tore the ironwood loose and rolled
it over. Gideon had no idea how long he was underwater, but
he knew it hadn't been long enough to kill him because the
tree had righted itself and he was half-drowned but still sucking air. Boulders ground beneath him. Slabs of sandstone were
hammered from the canyon walls. The ironwood tree was

dragged into the central current and propelled along with the rest of the debris. Its limbs kept it right, and the boy hung on, though he was beyond knowing how. He had no idea when the big ironwood banked off a rocky outcrop and sling-shot out into calmer waters; however, at some point he became aware that there was no more roaring in his ears and opened his eyes to find himself flowing gently along in the middle of a wide, deep river. It was golden, and Gideon wondered if this might be heaven until he became aware of the sun on his back. The smattering of dead leaves left on the ironwood had been ripped away by the floodwaters, so there was no shade, no relief. He hadn't drowned—he was still alive—but he was burning and couldn't get away from the fire. What was left of him continued to cling to the ironwood tree as it drifted.

Sunlight played over the boy's nearly naked body. On either side of him the canyon walls glowed with a trace of bronze. The water reflected back the color of beaten copper. But Gideon prayed for night and burned until the dark arrived with some relief, not relief from his hunger or the wound beginning to fester at his hip, just some few hours' relief from that relentless sun.

The great river carried the ironwood tree through the maze of colossal canyons and side canyons it had been cutting for thousands of millions of years. The silence was as massive as the stones. The tree rode the water as easily as a canoe, and the boy hung on. His back burned from the sun, but the boy hung on. He could have allowed himself to slip off the log, to finish the business, but the business was not finished, and that kernel of desire drove him to stay alive. At one point, though, he did slip from the tree, held on to a limb, and eased into the water.

It was gold and it was green, the water. It cooled the boy's body. He looked out at the sunlight dancing over the water and thought it very beautiful. At some point, Gideon heard the hushed and sensual laughter of teenagers sneaking away from a party. He looked over the tree and saw a boy and a girl running along the bank of the river. The boy was about his age, and so was she. They disrobed as they ran. Their clothing was left behind on the bushes. Gideon had never seen underpants as white as hers. They were naked as they dove into the water, arched like dolphins, and entered the river together. Gideon heard more laughter. It came from atop the cliff on the other side of the river. Another young couple, strong and naked, stood in the sun like a young god and goddess. They raised their arms above their heads, leaped toward the sun, jackknifed, and sliced through the water without a splash.

Gideon heard the intimate laughter of young couples all around him. He looked out across the water and saw someone swimming toward him. Her strokes were long and luxurious, her timing flawless. Her hair was long and thick, golden, platinum almost, like a princess in a fairy tale. She reached Gideon and dove below the surface, where she gently kissed his feet, his ankles and knees, thighs and groin, stomach, chest . . . tiny kisses . . . the nibbles of a goldfish. She surfaced in front of his face and smiled her most angelic smile, laughed her most seductive laugh. Gideon stared back with horror. It was Abilene, and she was as naked as the others. She put her arms around his neck and her legs around his waist. Her weight dragged him down, and he was incapable of stopping her. He tried to free himself and could not. Both of them went under. Linked together they turned round and round, slowly, until Abilene kissed him. Gideon kissed her in return, then wanted to vomit, pushed her away, tried to, but she laughed seductively and held on to him, and they sank deeper into the water. Death was on him again, and he was not ready! He fought and thrashed while his lungs threatened to burst on him, fought and thrashed and finally wrenched free, shot to the surface, gasped for air. Abilene's laughter seemed careless and coy but far away. It took all of Gideon's strength to pull himself back out of the river. It was his final effort, and it left the boy nothing. He clung to the trunk of the ironwood tree like a baby and cooked in the sun, and the ironwood tree continued to go wherever the river took it.

Some time after that, four boys racing their bicycles along the riverbank spotted something in a large tree that had been snagged by another tree that stuck out into the river. "Holy shit," said one of them when they got close. It was all shriveled up and looked like a dead monkey. It smelled worse than anything they'd ever smelled before, and nobody wanted to touch it.

The sheriff and the ambulance attendants arrived at the same time since the three of them had been having coffee in the Hidden Splendor when the call came. Whoever it was on that tree was dead. You could see that from behind the wheel. Burned to a crisp. Putrid. Christ, how long had it been out here? When the attendants tried to lift the body off the tree it stuck to it, but people knew that skin stuck to things, so at first neither attendant thought it was weird. Skin stuck. When somebody was dead a long time like with their face against the floor, for example, their skin stuck to that floor. But this wasn't that. The boy's legs were actually gripping the trunk of the tree, and his hands— black claws now—were actually holding on. Christ, he should be dead, and he would be, but he wasn't yet. "We're gonna help you, son," said the sheriff, knowing the boy was beyond hearing. His face and chest were imprinted with the bark of the tree. The sheriff didn't figure the kid to make it to the hospital alive, but he cleared a path for the ambulance and led the way to Edom, his siren screaming as if it could help. One of the emergency ward nurses recognized the boy as he was brought in, not by name, but she'd seen him up to the Hidden Splendor restaurant with Jack Savage and another man and a woman, must've been his parents. "Nice-looking boy," she said.

Abilene had been alert to trouble way before the ambulance came screaming into town. As soon as she'd discovered that Jack had taken off, she knew in her marrow that he had gone to the claim. She knew some kind of confrontation was coming—had to be—although Jack hadn't said anything to her. But when he didn't return, her bones told her he wouldn't, and she got scared. The sheriff had taken a helicopter out to the Angel, and what he found there didn't make her feel any better: no truck; one helicopter; no people. Cold ashes. Blood on the ground and more blood spattered against a boulder. It had been nearly a week. The ambulance with its police escort frightened her. She began to tremble and couldn't stop. Once the boy was identified, the sheriff sent a car to bring her to the hospital. Abilene seemed so shaken the deputy thought she might pass out from the shock, which is what he told the nurse when he brought her in. The nurse put her arm gently around Abilene and escorted her to Gideon's gurney. "Yes," said Abilene, "yes. That's the boy." But she couldn't answer any of the sheriff's questions, didn't know why or what or how this all happened. The sheriff kept his voice even and his face a perfect blank, but he'd seen too much in life to believe her, and he wondered what that nearly dead boy in there could tell. He'd also seen too much in life to bet on the boy pulling through. The river brought him back here to die. Why'd the river do that, he wondered, bring him back?

The nurses tended to his burns first. If they hadn't, septicemia would have raced through his system like mercury from a lit match. Abilene sat in the emergency waiting room with a paper bag of his belongings in her lap. An orderly had brought them to her. There wasn't much: a laminated Mississippi driver's license, his belt, a red can of Prince Albert, a few small stones, torn trousers, a jackknife. A nurse came by and asked if she wanted to see Gideon before they took him upstairs to surgery, and, of course, she did. She whispered in his ear, "Be strong, boy," meant it, and kissed his forehead. Then the surgical orderlies whisked him away, and another orderly walked Abilene to the waiting room outside of the intensive care ward.

She sat there and waited with Gideon's things in her lap. Her brain whirred like a kitchen blender. She looked at her future and couldn't see it anymore, and that scared her. She'd always had plans, backup plans, contingency plans, plans from column A and plans from column B. She told herself to sit still and think, but everything was out of control, so what did it matter what she came up with, and that struck her as a cosmic fact for the first time in her life. That's when she got scared. She floated somewhere in space. Whatever sounds got through were hollow. Everything was far away, and a fear filled her stomach such as she had never felt before. She saw the void and spotted herself in it.

"Sometimes the good Lord turns a blind eye, don't he?" said Charlie Nickel.

What? Was he talking to her? How long had he been there? "What'd you say?"

"How are you?" he asked.

"I'm not," she answered.

"Something went terribly wrong out there. They found the truck," he said. "It was at the bottom of a slot canyon too narrow to access. Looked like an atom bomb hit is what they say. They winched a man down from a helicopter. Nothing survived. Nothing's left."

She felt her heart stop and did not know if it would start again.

"I hear the boy's been beat up pretty bad," said Charlie.

"He's not supposed to be alive." She could barely get the words out.

"This country eats people. It's amazing he had the will to

hang on when most grown men would've been brushed away like a grasshopper off the sleeve of your shirt. Does he know what happened to his father?"

"I don't know what he knows," said Abilene.

"Of course. How could you?" said Charlie. "But my guess is he's got a story to tell. Hey, tell me if I'm right about something."

"About what?"

"There was a fourth person out there that night."

"Where?"

"The Dark Angel," he answered.

"Who?" she asked.

"You."

"You're crazy," she said, but she said it in a near whisper and without conviction. It hurt. It really hurt.

"An astute observation, but not one that alters the situation," said Charlie. "In any case, it's down to just the two of you now." She sat there and let that sink in.

The elevator doors slid open and two orderlies exited with Gideon on a gurney. The boy was still out. The surgeon got off just behind them and accompanied the stretcher to where Abilene sat.

"Ma'am?" asked the doctor. Abilene wondered at how young he looked. She jumped to her feet, spilling Gideon's belongings on the floor. Charlie Nickel stopped her from getting to her knees to retrieve the things.

"Talk to the doctor," he told her. "I'll get this stuff."

"He's a fighter," said the surgeon. "I'd want him on my side." Abilene thought the boy looked so young and so tender lying there. She reached out to touch him and pulled back in shock the instant she got it that his right leg was gone. "Gangrene," said the surgeon. "Shotgun wound. Nothing else would have saved him. Let's get him set up and then you can come in." When he saw the look of horror on Abilene's face, he said, "I'd still want him on my side," nodded to the orderlies, and disappeared through the swinging doors into the intensive care ward behind them.

"Tough," said Charlie. "Young kid like that." Abilene stared after the boy and tried to comprehend what was happening to her. "I think you'd best sit down before you fall down," he said as he helped ease Abilene back into her chair. "His things are right there," said Charlie, and indicated Gideon's belongings on the chair beside her. "Get you anything?" he asked.

"Bourbon," she said half-seriously. "No ice."

Charlie took a half pint of Wild Turkey from the inside pocket of his coat and offered it to Abilene.

"No shit?" she asked.

"No shit," he replied. "Good thing you don't want ice. Tell you what: you sit here and stand guard. I've got a couple things to do, then I'll come back and dinner's on me."

"I get it free, anyway," she said, though she didn't know why she said it.

"Fine. Then it's on you." He reached down and took two pebbles in his hand. "Mind if I take a couple of these things? Kind of like worry beads," he said, and shook them in his fist like dice.

"Take 'em," Abilene said, and tendered back the bourbon.

"Keep it," said Charlie. "I'll fetch a fresh one."

"Ma'am?" a nurse called out.

"Put it in your pocket, goddamnit," she whispered in what sounded more like a growl, and awkwardly shoved it in there for him.

"Mrs. Pickett?" the nurse called again impatiently.

"Coming," said Abilene, straightened her dress, and followed the nurse through the wide swinging doors into the intensive care ward.

She was surrounded by hospital beds filled with the barely breathing, the nearly dead. The nurse had told her that Gideon was becoming more alert, although he was still asleep when Abilene was allowed in to see him. So she stood there beside the boy's bed and started wondering, which set off a stream of thoughts, none of them promising much relief. Starting out after she left that bastard back in Oklahoma, what she felt was kind of heady because for the first time in a long time she was on her own, which was exactly where she wanted to be. Queen of the road. *Ándale!* Let's see where it goes and what goes with it. OK. This is where it went, and a crippled boy is what went with it. Didn't she meet them for the first time in a hospital? Maybe that was an omen. She should have paid more attention. Now what? The thing was, she did believe in God and it had occurred to her that maybe He had set all this up and maybe she ought to go along with it to find out what the hell she was supposed to do. She'd thought about being a nurse once; maybe this was it. Gideon'd be all grown up soon anyhow, so maybe she was here to get him through the hard part. Wouldn't be forever. Chalk up a good deed on the Lord's blackboard. She felt a little better.

Abilene had been staring at a spot on the wall, oblivious to her surroundings, while she went through the this-and-that of her situation. Whoa. Here's a thought: get Charlie Nickel to buy the Hidden Splendor and hire her to run it. Edom wasn't the worst place in the world, and she'd have a good job, maybe buy the whole shebang from Charlie someday. Get rich. Retire. Travel. Abilene began to see the makings of a plan in all this, but just as she did she felt a blow against the side of her head as real as if it was hammered by a piston. Gideon was awake. She knew this without even turning to look but when she did look, when she could no longer not look, she saw the blow had come from a set of eyes that seethed with a loathing so deep she could not fathom. One thing it did was answer a whole lot of questions. She couldn't stay in the same town as that boy because if she did . . . someday he would kill her. It would be his reason to live. That settled that. By the time he got out of the hospital she would be gone, maybe up to Salt Lake to work in a restaurant, although maybe that was too close. Here he is all bound up and stuff and still I feel like he's got his hands on my face, she thought to herself. "Back off, boy," she said, "I didn't hurt your daddy." It took a second, but he reached out his hand as best he could and moved his fingers like he was asking her to take them. He was reaching out to her, so how could she refuse him? Maybe he didn't even know who she was. Maybe he thought she was someone else. His mother, maybe. So Abilene took the boy's hand and curled her fingers comfortingly with his. Nothing he could do to her now, she was thinking, when she suddenly felt him clamp down on her. "Let go," she said, but he wouldn't. "I said, let go!" She tried hard to tear away but he held on like a python, squeezed, and pulled her toward him. She tried to pry his fingers from her hand and was half in the bed with him when the nurses ran over. The boy's blood pressure had spiked, and all of his monitors screamed in warning. "Get that woman out of here!" someone yelled. "Let go of him!" someone ordered. "He's got *me*," she wailed in explanation, but an orderly had already broken the grip and shoved her out the door like a drunk from a barroom. After that incident, the hospital barred her from seeing one Gideon Pickett, patient, while the boy remained in intensive care. The attack, for that's how Abilene thought of it, rattled her, that Gideon had a grip at all let alone the strength to grab and hang on. My God, how he must hate her! She did not want those hands around her neck.

Jesus.

She wanted to scream and cry and pound the walls. "I have lost things, too!"

He would have killed her if they hadn't stopped him.

Well, she came light, she'd leave light. One suitcase. She'd probably have to sit on it to close it, maybe ought to put a strap around it, too, but hell, she was bound and determined: one suitcase. Do a load of dirty clothes in the morning at the Laundromat, pick up her pay from the Hidden Splendor, buy some snacks, and be on the road before noon. Simple. Clean. Uncluttered. Go! The boy would be left with a trailer in reasonable shape, so he had resources, right? Sell it. Get Charlie Nickel to help him do it. It's not that the kid would have nothing in his pockets. She didn't know about wooden legs and that kind of stuff, but what she did know, sure as hell, was that the boy was going to live, and the further he lived from Abilene, the safer she would be. That night, for the first time since she moved to the wash, Abilene was too nervous to sleep. She knew nobody could sneak up on her, especially a kid mostly dead from exposure with one leg who was still in the hospital, but, even so, she remained awake on her back all night long with her finger on the trigger of her .25-caliber, semiautomatic pearl-handled pistol. Jack had made fun and told her it was nothing but a pop gun—fine, pop pop pop, a tight, three-shot group right between the eyes; you'd be dead by pop gun, no question about it. Regardless, she was out of the campsite by dawn and waited outside for the attendant to open up the Laundromat. She was about fifteen minutes away from dry clothes when Charlie Nickel walked in. She'd bought her snacks and picked up her pay during the wash cycle. Vanda said she'd give her a reference, no problem. Five minutes to fold, then she'd be gone. But Charlie walked in.

"Just in time to say good-bye, Charlie," she said.

"You know what they say about telling God your plans?" he asked.

"No. What?"

"You're just going to make Him laugh."

"And your point is?"

Charlie took an envelope from his jacket pocket and handed it to Abilene. "You might want to take a look," he said with a tone and expression that implied she'd better. There was no return address on the envelope, a standard business type, but the sheet of paper she took out of it said "Assay Report" at the top.

"What's this?" she asked.

"Read it," he replied. "I pulled a few strings. When you're rich, people don't just open doors for you, they kick 'em down. Fools fall all over themselves. OK. I'll shut up. You read." Although some of the report was technical jargon, Abilene thought she understood enough of it to wonder why Charlie Nickel had insisted she read the damn thing. *High-grade commercial ore.* That stood out. Great. So. "What's this got to do with me?" she asked. Charlie took a couple of pebbles out of his pocket and handed them to her. "Know what these are?" he asked.

"Stones."

"Close, but no cigar. Stones from the boy's pocket, to be exact." Abilene's mind raced ahead.

"What are you saying, Charlie?" she asked.

"High-grade commercial ore," he said, cradling the two pebbles in his palm. "I'm talking to a very rich lady. You're going to want to unpack that suitcase I saw in your car and stay around. That boy back there was on the mother lode."

———

Jesus.

———

Was a fortune worth the risk of your life? she asked herself; and the answer came back, what was life without it?; and the answer came back that life was a good thing; and the answer came back, not without a house and car and money it wasn't. She guessed she thought being dead was better than being poor. Time to back up then, lady. You're at a genuine crossroads and you'd better think about this one but good. According to Charlie Nickel he could walk her through the complexities of getting rich by the truckload. She'd need a good lawyer, and he'd introduce her to his. "It's been kind of lonely being the only millionaire in town," he said. "Welcome to the top one percent. You're about to pay more in taxes than most people make in a lifetime."

"And that's a good thing?" she asked.

"A patriot's duty. Let's put it this way: with what you got left you could buy your own country. It'd be a small one, of course, not one like China, but still . . ."

The beauty part of this was that she didn't need to do one thing more than she'd already done. She had a signed contract. The Dark Angel had paid off, and Abilene Breedlove was poor no more. Had that been a smart move or what?

Now, Charlie also pointed out that Gideon was a rightful heir, so there'd be a split, but that'd still leave plenty for them both. Charlie was sure she would want the boy to have his share, and that was true. She begrudged him nothing. That was not her problem. Being dead was her problem. According to Charlie, a mining company named American Pure bought his claim for more than the gross national product of the Belgian Congo and cut him a deal whereby he and his heirs got royalties for the rest of creation or as long as the company was in existence, whichever ended first. He was sure they'd make the same deal with her, and, since the company had the great good sense to stick him on its board of directors, he almost guaranteed it. "Maybe," Charlie said, "you 'n' me could take up golf. Of course, we'll have to build us a golf course first; cost just about what we make in fifteen minutes on a slow day."

She had to sit down.

"You might want to unpack," said Charlie.

———

He watched her as she spooned three sugars into her coffee and filled the cup nearly to the brim with cream. She looked wan and drawn and fixed on something only she could see. She found herself wanting to turn to Jack for help with her predicament, but there wasn't any Jack. He wasn't there, and he wouldn't be there, and his loss sent her tumbling. She really could have loved that man. He was so smart, knew so much stuff, her "gold mind." There hadn't been time enough for them to pick their favorite songs or special places. A few weeks ago she had no idea Jack was in the world. Now she couldn't think of the world without him. But it was without him and would stay that way. Son of a bitch, right? She brought the rim of the cup to her lips, then put it down again, afraid she'd spill it. "Charlie," she said, and took his hand across the banquette. "What am I gonna do?"

———

It wasn't 'til she was nearly through her third cup of coffee that Charlie Nickel asked Abilene, "What about the boy?" She stopped in midsip and stared at him over the rim of her cup.

"You given him much thought?" asked Charlie.

"He's got family back in Mississippi," said Abilene.

"I see you have," remarked Charlie.

"All that money going home in his pocket?" said Abilene. "They'll be thrilled to get him back."

"Just as well," said Charlie. "What the hell happened at the intensive care ward?"

"You heard about that?" she asked.

"One of the nurses." He nodded. "I play poker with her husband. She told him, and he told the table."

"He tried to drag me into the crib with him."

"Crib?"

"Hospital bed," she amended.

"I heard you were pretty near in there, too. Once you were out the door they had to strap his wrists to keep him from going after you. They thought he was half dead and then they couldn't get him to stay still. Finally had to give him a shot to calm him down."

"I think he'd kill me if he could," Abilene said.

"Why's that?" asked Charlie. Abilene didn't say. "He hate you that much?"

"I guess he must," she said, but she, too, felt grief. She, too, felt scared and alone, swamped, shredded, gutted like the carcass of a deer. Abilene was taken by a great, deep sadness. She felt bent as an old tree. She felt she'd never move from this spot again. She'd been staring out over Charlie's shoulder when she became aware that someone had stopped at their table.

"Abilene Breedlove," she heard Charlie say as if introducing her to someone. Her eyes returned to the table. "I want you to meet George Barrett." She saw a smiling young man, about thirty, with a good haircut, wearing a seersucker suit and a bow tie. He carried a hand-tooled leather briefcase. "George Barrett is going to be your new best friend," Charlie said.

"Mind if I sit down?" Barrett asked.

"Grab a chair," said Charlie, and George Barrett sat down at the table with them. "This ain't divine provenance," Charlie said to Abilene, "but it ought to be. I asked Mr. Barrett to stop by because I had a strong feeling you two should be talking to each other. George Barrett, meet Abilene Breedlove."

"A pleasure," said George, and held out his hand. Abilene took it and thought it felt soft and well cared for.

"He's my point man at American Pure," said Charlie. "We made each other rich, and I thought you might like to hear about it."

"Are you going to make me rich, too, Mr. Barrett?" asked Abilene.

"I will if you'll let me," he replied.

"Oh, I'll let you, all right," she said. "Where do I sign?"

Charlie thought her smile seemed especially dazzling at that moment.

———

Gideon got better faster than anybody on the hospital staff ever imagined he would. Should have been dead ten times over. When he was let out of intensive care and moved to a regular ward, the physical therapist rigged a trapeze over his bed so the boy could pull himself up and stretch out a little. Once Gideon got the knack of it he spent most of each waking hour pulling up pulling up pulling up and gradually lowering himself down again so that he felt it deep in the pit of his stomach muscles. Other muscles began to swell: the muscles of his back, his neck and shoulders, the sides of his arms. "You'll be ready for the Olympics soon," said one of the orderlies. "That's one boy eats all his breakfast," said another. The hospital dietician wanted to know, "What'd your momma feed you, son? Grizzly burgers?" Everybody on the staff was rooting for Gideon. He was the news at the beginning of each shift, and that meant throughout the entire hospital, the janitorial staff, too, how he was doing and whatnot. Sometimes one of the nurses reported they had seen what they thought might have been some kind of smile, some small twitch of the cheek muscles, but mostly the boy seemed without humor and doggedly earnest. His gaze remained fixed on something out there someplace, and sometimes a nurse would wonder whether he even knew she was in the room. Or cared. He wasn't a winning kid, and nobody rooted for him because they thought he was. They rooted for him because the boy had gone to the edge and back, and doing so had shown them it was possible, that you really could hammer your way out of a bad place. At least, that's what they thought, and they rooted for him because why wouldn't you? He was just a kid!

Vanda stopped by to see him a couple of times and brought him a box of almond rocha when she did, but the only person to visit Gideon regularly was Charlie Nickel. The old man explained the boy's circumstances to him in great detail, and Gideon appeared to understand. His eyes remained on Charlie, and Charlie had the distinct impression that the boy was listening, although, as usual, Gideon revealed nothing. At some point Charlie brought up Abilene and explained how, the two of them being legal partners, since there was business to be done here, it'd be a good idea to call a cease-fire. "I don't know what you got against her," said Charlie, "but I know it's in your best interest to set it aside." Charlie was sure he got through to the boy and reported this to Abilene, who claimed she was glad Charlie was so sure, because she wasn't. The only way she'd go anywhere near Gideon's room was if Charlie went with her, which, of course, he said he would. "I'm here to help," Charlie told her, and he was.

George Barrett was in Salt Lake on business, so it took a few days, but as soon as his helicopter landed, Charlie was waiting on the blacktop to take him to a meeting with Gideon and Abilene in Gideon's hospital room. "Do you mind if I take a whiz first?" asked Barrett.

"Listen up, amigo," Charlie said. "We're talking beaucoup sums of legal tender here. This is the first time they'll be in a room together since he tried to kill her."

"He really tried to kill her?" asked George incredulously.

"Nobody's denied it," answered Charlie.

"Anybody know why?"

"My guess is she does," said Charlie.

"Just give me a minute," said George as he headed for the men's room. Charlie took ahold of him and turned him around.

"Put a clothespin on it. We'll be at the hospital in five minutes," said Charlie. "Let's see what you're made of."

"You're getting to be a pest, Charlie," said Barrett.

"I know," said Charlie, and hustled George toward his truck. "Be prepared to give, and be prepared to get."

"Whose side are you on, Charlie?" asked Barrett.

"The side of the righteous," said Charlie, and winked. They reached the truck, and Charlie held the passenger door open for Barrett. "Let's ride," he said.

"Come on, Charlie," said Barrett once Charlie was behind the wheel. "What's your deal? Are you expecting some kind of cut?"

"No deal. Not a penny," said Charlie.

"Consulting fee?"

"Nada."

"Case of Jack?"

"Nope."

"So why do it?"

"Because it's fun," the old man answered, and peeled out like a teenager at the Dairy Queen.

Abilene stopped by the hospital newsstand to buy some magazines for Gideon, but what she was really buying was time. George and Charlie had already gone up to Gideon's room. They were to get things started, then she'd come in with magazines and Baby Ruth bars, keep George and Charlie between her and the bed, and hope for the best. She had come to care about the boy and sure didn't wish him any harm, but she didn't wish herself any harm either. Abilene wanted to look good, too, bright and chirpy, so she dressed as she had when she first applied for the job at the Hidden Splendor,

and when she finally did enter the room (after hesitating outside the door until she hated herself for being such a coward),
her big smile was right out in front of her. Charlie was impressed. He had her as a woman with assets who made the
best of them. That smile of hers could stop a train right in its
tracks.

"Buenos dios, gents," said Abilene as she entered the room.
She deftly flipped a candy bar behind her back to Gideon, who
snatched it in midair. "Johnny Unitas to Ray Berry. Touchdown! Are we a team or what?" she asked. "Also brought you
stuff to read." She handed the magazines to Charlie. "Give
these to him, will you, Charlie?" she said, wary of approaching
the bed.

But Charlie shook his head and said, "He won't bite. I
promise."

"You sweet-talking daddy, you," she said, stowed her fear,
and approached the side of Gideon's bed with the magazines.
"How y' doin', kiddo?" she asked, and brushed his hair back
from his forehead. He let her do it. Abilene tried to read his
face for danger when Gideon looked at her. This time she
didn't see it. "OK. Here we got your *Boys' Life,*" she said,
and handed him the magazine. "We got *Argosy,*" and handed
him a second. "Plus, *Mad* magazine. It's a riot." Gideon took
them from her. "Thanks a bunch, Abilene," she said, trying
to get a response from him. "At least tell me I've got nice
teeth." She flashed her most dazzling smile, then raised her
eyebrows in a question. Gideon didn't respond. She turned to
George and Charlie. "What about you gentlemen? Is he like
this with you, too?"

"We got an understanding," said Charlie.

"Can a girl get in on it?" asked Abilene.

"You're in on it," he said.

The deal offered by Mr. Barrett of American Pure was, as he explained it, identical in principle to the one given to Charlie Nickel: a large sum that would secure ownership of the real estate itself plus a royalty per ton once the mine began to operate.

"Which would be when?" Abilene wanted to know.

"My guess is early next year," answered Barrett.

"You were talking about a lump sum, Mr. Barrett?" she continued.

"Yes, ma'am," he said.

"Which would be what?"

Barrett shuffled through his papers or pretended to, found the one he wanted, and seemed to give it a quick review.

"I am authorized to offer you thirty thousand dollars," said Barrett.

"And I am authorized to tell you to stick it where the sun don't shine. What about you, kiddo?" she said to Gideon. "Fifteen apiece sound good to you? I didn't think so." Abilene winked at Charlie. "We got an understanding," she said.

"What sounds good to you?" asked Barrett.

"One hundred thousand," she replied.

"No can do."

"My guess is there's more than American Pure out there waiting to jump on this," she offered.

"Fifty," said Barrett.

"I came here poor, and I'll leave here poor unless I get my price," said Abilene.

"A hundred thousand?" Barrett asked.

"One twenty-five," she said.

"Jesus!" he exclaimed.

"Think of me as a poor widow with a stepson who's a cripple," she said. "That's what you're looking at."

"One fifteen."

"One fifty."

"Shit!"

"I take it that's a yes?" she asked.

"Come on, Georgie," needled Charlie, "it ain't your money."

"Hell, then!" squealed Abilene. "Make it one sixty."

"One fifty."

"Ten thousand is chump change, Abby," said Charlie. "Take the deal."

"One sixty," she said, and smiled.

"Ma'am," said Mr. Barrett, "you just bought yourself a bright future."

"Done!" she exclaimed with a whoop, spat in the palm of her right hand, and stuck it out to shake with Barrett.

"Go on, Georgie, spit!" Charlie urged. To Barrett, a meticulous man, the thought of shaking a handful of saliva was truly repugnant, even if that hand was attached to an intoxicating woman, which, in his opinion, it was. "Tick tock tick tock," counted Charlie. "Take the lady's hand." So he did. Barrett spit and shook like he meant it. "How 'bout you, junior?" Charlie said to Gideon, and flashed a thumb up or a thumb down. Gideon looked at Charlie, at George Barrett, and, finally, at Abilene. He held her eyes and turned his thumb up.

"We've got a deal," said George Barrett, flashed a smile, and shook hands all the way around.

"This calls for a drink!" cheered Charlie, and ran out to buy some Cokes at the newsstand. Abilene shivered, although not so much that anybody would notice it. Charlie was happy. She had turned her smile on Barrett and weakened that man's knees. She was rich, and the boy had not tried to drag her into the bed with him. In fact, he was acting kind of normal. For him. Still, Abilene shivered. That old ghost-on-her-grave routine. Jesus. Why couldn't she just feel good and celebrate like everybody else? Well, hold on a minute. Just wait and be honest. The kid wasn't celebrating, either, but you'd expect that, right? Losing your father and all, plus the fact that he wasn't old enough to suffer being broke.

George explained the paperwork would take a week or ten days to put together. Things had to go to corporate headquarters in Salt Lake. He'd take them himself since he was flying to Salt Lake in the morning. Once they were signed it would take only a few days for Abilene and Gideon to get their first two checks: $80,000 each. He said he assumed they could prove who they were—drivers' licenses would do it—and he requested a copy of the Dark Angel contract the principals had drawn up between them. Charlie Nickel could recommend a good lawyer for them because they'd need one when the papers came back. Other than that, declared Barrett, the deed was done. "Just in time," said Charlie as he bustled back into the room with his arms full of Coke bottles and vending-machine packets of potato chips, pretzels, peanuts, and pistachios. He dumped the packets on the bed in Gideon's lap and handed out the cold Cokes.

"And for the adults in the room . . ." He took a pint of bourbon from his coat pocket and offered it around. "It's not every day I find myself in such rich company," he said. He poured half his Coke into the sink and refilled the bottle with bourbon. "To the Dark Angel Mineral Development Company," he toasted. "May good come out of her." Barrett said, "Cheers." Abilene said, "Amen."

———

It was agreed that Charlie Nickel would find Gideon's family back in Mississippi and see that the boy got there once he could travel. George Barrett said he would fix Gideon's account so that no one back in Mississippi could ever take his money from him, and it was also agreed that Charlie and Abilene would watch out for Gideon for the foreseeable future. She had her misgivings, but so far things had mostly gone her way, and she figured for the foreseeable future Gideon would be in the hospital anyway. Abilene also truly felt Charlie Nickel was a man to be trusted. A terrible thing had happened, and an extraordinary thing had come out of that. "If I don't celebrate now, when do I?" she asked herself. Still, she didn't feel right, and the feeling followed her like a swarm of black flies she could not flick away.

———

A week passed without anything much going on except that Gideon got better by the minute. His skin was still tender where the sun had burned it, but he was out of bed and on crutches way before he should have been. With his strong arms and one good leg, he could scoot faster than a fat man chasing a cherry pie, and the medical staff speculated that he might just go home soon. It seemed to Charlie that Abilene got agitated at the news, but he assured her he'd come out and do his part, give her a break, take the boy for rides and whatnot. Abilene wondered if he'd heard from George Barrett, and Charlie told her she'd have to be patient; these things take time. "They got a battalion of lawyers and accountants working on it, believe me," he said. Talk of lawyers reminded Abilene she had to get the Angel contract from her safe-deposit box. "What time is it, Charlie?" she asked. "Two thirty," he answered. Time enough for Abilene to get to the bank. Uh-uh. Nope. She'd left the safe-deposit box key at home. She'd have to do it first thing the next day. Don't forget, she told herself.

———

Everybody in the bank that morning as well as those passing by heard her scream. The guards ran to the locked cubicle where Abilene had taken the safe-deposit box and demanded she open the door. When she didn't, they splintered the flimsy thing and found her sitting dumbstruck on a folding chair staring at an empty safe-deposit box in her lap.

"Son of a bitch," she said.

"What'd you call me?" asked one of the guards.

"Not you, bonehead!" she yelled, pushed through, and stomped out.

"What about your box?" an officer yelled after her.

"Ram it," she said.

The goddamn thing was empty. Abilene raced back to the trailer and ransacked the place—she'd have torn the wallpaper from the wall if there'd been any—but no contract turned up. Gideon had to know something about this. Had to! He never left his father's side, for Christ's sake! She turned around and drove back to the hospital so fast she was lucky not to be arrested. Just get there was what mattered. But once she got there she saw Charlie was already in the room—he and Gideon were playing a game of chess on the bed; Charlie was teaching him—so she had to make believe nothing was wrong until the goddamn game was over and he left. It was torture. Inside she was screaming, "Get the hell out of here, Charlie! Scram! Go, goddamnit!" But as far as anybody could tell on the outside, Abilene Breedlove was all fine and dandy, considering her loss. Then the doctor came by and said he saw no reason to keep Gideon in the hospital beyond the end of the week, so Abilene had to pretend she was glad about that, too. One of her favorite TV shows was *The Life of Riley,* starring William Bendix. When Riley got himself into a pickle, which was all the time, he'd look at the camera and declare in his gravelly voice, "What a revoltin' predicament this is!" What would Riley say about her mess? she wondered. Charlie! Jesus, man! Cram it and go! Lunch? "Uh, let me have a rain check on that, Charlie. Gideon and me have some points to talk about. Family stuff." She noticed Gideon looked at her when she said it. Good, she thought, got his attention. Charlie said he was going to send somebody out to build a ramp over the trailer steps so Gideon could more easily go in and out.

"This OK with you, me going?" he asked Gideon, then left once the boy nodded.

Abilene stood at the door to Gideon's hospital room and watched Charlie walk up the hall and turn right at the arrow toward the elevators. She didn't move until he disappeared around the corner, and when she turned back to Gideon the boy was doing pull-ups on the trapeze. Abilene stood at the foot of the bed, where she knew he couldn't reach her. "We got business, boy," she said. Gideon gave no sign of having heard her, although he dropped his right arm and continued doing one-arm pull-ups with his left. His bicep tightened to the size of a baseball, and she marveled at the boy's strength. He got that from his father, of course. That man was strong as a bull. He'd been a really good father, too. She didn't grieve for him but she did feel sorrow. Jubal had been a good guy. Nothing wrong with the man. She liked him; he was fun; she was here because of him, and she was sorry Gideon no longer had him. She cared. It wasn't that she didn't. You can't have a man inside you one day and dead the next without feelings about it. Whatever happened out in the desert that night was never her intention. What could the boy tell her? she wondered. "If you could talk," Abilene said to Gideon, "what could you tell me?" Gideon said nothing, of course, but he switched arms and continued doing one-arm pull-ups with his right. That bicep was like a baseball, too.

"Well, OK, my little friend, since only one of us intends to do the talking, I guess I better get started," said Abilene.

"Something's missing, and I want it back. You got any idea what I'm talking about?" Gideon grabbed the trapeze with both hands again and pulled himself up so high his stump raised up off the bed, then he lowered himself slowly until he was settled back down again. He crossed his arms over his chest and locked himself down, but Abilene suspected she saw something that resembled a smile flit across his face. His eyes had widened, and his mouth had twitched. "You do know what I'm talking about, don't you? Piece of paper, eight and a half by eleven, small print?" Gideon's eyes narrowed again. He never stopped watching Abilene, never took his eyes off her, like those pictures of Jesus. So Abilene was dead sure Gideon knew exactly what she was talking about, because most of the time he barely looked at her. Now he didn't look anyplace else.

"You and me don't want to be locked in mortal combat, son, do we? I mean, come on, haven't the past few weeks shown us how dangerous it is out there? Turn the wrong way and some-body comes at you with a two-by-four. Busts your skull. It's bad, Gideon. I don't need to tell you how. So here's the deal as I see it: we're family. Forget about those people back in Missis-sippi who were glad to see you go. I'm what you got, and here's the good part: I'm not going to be after your money. We're both rich. All we got to do is produce that contract for the man at American Pure, and we go to the bank. Hell, we'll buy the bank! Look, buddy, we might not have chosen each other but we got each other anyway. Ever see Siamese twins in a circus? You and me. But all we got to do is produce one flimsy piece of paper, and you and me can each go any way we want. Of course, the bottom line is if I don't get a dime neither will you. We'll both be rich or we'll both stay poor, and what's the point of that? So, here's my best offer: you might be coming home but you still ain't better by half, and you're going to need a lot of care to get back on your feet. You stay with me until you can manage on your own. I'll do my best by you, but you've got to tell me what your daddy did with that contract." Abilene had no idea whether she reached him or not. "One piece of paper, buddy. That's all." She wanted to slap him.

When Charlie came back for his afternoon visit he heard Abilene's voice and stopped this side of the door to listen. It sounded like she was reading out loud from the newspaper. Charlie was sure of it, especially when he heard the newsprint rustle.

"What's going on in the world is, let me see," she said, "um, Christine Jorgenson is the most widely recognized transexual in the world today. I guess so. *The Robe* is the first movie picture filmed in CinemaScope, wide-screen. We gotta go. Last year was the first year in seventy-one years that there wasn't a lynching in the United States. Whoa. Get this one: Gideon Pickett defies medical science and stays silent. There's a story we ought to follow. Come on in here and stop eavesdropping, Charlie. I see your shoes."

"I didn't want to disturb anybody," Charlie said as he walked into the room.

"You didn't want to miss anything is what you didn't want," said Abilene.

"I stand in awe of your resources," he replied as he looked around Gideon's room. Abilene sat in a chair alongside Gideon's bed looking quite composed, with a newspaper in her hands. A vase of fresh flowers stood on the bedside table. On the tray table across his bed were about a dozen assorted snacks and a glass of orange soda with ice. Charlie couldn't help but observe to himself that the tray table stood between Gideon and Abilene. He didn't know if she'd meant it that way but there it was. "Santa come early?" he asked. "New pj's? Pretty snappy."

"Just like his father's," said Abilene.

"Well, you seem to have things under control," offered Charlie.

"I told you. Me and Gideon got an understanding," she said with a smile on her face as if she believed it. Charlie wondered if she really did. He reached over and took an orange box of cereal from Gideon's tray table and examined it as if it were a foreign artifact.

"Kellogg's Sugar Frosted Flakes," she informed him. "Just come on the market."

Whatever she's doing, she sure is doing it right, thought Charlie.

PART 11

Abilene stood outside behind the trailer in the oven of another desert day and thought how she'd suffocate if she didn't get out of here soon. She stood over the open pit that functioned as their latrine with Gideon's bedpan in her hand and never felt so like a drudge in her entire life. She washed it out with water from a bucket she had brought for that purpose and placed it on a rock to dry and fumigate in the sun. Weary. That's what she was: weary. What was worse than weary? Nothing Abilene could come up with. She always seemed too busy, yet she never imagined time could move so slowly. Taking care of Gideon was both tedious and nerve-racking. Gideon made the task even more thankless because almost as soon as he was back in the trailer and alone with Abilene he began to brood again. At first she tried not to let it bother her, tried to busy herself with tasks she hoped would make Gideon's recuperation easier, but his brooding intensified, and her fear returned. He was always watching her. What the hell was he looking for? What could he see now that he couldn't see yesterday? As well as a ramp to help him get in and out of the trailer, Charlie rigged a trapeze over his bed so he could pull himself up like in the hospital, and Gideon did pull-ups like he was possessed. They'd been back at the trailer for a week now, and Abilene was no closer to that contract than she was to the goddamn pope in Rome. She rolled her eyes up to the sky and let out a moan. "Thanks a lot," she said, and shook her fist and dropped it wearily at her side.

In truth, Abilene never expected the loss would be so great. Each man had dreams and was eager to share them with her, and she had hitched her dreams to theirs until everybody had the same one. Now they were dead, and she was left without any dreams of her own. It was like slowly dying from starvation. More of her was gone each day. Jubal was a good Joe, kind and generous, and she missed him, and, no, she did not forget how Jubal had brought her to this place. But Jack was like a sneaky right she never saw coming. He took her to another level. She'd said all kinds of things to all kinds of men, but she never called a man "my love" before. To remember this was agony.

Abilene's attention was taken by the distant purr of a well-tuned motor engine. She recognized Charlie's Cadillac when she heard it, but this wasn't his, and no one else had been out there. She walked around to the front of the trailer and waited to see who it was. When the automobile came into view she saw it was a dark green Buick but not who was driving it. She always liked Buicks. People who were rich but didn't want to show off drove Buicks. Now, who's driving this one? When he first pulled up she didn't recognize him through the window, but when he got out of the car she saw it was that nice guy from American Pure, George Barrett. Abilene knew he was in Salt Lake but not when he was coming back.

"Hey, Miss Breedlove, how are you doing?" he said, and touched two fingers to the brim of his summer straw Borsalino. Nice car. Nice hat.

"Hey, Mr. Barrett, you don't need to salute me," she said, and smiled. "I'm just a private in this man's army." Then she curtsied. "Give me an order," she said, and smiled again.

"Huh?" He didn't get it.

"Just a joke. To what do we owe the honor of this visit, Mr. B?" she asked.

"How's the boy?" he asked.

"Asleep," she said curtly, her guard immediately up.

"I won't disturb him," Barrett said. "How are you doing?"

"It's a full-time job," she answered.

"You seem tired," he said. "Who's taking care of you?"

"The only person who ever did—me." She didn't know whether she sounded proud or desperate; she hoped the former.

"Well," said Barrett, "when you produce the contract you can hire an army of servants to do anything you want."

"I think I'd rather travel, to tell you the truth," she said.

"Travel with them."

"I'll give it some thought," she said, and laughed. "When did you get back from Salt Lake?"

"Last night," he answered.

"And out here bright and early? When do you sleep?"

"I don't need much."

"Hell, I need a truckload."

"So, do you have it?" he asked.

"What?" she asked.

"The contract."

"On me? No. Of course not. It's in the safe-deposit box, but I've been so busy I haven't had a chance to go to the bank yet." Could he see right through her?

"The T's are crossed; the I's are dotted. All we need is that contract."

"I'll go to town this week and get it," she assured him.

"If you want," he offered, "I can bring a nurse for Gideon while I drive you into town and back. Get the contract. Do some shopping. Make a day of it."

"I don't need to do any shopping, but he's getting to a point where he can mind himself for two hours. Give me a couple of days. Then I'll meet you at your office, and you can buy me coffee," she said.

"I'll even throw in a doughnut," he said, and laughed.

"Make sure it's got jelly in it," she said as he walked back to his car.

"You like éclairs?"

"Never had one."

"On me," he said, and waved as he drove away. "Tell Gideon I was by but didn't want to wake him up."

He was good company, and she wished he could have stayed around. She watched him go and felt some sadness as he did.

Gideon watched him go as well. He stood on crutches inside the trailer, hidden by the door, though he could still see and hear them. When he saw Abilene turn back toward the trailer, Gideon vaulted across the floor and into bed like he'd never left.

The moon was full, and there was a ring around it. Time for witchcraft. Abilene washed in the shallows of the pool, her hair piled atop her head, and made up her face in a mirror she held in her hand. She dabbed perfume on all her special places, and then she dressed in the moonlight. First she put on the cherry-red Frederick's of Hollywood bra and garter belt she kept in a silk bag she'd brought with her in case of emergency. Her nylons were next, and finally she stepped into a tight red skirt and put on an ivory blouse that buttoned up the front. As she buttoned it she wished she had a full-length mirror, but, still, she had a good idea of the effect. "Geronimo!" she said to herself when the last button was done, and crossed the desert floor from the pool to the trailer, her high heels in her hand. Abilene put them on right outside the trailer. She liked the clickety sound they made when she walked up the ramp. Before Abilene opened the door she checked her seams to see if they were straight, although she was experienced enough to know that if the object of your affection was checking out your seams something was seriously wrong. Abilene opened the door and eased inside.

Gideon was asleep with an open magazine across his chest, although a kerosene lantern was full up. Abilene turned the wick down to a glow—it was more like a dream that way—stared at the sleeping boy a moment, then gently sat beside him on the bed. She was aware that she sat where his leg had been. "Are you really asleep, boy?" she whispered. His breathing assured her he was. Abilene reached under the covers and through the fly of his pajamas took his fine strong penis in her hand. She let her fingers flutter on it as if it were a flute, then she held him firmly and worked him up and down. What does a boy who never speaks sound like when he comes? Abilene wondered, and smiled. A few seconds more and Gideon lurched awake. He came up on his elbows. "What took you so long?" she asked. "Got any plans for this thing?" He stared at her, unable to move. "Don't worry, Gideon, I'm not going to do anything you don't want me to do. I know you think about girls. I know you think about me. Here I am." She stood up so he could get a good look at her. "I'm the teacher you always wished you'd had." Abilene unbuttoned the top two buttons of her blouse. "Tell me to stop." She undid another button. "Tell me," she said again. "Tell me to stop." But Gideon didn't do it. His eyes went from her face to her breasts as she undid the rest of the buttons and pulled the ivory blouse out of the band of her red skirt. She shrugged out of it. "Will you undo my bra?" she asked. "Want me to come over there? Is that a yes?" Without waiting for an answer she walked over and sat on the bed facing him. "Go on. Undo it," she said. "It hooks here," and guided his hand to the right place. Gideon reached out with fingers that trembled and fumbled with the clasp. He couldn't do it. She laughed softly. "You'll learn. We have lots of time." She unhooked the bra herself. "Now you do the rest," she said. He reached out and pulled the red bra from her body. Her breasts were so close he could kiss them. "Why don't you?" she urged. She took his cheeks in her hands and pressed his lips to her breasts. "I feel like I'm going to explode. Do you?" she asked. "I want you, little baby, and I know you want me." She lifted his face up to her and ran the tip of her tongue around his lips, but when he reached for her she moved away. "You can have it all, Gideon. Love, money, you can have it all." Abilene reached behind her and unzipped her skirt. "Tell me to stop." And, when he didn't, she stepped out of it and stood before him naked except for the stockings and garter belt. She wore no panties. "Some men like it when you leave these things on. What about you? Do you want me to take them off? I don't think you do, young man," she said, walked to the bed, pulled down the covers, and straddled Gideon's belly. With her hands she kneaded the muscles of his arms and shoulders and chest. "God, you're so strong," she marveled, and meant it. Abilene reached back, undid her hair, and shook it down. She brushed it slowly across his face, back and forth. "Just tell me where the contract is, and you can have it all, my big strong baby boy." She moved against his belly and whispered in his ear, "Tell me, sweet Gideon, tell me where it is." He thrust up against her but she stopped him. "Tell me. Tell me where it is." Gideon tried to thrust into her again but again she stopped him. "Tell me, boy," she said, and slapped him across the face. Then, with all his strength he lifted Abilene off his stomach, rolled and flipped her under, pinned her there with her legs held apart by the weight of him, plunged and drained inside her, and went limp. Something guttural came from deep inside him, but her own cry eclipsed whatever she had heard.

He let her crawl out from under him. She felt humiliated and very frightened, confused and shaken to her core. She trembled as she picked up her lilac chenille robe, then sat in a chair because she didn't know what to do. A scorpion crawled down the sleeve of the robe. When she saw it she slapped it away with a scream, grabbed the broom, and smashed it flat where it fell to the floor. With the broom still in her hand, she leaned against the wall and tried to stop shaking. She saw that Gideon stared at her with the coldest eyes, and she snapped and came at him with the broom. Abilene swung at him as if he were the deadly insect. He grabbed the broom and pulled her onto the bed again, where he got his hands around her throat. Abilene couldn't tear them loose. She slapped and scratched his face, tore at his hands, tried to bite, but could not stop him. She felt her eyeballs popping in her head, and she knew then that he would kill her.

Suddenly he stopped and pushed her off him. They lay there side by side. Her hands went to her throat. Her breath came back painfully. Finally, she asked, "Why didn't you kill me?" He turned to her and punched her in the face with all his might. Abilene went black and fell to the floor.

When Abilene regained consciousness she decided she must still be alive because dead couldn't hurt this much. Gideon was gone. She looked to the corner. So were his crutches. He had to be out there somewhere. She wasn't sure why but she had to get him. Abilene was still groggy when she put on her lilac robe and staggered out the door, but she made

Gideon out about fifty feet ahead, vaulting toward the pool on his crutches. Jesus, he was fast! He outdistanced her easily, and she began to fall back when the tip of one crutch slipped off a stone and Gideon tumbled to the ground. He couldn't get up again; Abilene was closing in. He propelled himself along with powerful arms and his one leg, like a seal, until he reached the rock wall beyond the pool, pulled himself up to his good leg, stretched and reached for a fingerhold ledge, and began to pull himself up the rocky face. He was nearly out of reach when Abilene jumped and grabbed at his leg. He wrenched free and used his powerful hands and fingers to work his way up the wall.

"What the hell are you doing? You're going to kill yourself," she yelled as Gideon continued his climb. Abilene threw her hands over her head in frustration—"Come back here, Gideon, goddamnit!"—and then she remembered the .25, the pearl-handled popgun. She snatched it from the pocket of her robe and fired wildly up at him. She could hear the ricochets twanging off the rocks, so she knew she hadn't hit him, and fired again. This time she heard no ricochet, squeezed the trigger one more time, and heard the metallic click of an empty gun.

When the firing stopped he knew he would make it. He had taken the one shot in his stump like a bee sting. That little bullet didn't do much to stop him as he reached the ledge where the cave was and pulled himself up to a sitting position. His leg dangled over the side. He saw Abilene way below yelling at him. He couldn't make out what she was saying and wasn't trying to. Instead, he rested.

Him just sitting there with that one leg dangling over the edge drove her crazy. What's he going to do, sit up there forever? That's what it looked like, but it defied common sense. The boy had to come down sometime, but he didn't act like he was in any hurry, and the instant he took that red tin of Prince Albert tobacco from his shirt pocket, she knew where the contract was. Clever, she thought. Smart. Well, hell, like she said, he had to come down sometime. Maybe he thought he'd put the contract where she couldn't get at it. In the meantime, she knew where it was, so that was really a relief, in a way. She watched him open the lid to the tobacco tin and remove a piece of paper folded many times to fit. She watched with some satisfaction as he unfolded the paper to its proper size and let it flap in the wind, took a few steps and leaned backward at the edge of the water so she could see better. That was it. That had to be it. She flushed with excitement. She was going to be all right. But as he tore off a strip of paper her heart shuddered when it came to her what he planned to do, and she watched in horror as he tore the paper into as many skinny strips as he could. "Don't be crazy!" she yelled. If he heard her at all Gideon ignored her and took a packet of matches from his shirt pocket. He tried to light the ribbons of paper but the wind kept blowing out the flame, so instead he began to drop them one by one over the ledge before he let them all go at once like a handful of confetti. The wind took them and carried them beyond the cliff, back where the twisted canyons were, back toward the

Dark Angel, but still some were caught in a downdraft and scattered at the base of the cliff around the pool.

In a frenzy, Abilene raced around and jumped up to grab what she could, and when she saw some of the pieces land on the water she lunged into the pothole to get them. One by one she snatched pieces from the water, followed them thoughtlessly like a pigeon on a bread trail, forgetting in her frenzy where she was and grabbing what she could until she lost her balance and began to flounder in the center of the pool, began to drown as water poured down her throat. She gagged. Panic took her guts like a shot. She flailed desperately and sputtered, "Help me! Gideon, please help me! Don't let me die!" Most of her words were swallowed with the water, but Gideon heard some of them. They rode the thermals upward like buzzards, but by the time Gideon heard them, they were merely sounds in the wind stripped of their pain and meaning.

Gideon watched without emotion as Abilene's lilac chenille robe became soaked with water and the weight of it began to drag her under. She fought death as long as she could, even as her lungs filled and water closed over her head like the lid of a coffin. She kept her eyes open until that final and eternal second when it all went black, and then they stared at nothing. He watched the air bubbles rise to the surface, watched without expression as the rings washed toward the edge of the pool, and, when the surface calmed again, he saw it was as if nothing had happened.

Gideon sat for a moment more, and then he began to tremble. He missed his father and didn't want to be alone. His face twisted and his mouth opened and he tried to scream, ached to scream, except only caws came out, like crows, and shrieks like jays, and whinnies and bleats—the lacerating cries of the slaughterhouse—a buzz saw through bone, but even that was not enough, so he had to reach down deeper than ever until he touched off a truly terrible thing that erupted from his aching chest and echoed back and forth across the wash. He did it again and again and again.

<u>ACKNOWLEDGMENTS</u>

The Adams sisters, Brooke and Lynne, and their husbands, Tony Shalhoub and George Fifield, for the love and care of my family.

Ellen Stern and Peter Stern—for early reads and constant encouragement.

Joel Foreman and Ellen Sack—übersiblings.

Lenny Bee, the Sage of Aquarius, Patron Saint of Starving Artists.

Max Pushman—for that endless cup of coffee.

Debra McGuire and Lynne Schwabe—ladies who walk the walk.

The Hunter Village Square bookstore and Carol Bennett— another lady who walks the walk.

Finally, I feel blessed to have had the advice and encouragement of my agent, Claudia Ballard, from the William Morris Agency and the tender guidance of my editor, Nina Schwartz.

Thank you all.

ABOUT THE AUTHOR

Stephen Foreman received a BA from Morgan State University and an MFA from the Yale School of Drama, and taught writing at various universities before moving to California to work as a screenwriter and director. Having trekked across the Alaskan wilderness, bushwhacked through tropical rain forests, and hunted for gold in the Arizona desert, he now makes his home in the Catskill Mountains with his wife and two children.